Center Hill

MAURY M. HARAWAY

authorHOUSE®

AuthorHouse™
1663 Liberty Drive
Bloomington, IN 47403
www.authorhouse.com
Phone: 1-800-839-8640

First published by AuthorHouse 5/17/2011

ISBN: 978-1-4567-6553-8 (e)
ISBN: 978-1-4567-6552-1 (dj)
ISBN: 978-1-4567-6551-4 (sc)

Library of Congress Control Number: 2011906946

Printed in the United States of America

Acknowledgement

I gratefully acknowledge the help of my good friend Margaret Truly during the preparation of this book. Her advice, interest, and constant encouragement eased the process and improved the product.

Chapter One. April, 1844.

One afternoon in the spring when he was nearing five years of age, Herndon Henshaw saw a movement within the depths of a large copse of shrubs at the edge of the yard. He walked over and peered into the darkness of the shrubs but was unable to locate the source of the movement, so he got down on hands and knees and crawled slowly into the shrubbery. The canopy was thick and closed so that the shaded floor of the copse was open soil covered with a light sprinkling of long-fallen leaves. Across the open chamber beneath the ceiling of leaves, among the supporting pillars of the shrubbery trunks, he saw a rabbit. The rabbit seemed to be an extraordinarily large one. Hern sat down to watch it.

The animal was only ten feet away and was looking directly at him, yet instead of running away, it took three small hops toward him and continued to look at him calmly. Within the dim light of the shaded chamber, its liquid, deep brown eye glowed softly and seemed to extend inward to a great depth. The guard hairs of the rabbit's coat stood in splendid separation, individual and vibrant as though each had its own life. They shone with a light that seemed not merely reflected but immanent, generated from within. The entire creature seemed the center of a palpable energy field that radiated its force like the rays of sun shining out from behind a cloud.

As Hern sat enthralled with the first rabbit, a second just like it hopped forward from the depths of the chamber and kept coming until it sat beside the first. It, too, seemed perfectly calm in its nearness to Hern. The atmosphere around Hern seemed charged and alive with energy emanating from the rabbits, the shrubbery trunks and leaves, from the very soil around him. The world had become a place far more strange and exciting than he had experienced before, though his previous experience had seemed extravagant.

He felt now that he could crawl over and touch the rabbits, feel their soft and vibrant fur, look more closely into the depths of their liquid eyes. They sat looking as he approached, as calm as before, and he believed they would sit for him, that they had been changed from wild animals to his friends by a transformation of the surrounding world. He felt the usual rules wouldn't apply anymore. Yet the relations of predator and prey are ancient and iron clad and felt with special acuteness on the prey side of the issue, and though the animals allowed him a close approach and only hopped away, finally, in a calm and leisurely manner, but hop away they surely did.

Hern didn't mind their leaving but recognized it, instead, as the proper outcome of the adventure. Regardless of the strangeness and depth of this new world of infinite things, there was nowhere wild rabbits could afford to let people come up and take hold of them. Hern said none of this to himself—indeed, throughout the episode he had said nothing whatever to himself—yet he understood it implicitly. He looked around the chamber once more in the vibrant light, then turned and crawled back into the familiar dooryard that would never again seem quite so ordinary.

It was in the fall of that same year that Hern first realized he was going to die. Not that he would die in the next few days or weeks or even years—but he was going to die just the same, and there was no way he could avoid it. This was a terrible revelation to him. He had lived previously with an implicit sense that he would go on living forever. The realization that he would not was a cold and harsh blow that he felt in his stomach with a keen sense of sadness and loss.

Hern didn't remember just what had happened to start the process, but he began thinking about dead animals. He knew he was a young person, but already he had seen many dead animals in his life. He also knew he had heard his parents speak of loved family members who had died. These facts came together in his mind to evoke a simple act of logical deduction—a simple deduction, but surely the most complicated and far reaching of his young life. Animals died. This seemed to apply to all animals. It made a rule. People were like animals, and people died, too. All people. Including him. He examined the thoughts that brought the conclusion of his coming death, and he could find no escape. He was hesitant to believe it and hoped somehow it was not true. Yet he knew it was. He could feel the certainty of that truth in the pit of his stomach. The knowledge was almost devastating.

He wandered the yard in desolation, hesitant to leave the field a loser. He longed for a reprieve from condemnation. But he knew none would come. Still he waited, until he could gain a degree of control over his dejection and heartsickness. He didn't want Mama to see him so distraught when, outwardly at least, it seemed that nothing at all had happened. Yet he knew very well that a huge change had occurred in his understanding of life and the world.

He asked Mama about it, hoping somehow his conclusions could be wrong, yet she had to confirm them, instead. At least she took his concern seriously, was gentle, sympathetic, genuinely saddened by his grief at the discovery. She told him not to worry about it. That everybody died, and it was alright. And when they did die, they could go to heaven to live with God forever. And that she just knew he wouldn't die for a very long, long time and so needn't worry about it for a long, long time. And needn't worry about it even then because of God taking his soul home to heaven.

Hern felt much better after talking with Mama. He believed everything Mama told him. He realized Mama and Pa knew they were going to die, yet they bore up to it with no trouble. They seemed immensely powerful to Hern. They could do anything they wanted. They seemed to control so much about the world they lived in. Hern could hardly imagine becoming a being as powerful as Mama and Pa. If beings as powerful as that could stand as they did in the face of death, then Hern didn't mind trying it, too.

He felt better about his own death after that, although he thought about it from time to time. He no longer had the sick feeling in his stomach at the thought. But having expressed to himself the knowledge of his parents' impending deaths, he began to have dreams based in his unwillingness to be parted with them, his fear of their loss, his sadness over their demise. In his dreams, Mama was lost somewhere in the woods and no one could find her. He knew something no one else knew that could save Mama, but he could never remember what it was. Or Pa was out swimming in a lake and he was about to go under. He was going to drown and only Hern could save him. Hern started into the water. He knew he was going to save Papa. Then he realized he couldn't swim, that after all he could really do nothing.

These dreams troubled Hern for only a year or so, then faded away. His personal concerns about death had faded much sooner. Yet from time to time throughout his childhood, in his waking thoughts and in his dreams, he returned to the revelation of the world he had discovered with the rabbits in the chamber of the shrubs.

Chapter Two. July, 1856.

Hern awoke in his bed in his father's big log house at the farm in Center Hill. His brothers Bob and Ben in the bed across the room and his sister Lisa in the adjoining bedroom still slept. On the other side of the house, his parents had just awakened and were getting dressed. It was early daylight and nearing sunup.

Hern had grown rapidly in the past four and a half years, since he was twelve, and he now stood just over five-foot ten. He was compactly but strongly built. His face was attractive, and although his prominent nose fit in nicely with his other features, it kept him from being conventionally handsome. He had a firm chin creased with a sharp cleft. His hair was light brown and wavy, and his hazel eyes were bright and lively–the sort sometimes described as being full of the devil.

He dressed quickly and went out to the kitchen where Aunt Lucy was rolling-out biscuit dough and preparing to cook breakfast for the family. Aunt Lucy was a large woman, though not tall, and had pleasing features that looked capable of warm affection. She had been a house servant to members of the Henshaw family for over forty years. Along with the other Henshaw slaves, she had moved here with Mitchell Henshaw and his wife from Limestone County, Alabama more than two years before Hern was born.

"Good morning, Aunt Lucy," he said. "Sure looks like a fine day coming in."

"That it do, Hern," she said, "You's up mighty early this mawnin'."

"Guess I was restless this morning to see the whole day from the beginning," he said. "What are you fixing for breakfast?" he asked.

"We 's havin' scrambled eggs and bacon, biscuits and grits." she answered. "Don't you be wanderin' off so far you misses it, you hear?"

"I'll be here for it, alright," he said.

Hern reached into the cool cabinet on the far side of the room and fetched a pitcher of milk, poured a glass and drank it, and went out the back door toward the barn.

"See you later, Aunt Lucy," he called back. "Don't be burning those biscuits."

"You hush up, child," she called after him. "I ain't study'n' you no further."

The sun was just about to come over the horizon and the sky was covered over with the warm, yellow-gold light of a dawn in early summer. The robins that had been singing loudly when Hern awakened, and as he dressed, had stopped now and been replaced by the redbirds. Three different males, already glowing a deep rich red in the early light, were singing now from high branches of trees around the edge of the open yard surrounding the house. The birds were evenly spaced about the area so that they were almost equidistant from one another, like three points of a triangle.

Hern walked down the slight slope from the house to where the big barn stood above the creek on level ground. George was in the milking parlor at work, halfway through with milking the four cows, as it was his early job to do every day. George had a pleasant face and a pleasant disposition. He was a small man, more narrow than broad and rather short of stature, but he was very strong even so, and was easily the most productive working man on the place.

"Morning, George. How does everything look to you this morning?" Hern said.

"Mawnin' Mr. Hern. Hit look 'bout the way it do ne'ly every mawnin' this time of year. How it look to you?"

"Why, I think it must be one of the finest mornings I ever saw, George. Looks like you've still got two cows to go. What do you say I 'tend to Mollie for you and you can finish up early?"

"I say that'd be mighty fine, Mr. Hern, mighty fine indeed. You got to watch Mollie 'bout bringing up that right foot an' kicking over the bucket." George said.

"I remember, George, but thanks for reminding me, anyway."

"George, I don't see why you need to call me *Mister* Hern. Just plain Hern suits me alright. You've known me since I was a baby, might say you had a good part in raising me to where I am now."

"I know, Hern, but you's almost a man now and it's proper I should be calling you Mister. Don't make much diff'ence down here in the barn, just us, but if we was to be out someplace where there was folks around, hit wouldn't sound right was I to call you Hern 'stead o' Mister Hern. I best be gettin' in the habit now. Hit won't make no diff'ence between us no way. Maybe it won't never make no diff'ence." George said.

Hern pulled a short milking-stool over to Mollie and slid up under her right side. He washed down her udder with a damp cloth, positioned his bucket, and started milking. He liked the sounds of the keen streams of milk hitting the empty bucket as he squeezed and noticed that George's bucket had stopped ringing and was producing instead the soft, foamy sound of a bucket that was half-full. Hern liked the smells of the milking parlor, smells of the cow's feed, the cows themselves, the fresh milk, even the dried and not-so-dried manure George had raked up next to the wall. It was a place Hern always liked to be, especially early in the morning when George was at work.

After a while, Mollie tried to kick at the bucket with her right foot, but Hern was ready for her and casually blocked her with his right leg.

"These biscuits are sure good this morning," Bob said.

"I got up early and made sure Aunt Lucy didn't burn them," Hern said.

"She don't never burn 'em anyway," Bob said.

"Say *doesn't ever burn them*, Bob, not *don't never burn 'em*," his mother Elise said.

"Yes'm," Bob said, "but she doesn't ever."

"That's much better," his mother said. She was a very pretty woman, beautiful in a friendly and warm-spirited way, and the boys adored her, as did her husband. She had light brown hair that was almost blonde, and very warm, deep brown eyes. Mitchell Henshaw was a well built man about six feet tall. He had strong features, with eyes of a deep blue and hair that was pure black.

"Bob took the last piece of bacon, Mama!" Ben said. He was five years old and the baby of the family. "He already ate three pieces and I didn't get but one."

"It's alright, honey. You go out to the kitchen and see if Aunt Lucy didn't hold some back. She knows how you boys are."

"Well Bob always takes more than he should. He always gets more than I do," Ben said.

"Bob is bigger than you are and maybe he's growing faster," his mother said. "You go on out to the kitchen, now, and see if Aunt Lucy doesn't have something for you."

- -

Hern and his brother Bob rode over to Olive Branch in the early afternoon to attend the Fourth of July celebration. There was a big crowd of folks gathered in the town square, everyone dressed in their nicest clothes. There were tables set up with sandwiches and fried chicken and pies and cakes. People were gathered around punch bowls, and there was a politician giving a speech to a small group over near Mr. West's general store.

Bob went over to get some fried chicken, and Hern stepped up to one of the tables to get a cup of punch. A striking young woman stepped forward out of the group at the punch bowl; she walked with apparent purpose right toward Hern. She had chestnut hair and big brown eyes. She was coming right for him, alright.

"Why Mr. Herndon Henshaw," she said with a brilliant smile. "I don't believe you even recognize me."

"Please forgive me, Miss Madelyn," Hern managed to say. "I guess I'll have to admit I didn't recognize you for a minute, there. The last time I saw you, you were a little girl and now you're all grown up into a fine lady."

"Why, thank you, Mr. Henshaw. But I dare say you've changed more than I have. You must be a foot taller than when you last visited us at Robertson's."

"Well, this is fine. I'm so happy to see you again, Miss Madelyn. Tell me, how are you doing? Are your family all well, may I ask?"

"Yes, we're all fine, thank you, and may I say I hope yours are the same?"

"Yes ma'am, thank you, they are," Hern said.

"Isn't this a fine celebration, Mr. Henshaw? I'm so glad I came."

"Yes ma'am, I'm mighty glad you came, too. May I ask if you would have a cup of punch with me?"

"Why, thank you, Mr. Henshaw. I think that would be very agreeable, indeed."

"What's the matter with you, Hern? You act kind of distracted," Bob said. They were back on their horses, just starting on their way back home to Center Hill. "Who was that lady you were talking to, anyway?"

"That was Miss Madelyn McCall," Hern said. "She lives over at Robertson's Crossroads. I hadn't seen her since Pa and I stopped at her house to visit a couple of years ago. She was just a little girl then. She and I walked around her Pa's place some and threw bread crumbs to some tame ducks in her pond. That's about all I remember about it. She was just a little spit of a girl."

"Well she ain't a little spit of a girl any longer," Bob said. "Seems to me you were looking at her kind of funny. Come to think of it, you been acting funny ever since."

"I was surprised to see her, that's all. I was surprised to see how much she's grown up."

"Well I think there's more to it than that. Say, you ain't gettin' stuck on her already are you?" Bob said. He had a big grin on his face.

"Don't be foolish, now, Bob. I only talked to her a few minutes. I was just being neighborly and polite."

"That's what you say. And what I say is it might not take you even that long to get stuck on her," Bob said, still grinning.

Chapter Three. October, 1856.

The sun was just clearing the horizon behind them as Mitchell and Herndon Henshaw rode their horses up the last rise and onto the broad ridge top on which Olive Branch was built. Within five minutes they crossed the railroad track and the road to Memphis, and came to the center of town–what everyone called 'the square,' though it might have been more accurate to call it a triangle. They passed Jameson's Hardware on the near corner, crossed the open space at the center, then passed between West's and Brown's general stores, sitting across from each other at the far corner. The doc's office and Appling's eatery were located off to the north end, where the square narrowed down and pointed away toward the cow pens and on toward Memphis. This morning Mitchell and Hern rode straight through town without stopping. When they came to where the road divided on the far edge of town, they took the west fork toward Horn Lake and the Mississippi River.

They crossed through a shallow hollow, climbed a rise to the sharp edge of the ridge top, and dropped off the ridge into the floodplain of Camp Creek. The creek came down from northeast of town and made a line to the south toward it's confluence with the Coldwater River twelve miles away. The creek carried enough water to have made a plain nearly a mile wide down much of its length, and in many places, as here at Olive Branch, the plain was farmed on both sides of the creek.

Mitchell and Hern crossed the flat and continued on the Horn Lake road three more miles, then took the road south, through Robertson's Crossroads and on to Hernando. As they passed the turn-off for the McCall place, Hern cast a long and wistful look in that direction. Just over there, less than a mile away, Miss Madelyn McCall was eating breakfast, or maybe feeding her pet ducks. Maybe she was sleeping late and was just opening her eyes, still dressed in her nightgown. He wondered what her nightgown looked like, imagined he was looking at her in her nightgown. The thought didn't seem proper and caused him to blush slightly. Miss Madelyn McCall was right over there, just breathing, blinking her eyes, moving around, and here he was riding right past her turn without a pause. It didn't seem right.

Mitchell noticed Hern's long look toward the McCall place. "Maybe we'll have time to stop by the McCall's on the way back from Hernando. I'd like to see Matthew for a few minutes as long as we're this close," he said.

"I hope we do, Pa," Hern said. "I ran into Miss Madelyn at the Fourth of July celebration and had a good visit with her. I'd sure like to see her again."

Mitchell glanced sharply at his son, then turned back to the road, a grin spreading across his face, "Why then, we'll just make it a point to take time for a short visit whether we have it to spare or not," Mitchell said.

Shortly after mid morning Mitchell and Hern passed through the town square of Hernando, which really was laid out in a square surrounding the grounds and courthouse of the county seat. They continued on without pause until they came to a large farm in the gently rolling hills south of town. The main business of this farm was the breeding, raising, training, and selling of mules. Mitchell and Hern had arrived at the destination of their morning's journey.

A series of quarter-acre holding pens and training pens ran along the right side and the back of a large barn. A pasture stretched from the rear of the barn across a broad hilltop for a distance of over a quarter of a mile down a gently falling slope. The pasture was divided into twelve rectangular plots by six fences that ran longitudinally down its length and a single fence that ran from side to side at the midpoint. The individual plots were useful in keeping separate the various classes of animals involved in the operation of the farm.

The breeding Jacks were extremely large male donkeys, whose heritage could be traced back to Royal Gift, the giant black Jack presented to George Washington by the King of Spain in 1785. Breeders in Spain had produced an exceptionally large line of Jacks in the eighteenth century, establishing that country as the world center of mule production. But the exportation of Spanish Jacks was banned until the year 1813. Thus, Washington's possession of his Gift in 1785 presented him with a unique opportunity that he was quick to exploit. He arranged for the Gift to be bred both to numerous female horses and to numerous donkeys, thereby establishing himself not only as the father of his country but also as the father of the its mule-breeding industry.

The separate pasture plots of the farm kept the breeding Jacks apart from the brood-mare horses except under controlled conditions when a selected breeding was to take place. Since the whole purpose of this farm was to produce large mules for field work and draft use, the brood-mares, too, were exceptionally large animals, selected primarily for their size and strength, and secondarily for their gentleness and tractability.

It was also convenient to keep mares and their young foals together in their own plot, and to have plots, as well, for mature foals grown independent of their dams and undergoing training as working animals. In addition to these three animal communities, there were also the mules used for working the farm's own corn and clover fields and a small group of horses used by the farm's residents for riding and for pulling in harness.

The beauty of the farm and the animals, as well as the complexity of the necessary arrangements, made a fast and strong impression on Hern. He immediately began to have visions of himself as a mule-breeder. He knew of no mule-breeding operations located in the east half of the county; it seemed possible that he might hope to generate enough sales locally to keep an operation afloat for a few years, until he had a chance to establish a broader reputation. He knew expert training would be needed to transform mature foals into useful and dependable working animals, and he immediately thought of his Chickasaw friend, Push-pun-tubby, as a potential ally. Push alone had raised not only his dog but his two horses to a remarkable degree of training and dependability that Hern had seen nowhere else in his experience. If Push could do these things, maybe he could and would teach Hern to do them for himself. These possibilities filled his mind with the rich dream of a youth envisioning the advent of his independence, the establishment of a working operation that to him seemed as vast as an empire. "Pa," he said, "this farm is about the most interesting thing I've ever seen. I'd sure like to know more about it."

"Well, maybe we can do something about that," his father answered. "At the least I expect we'll get a closer look around it in a few minutes."

Mitchell and Hern rode up to the big barn and got down from their horses. Mitchell told a young man who had come out of the barn to meet them that they were interested in buying a mule. They wanted a young, well-broken male of good size and strength.

"Yes, sir. We're sure to have what you want here somewhere. Selling mules is what we're all about. Have you gentlemen come far this morning?" he asked.

"Not so terribly far," said Mitchell. "We just rode over from Center Hill, near Olive Branch. I'm Mitchell Henshaw and this is my son, Hern."

"Pleased to meet you both, Mr. Henshaw," the young man said, reaching out to shake hands, "I'm Jody Mimms, this is my father's farm. Let's go up to the house and get you gentlemen something to quench your thirst. I'll get Pa, and then we'll go have a look at some mules.

"You gentlemen make yourselves comfortable here on the porch and I'll get your drinks," he said, as they stepped up to the front of the house. "How about a cool glass of lemonade?"

"Thank you, that would be welcome, indeed," Mitchell answered.

Mitchell and Hern took a seat in two of the comfortable rocking chairs at one end of the long porch. In a short time Jody returned with a pitcher of lemonade and glasses. He was accompanied by a large man who looked to be in his mid forties.

"Pa," he said, "I'd like you to meet Mr. Mitchell Henshaw and Mr. Hern Henshaw. They rode over from Center Hill this morning and they'd like to look at some mules."

"Pleased to meet you Mr. Mitchell, Mr. Hern," the big man said. "I'm Ab Mimms. Maybe we can find something you like. Take your ease here for a few minutes and drink some lemonade. Then we'll ride out to the pasture."

"Pa, while these gentlemen rest, I'll go saddle up a couple of horses for us," Jody said, and walked off toward the barn.

"Ab, Hern here has taken a big interest in mules since seeing your farm. How about running over a few of their special qualities for him while we sit?"

A big smile spread across Ab's face. "Well, I'd be mighty glad to do that, Mitchell," he said. "You've just raised one of my favorite subjects.

"Mules are strong, stronger than horses or oxen. They're much quicker than oxen at doing their work, and they have great stamina. You can work 'em all day if you give them a rest and a little feed at noon. They're very intelligent. I think they're smarter than horses. Most of them are calm and tractable, easy to work with. They need less fancy feed than a horse, and they live dang near forever. Seems to me they're the perfect work animal, and they're good company for a man to spend his day with. Far as I'm concerned, they don't have any faults."

"What about the idea they're stubborn?" Hern asked. "You hear that said quite a bit."

"It's true a lot of people will say that," Mr. Mimms admitted, "but I think it's a big exaggeration. I think it's based on the fact that a mule won't hurt himself. He's too smart to work until he collapses, like a horse will do. If he reaches the point where he shouldn't go any further, he just quits. You can't get him to do any more and you shouldn't try. He is stubborn about not killing himself for you, but as far as I'm concerned, that's another of his good qualities. His master may be stupid enough to work a mule to death, but the mule is too smart to let him do it. If a mule is well trained, well treated, and handled properly, that's the only thing he'll be stubborn about."

Jody had come back up to the porch leading Mitchell's and Hern's horses and two for himself and Mr. Mimms.

"Well, if you gentlemen are ready, let's go out to the pasture," said Mr. Mimms.

They rode out to a plot toward the back of the big pasture that contained two dozen young male mules. Mr. Mimms said they were all three years old and all had been gelded.

"All mules are supposed to be sterile, anyway," he said to Hern, "that's part of their hybrid heritage. But they're sexually active, anyway, unless they're gelded. Besides, gelding makes the males more easy going and handier to work with."

After a while, Mitchell's attention settled on a large, black mule–black all the way out to his points and his dark muzzle. He was tall, at fifteen-and-a-half hands, and was heavily muscled. He looked like he could pull a breaking plow all by himself.

"Ab, I'm getting partial to that black animal there. I think I'll take him off your hands if you don't have too high a price on him," Mitchell said.

"Mitchell, you know those 'blue nosed' mules are kind of rare," Mr. Mimms answered. "I could let you have one of the others for a lower price."

"I appreciate that, Ab. But I intended to pick the best mule in the lot. I have to expect you know your own animals better than I do."

"He's well trained, too. He can do it all. I'll be glad to take him up to the barn and show him off for you," Mr. Mimms said.

"No, I'm confident you know your animals," Mitchell answered.

"Well then, there's two ways we can go about this. I can start a little high and we can dance around a while and work the price down, or I can just give you my best price up front and you can decide whether to go with it or not. Now I prefer the second route, but I can do it either way that pleases you."

"No, I entirely agree with you, Ab. Just start off with your best price and we'll see what we can do."

"Alright then, I figure I need three-hundred dollars to let him leave the place," said Ab. "That's a good price for me, but I figure I'll get it for him within the next few months whether you take him or not. I don't feel like I can let him go for less."

"Done," said Mitchell.

Across the fence in the next plot were a number of mature foals a year or more old. While the others had been studying the three-year-olds, Hern had drifted over to the fence where he had been watching the young mules in the adjoining plot. Seeing that Pa had concluded his deal for the black mule, Hern called out to him.

"Pa, could I speak to you for a minute, please?" he asked.

Mitchell rode over to where Hern waited while Mr. Mimms and Jody kept their distance. "What is it, Hern? I see you've been studying that bunch of youngsters," he said.

"Yes sir, I have. Pa, I'd sure like to have one of those to take home and train. I want to train it myself. I want to get the experience. I could get plenty of help from Push, I think. I've never seen animals that behaved as well as his do."

"Well I think that's a mighty good idea, Hern. I'm pleased you thought of it." Mitchell turned and called back to Mr. Mimms, "Say Ab, I think we'd like to take one of these youngsters along with us, too. Let's see if we can work out a price on one."

Ab Mimms rode over while Jody called up the black mule, gave him a handful of the feed he'd stuck in his pocket back at the barn, and slipped a halter over his head.

"Do you have one picked out, son?" Mitchell asked Hern.

"Yes sir. I like that brown one with the light tan forehead and points, if he's alright with you."

15

"He looks fine to me, son. What do you need to get for him, Ab?"

"He looks good to me, too, Hern," said Mr. Mimms. Then turning to Mitchell, "All those youngsters are broken to lead, but nothing else. I'll take seventy-five dollars for him, Mitch."

"Done again," said Mitchell.

It was nearing mid afternoon when Mitchell and Hern turned into the lane leading to the McCall house just outside Robertson's Crossroads. The house was on the top of a tall hill above Camp Creek. The view from the hill across Camp Creek Bottom, where Mr. McCall farmed, bordered on the spectacular. Hern took in the view, thought it a proper back-drop for Miss Madelyn McCall. Mitchell and Hern tied their stock to a fence beside the lane and walked up the steps and onto the porch. The house itself was of log construction, very similar to their own.

Mrs. Martha McCall met them at the door, having seen them ride up. "Why Mitch Henshaw, we haven't seen you around here since The Flood, it seems! How good it is to see you! Matthew will be so pleased."

"Hello, Martha," Mitchell replied. "Lord, it's good to see you. You look like a ray of sunshine. You remember my son Hern, I'm sure."

"Well I certainly remember the Hern Henshaw I last saw, but can this be the same fellow? Why I can see that it must be, but my goodness, Hern, you've grown into a fine, tall man while I wasn't looking. It's very nice to see you again.

"Come into the house, you two, and we'll have some tea. Maddie, oh Maddie, come and see who's come to visit. You won't believe it. It's the two Henshaw men."

Madelyn managed a graceful entry into the room, but her face clearly bore a flush of excitement. "Why Mr. Mitchell Henshaw, Mr. Herndon Henshaw, what a pleasure it is to see you both!" she said. "I'm so happy you came to visit."

"Good afternoon, Miss Madelyn," said Mitchell, taking her outstretched hands into his own. "My, what a fine young lady you've become! I can see now why Hern's been pushing the pace this last hour."

"Aw, Pa. Well, maybe I did push the pace just a little, Miss Madelyn. It's very good to see you again," said Hern. He delighted in taking her outstretched hands, as his father had done, and he managed to hold them just a bit longer than usual for such a greeting. No one appeared to take notice of this, but in fact, all had noticed it, Madelyn with secret pleasure, Mitchell and Martha with eye-twinkling amusement.

"Well come and have a seat," Martha said, "we'll have some tea. How are Elise and the other children? Have you just ridden over from Center Hill?"

"Everyone's just fine, Martha. We've just been over to Hernando to pick up a couple of mules. Where is old Matthew? I trust he is well."

"Oh he's as fine as ever. He's just over in the near field. They're turning under the corn stalks over there. You can ride down to see him in a few minutes if he didn't see you come in. Hern can stay here and entertain Maddie and me."

"I don't know how much entertainment I'll be, Miss Martha, but I'll be glad to try," Hern said.

"Nonsense, Hern, I'm sure you'll do very nicely," she replied.

"Would you read something for us, Mr. Henshaw?" Madelyn asked. Mitchell had ridden down the hill to visit Matthew McCall, and the three of them still sat in the living room. A fire burned cheerfully in the big fireplace at the end of the room, although the day was only comfortably cool.

"Why I'd be happy to," said Hern. "There is a piece in *Romeo and Juliet*, I've always liked it, but lately I find I like it even more."

"Yes, I think we can find that one," Mrs. McCall said. Hern accompanied her to the bookcase. "Yes, here it is. Here you are Hern."

Mrs. McCall returned to her seat. Hern remained standing before the two of them, sought out his passage and began to read.

> He jests at scars that never felt a wound.
> But, soft! What light through yonder window breaks?
> It is the east, and Juliet is the sun!
> Arise, fair sun, and kill the envious moon,
> Who is already sick and pale with grief
> That thou her maid art far more fair than she.
> Be not her maid, since she is envious.
> Her vestal livery is but sick and green,
> And none but fools do wear it. Cast it off.
> It is my lady, oh, it is my love!
> Oh, that she knew she were!
> She speaks, yet she says nothing. What of that?
> Her eye discourses, I will answer it.
> I am too bold, 'tis not to me she speaks.
> Two of the fairest stars in all the heaven,

> Having some business, do entreat her eyes
> To twinkle in their spheres till they return.
> What if her eyes were there, they in her head?
> The brightness of her cheek would shame those stars
> As daylight doth a lamp; her eyes in heaven
> Would through the airy region stream so bright
> That birds would sing and think it were not night.
> See how she leans her cheek upon her hand!
> Oh, that I were a glove upon that hand,
> That I might touch that cheek!

"A gallant choice, indeed, Hern. That was quite lovely," said Mrs. McCall.

"What a wonderful choice, Mr. Henshaw!" exclaimed Madelyn. "That has always been one of my favorites. It is so romantic. I can only dream that someday, perhaps someone might feel that way about me. Oh, it is too wonderful to be true."

"No, Miss Madelyn, it certainly is not too wonderful to be true. I would scarcely be surprised to find that someone does feel that way about you," Hern said softly.

"Would you take a turn of the grounds with me, Miss Madelyn? Would it be alright, Mrs. McCall?"

"Of course, Hern. I think that is an excellent idea. Maddie?"

"I would be delighted, Mr. Henshaw. Just let me get my shawl," said Madelyn, a radiant smile lighting her face.

The couple stepped to the door. "Do you still have those pet ducks, Miss Madelyn?" Hern asked.

"Why, Mr. Henshaw. Of course I do."

Chapter Four. November, 1856.

The riders were three hours out from Center Hill and nearing the head-waters of Little Coldwater Creek, where they would make camp for a three-day hunting trip. It was a bright day in late fall. Most of the leaves had left the trees by now, but here and there were bright pockets of red and yellow maples, wine-colored white oaks, and gums in various colors from yellow to orange to deep red. The air was singing and snapping with life. They had ridden through wild country for many miles now, trailing through the hills in a long line behind their leader and guide, Push-pun-tubby. Their way wound along rough pathways that were little more than traces, lines of scant opening through unmarked forest.

Push-pun-tubby was a full-blood Chickasaw, nephew of the clan chief Lush-pun-tubby, who had sold much of the land here to speculators, from whom the men in the hunting party had bought it, in turn. Push had stayed behind when almost the entire Chickasaw tribe had emigrated from their homeland to Oklahoma territory back in '36 and '37 under pressure from the National Government. He stayed much to himself on an 80-acre tract his uncle had held back for him at the time of the land deals. His place lay in rough country along the bluff above the Coldwater River Bottom three miles east of the white-settled land around the community of Center Hill.

Push had taken care to extend a hand to the white settlers a few years ago when they had struggled to carve out their farms from the wild land.

He had become friends with many of the families and often accompanied the men when they went out into the wilderness for deer in the late fall. He was particularly close to the Henshaw family.

They were nine men in all, six horses and six mules, nine of the animals carrying riders and three of the mules carrying packs of camping gear, provisions, and their own feed. There were Push and his dog Rube, in the lead, followed by Mitchell Henshaw and two of his neighbors, Dave Wilson and Ed Oakley, then Bob and Hern Henshaw, all on horses, then George, his son Zak, and Price, all Henshaw-family slaves, each riding a mule and holding the lead rope of one of the pack mules. Five of Wilson's large hounds and three of Oakley's trailed along behind the riders at their own pace. The dogs were used to hunting together, and with these men. Different individuals among them moved off the path from time to time to investigate a sight or smell but always hurried back to rejoin the group.

Push led the riders across and down a steep slope onto a bench of open woodland above a tributary of Little Coldwater Creek. The spot was a mile above where the tributary joined the Creek and about two miles above the confluence of the Creek with the Coldwater River, itself. The confluence was only a few miles downstream from the origin of the River in springs emerging from the base of a tall ridge of hills to the east. Little Coldwater Creek extended three miles north of the River in a tall Y to its own origins in two streams that also began with the outflow of springs at the base of the ridge. The rough curvature of the ridge around a huge semicircle formed an enclosed bowl of bottomland four miles wide and four miles deep. It was a place the men came every two years or so to hunt, as they had been doing for many years before Hern was old enough to accompany them.

The men selected spots where the heavy tarpaulins would be hung, where the fire would be, and where the stock would be tethered on picket lines tied shoulder-high from convenient trees. As the others went about the tasks of setting up camp, Push took up his bow, and with Rube at his side, slipped on foot up into the hills above camp to try for a young deer they could butcher for supper. He hoped to supply proper food for the hunters' first night and to set the stage for a successful hunt over the next three days. His use of the bow would avoid disturbing animals in the area where the main hunt was to be made and, besides, was a personal preference that would start his own hunt in the way he most respected.

Push worked his way uphill, past the spot where the stream along which they were camped emerged as a series of springs, and moved silently along the ridge of a hollow that fed down toward the head of the stream.

He came upon a faint deer trail that lead onto a small bench columned with the large, widely distributed trunks of white oaks. The ground was heavily strewn with large acorns, and the leaf-mold was scratched about and disturbed from the feeding of deer and squirrels. He strung a 30-inch hunting arrow armed with a two-inch flint arrowhead onto his bow and took a stance against a tree so that the outline of his body was merged into that of the tree, hidden from the view of an approaching animal, and settled in to wait. Rube lay against the tree at his side.

Now that he had ceased his own movement, the sounds of the forest around him began to speak more clearly to his senses. He heard the slight rustling of leaves as squirrels fed on the ground not far away. The timing of the sounds, signifying small hops as the animals moved about over the ground, told him they were squirrels, not deer. He heard the cheerful whistles exchanged by a group of chickadees as they fed in the trees nearby. A large gray squirrel hopped into the floor of leaves and acorns before him and he watched as it fed.

After a while, Push heard the sound of another animal approaching along the deer trail crossing the hollow below him. The sound was so low and subtle that it was almost like imagination, but Push had no doubt of its reality–the intermittent, faint crunching of leaves made by an approaching deer. He slowly tightened his bowstring to half draw, the arrow still pointing to the ground, and waited. The deer stepped into the open before him, a young six-point buck in prime condition. The deer stood for a few moments listening to the forest, alert for a sound or smell of danger, for a flash of nearby movement; then it shook its tail in what looked like a gesture of relaxation and began to feed on the acorns. Rube remained perfectly still and quiet, looking at the deer.

As the deer fed, Push slowly, slowly raised his bow and oriented it toward the deer; his movement, slight as it was, was made at times when the deer itself moved about in its feeding. By the time his arrow lined up on the deer's right shoulder, Push had pulled his bow to full draw. The deer made a slight move that afforded nearly a straight side-on shot and Push released his bowstring. The arrow drove in behind the deer's shoulder to the depth of the feathers.

The deer leapt straight in the air, then bounded away back in the direction from which it had come. Push noted the direction of movement and listened to the faint sounds of the deer's passage but otherwise was still. He didn't bother to string another arrow but merely stood quietly for a few minutes, then he and Rube walked over to the spot where the deer had been shot. He looked with satisfaction at the bright arterial blood that trailed away along the deer's path of escape. Rube led the way as he and Push followed the trail easily for seventy yards to where the deer lay dead in the path, just over the ridge of the little hollow from which it had approached.

"Nice going, Push," Mitchell called, looking up as Push approached the camp, dragging the field-dressed buck behind him by the antlers, "I figured we could count on you for some meat."

"Here, Push, let me help you hang that buck," Dave Wilson said. "Then I'll help you skin him and butcher him."

Dusk settled in the camp on the bench above the small creek in the woods. Smoke from the fire drifted above the men's heads on a breeze so light and casual as to be seen more in the easy drift of smoke than felt. Horses and mules rested easily on their tethers, as the hunting hounds did on theirs. Several of the dogs lay curled up, seemingly sleeping. Deer steaks sputtered in bacon grease in a big cast iron skillet on the fire, and beans charged with slices of bacon simmered in a half-gallon pot.

"You make good whiskey, Ed, just like always," said Mitchell Henshaw.

"I ain't tasted the like of it since I left Tennessee," Dave Wilson said.

"Thank you, boys, it does go down good, if I say so myself," Ed Oakley said. Ed was sitting at his ease on a big log a little back from the fire. On his feet, he stood six-foot-five and towered above most any company. Dave Wilson was of medium height, lean and wiry, tough as a piece of dried leather.

"Bring your cups over here, George, Price. I'll pour you a drink from the jug. Hell, we got plenty," Ed Oakley said.

"Why thank you, suh," George said, "that'd be mighty fine, indeed." He and Price walked over and held their cups out to the jug.

"How should we hunt tomorrow, Push?" Mitchell asked.

"I think maybe we should make a drive down the west fork at the head of Coldwater Creek. Let George and Price and Zak start the dogs from a little ways up the hill and let them work down along both sides of the stream toward the junction with the east fork. Set half the dogs on either side of the stream. George and them can stay alert on the upstream side to catch anything that turns back in their direction. The rest of us can take up stands downstream and try to cut off anything that drives toward us.

"Day after tomorrow we can drive down the east fork of the Y. The last day we can hunt the lower part of the Creek down to where it joins up with the River."

"That sounds good enough to me. What do you think Dave, Ed?" Mitchell said.

"Sounds like a good plan. Fine," they said.

"If it stays clear, we'll have plenty of moonlight in the morning and can get into place before daybreak, then they can set the dogs on the trail at first sunlight," Mitchell said.

"It'll stay clear," Push said.

The men sat spread around the fire after supper, sipping on Oakley's whiskey. Oakley smoked a pipe and Wilson a cigar. A great-horned owl spoke from the ridge above them, answered shortly by another, probably its mate. Barred owls talked back and forth from the depths of the bottomland woods before them. After a while they heard the slow, deep howl of a wolf from a good distance away, probably on the other side of the Coldwater River south and east of them. A few seconds later came the answering howl of another member of its pack. The howls seemed to reverberate for a long time through the cold air and the dark forest. Ed Oakley expressed an appreciation that was shared by the group. "That's a fine, wild sound," he said. "I'd ride a long way to hear that."

Push sat off a little distance from the rest of the hunters, listening to the night and sipping whiskey. Hern walked over to join him. "Would it be a bother if I sat with you for a minute, Push? There's something I've been wanting to ask you about," he said.

"No, Hern. I'm glad to have your company," Push answered.

"I've been thinking I'd like to learn to train mules, Push. Pa and I brought back a young gelding from Hernando the other day, and I hope to train him myself. Only I don't know the first thing about training. I've been thinking I'd like to run my own mule-breeding operation in a few years. Training the young mules would be a big part of it. If I can learn to do that, it'll be a good start on my plans," Hern said.

"You're the best trainer I know, Push. I wonder if you'd be willing to help me learn. I know it's a lot to ask."

"It's not much to ask, Hern, not between us, anyway. I figure we're pretty good friends," Push said. "But I have to tell you I don't think of myself as an animal trainer. Not at all."

"But I don't understand, Push!" Hern said. "Your animals are the best

---

behaved I've ever seen! It seems like they'll do anything you want them to. Surely you trained them. Didn't you?"

"Well, it's true we worked together a lot, and they've learned to work with me," Push said. "I guess they'd do about anything I'd suggest. But I didn't have to train them to do those things. Mostly they just do things that pretty near all dogs and horses already know how to do. The difference is they've learned to do those things in cooperation with me. It's about forming partnerships far more than training.

"I had to learn how to let them know what I'd like for us to do, and I had to give them a chance to learn confidence in my leadership. I had to try to think like a dog and to think like a horse. That's what you'll have to learn, too. It takes time and patience, but if you have those, you can learn it as well as I did.

"Horses and dogs are both sociable by nature, and both of them like to have ties with us. Part of their nature is that they'll follow a leader. All we have to do is to be good leaders and make sure they have reasons to learn confidence in our leadership."

"I never thought about it like that, Push," Hern said.

"No reason you should have," said Push. "Few people ever do. But that's how you want to start thinking.

"Dogs and horses are alike in being sociable but opposite in the roles they play in the world. Dogs are predators, like their cousins the wolves. Horses, on the other hand, are prey animals. When you work with them you have to think about the fears of a prey animal–fears that keep them alive when predators everywhere want to kill them. You can't ask them to do things a prey animal can't do if it expects to keep living–not unless you find a way to give them so much confidence in you that it overrides their natural fear."

"Well, I knew I'd have a lot to learn," Hern said. "I just hope I can do it."

"You can do it, alright. It'll be fun. I'll help you."

The sky began to gray and lighten where Hern stood in a cathedral-like area of the big woods on the camp side of the creek down which they were hunting. He was surrounded by huge timber of water oak, overcup oak, willow oak and, along the borders of the creek, cow oak. The creek itself lay a dozen yards east, to his right. He and Push were in the final line of hunters who had distributed themselves in concentric rings along the projected course of the day's drive down the west fork of Little Coldwater

Creek. Push had taken a position somewhere on the far side of the creek a half mile or so east of Hern.

Hern heard the distant cawing of crows and the twittering of birds with the strengthening of light across the forest. Despite his full knowledge of the hunters arrayed above him for two miles upstream along the creek, he had the feeling that he was utterly alone in the wilderness. Just then he heard the first voices of the hounds as they struck a trail in the distance to the north. It seemed likely they were on his side of the creek. Within the first two minutes he could tell the chase was going as they had hoped, proceeding downstream through the bottomland where the hunters had taken their stands.

Then he heard a chase begin on the far side of the creek. It, too, seemed to be heading downstream for the first couple of minutes, then turned to the east and on around back to the north, toward the area where George or Price or Zak had released the dogs. Hern heard the crack of a rifle, its sharpness dulled by distance, then a minute or two later, the excited jabber of the dogs as they closed on the site of the kill.

Meanwhile, the chase continued down his side of the stream, now halfway to him from where it had started. He thought it may already have passed the first tier of hunters, his brother Bob and Mr. Wilson. Then he heard the sharp bark of a rifle, and knew that another deer was likely down. After a while, he heard the dogs close in at the culmination of the chase.

Hern relaxed and dug a biscuit from his coat pocket and began to eat. It seemed they had two deer down already in the first hour of day, and there would be at least a short delay before the dogs could be set on a fresh chase. He finished the biscuit and stood listening to the vast silence of the woods that seemed to be waiting for something, maybe for him to make some response to its huge presence—at once challenging and implacable. Without conscious thought, he assayed for a path of direct relation to that presence, a way to enter companionship with the force that confronted him. His response seemed inadequate—he had hardly done anything at all—yet immediately he felt a sense of elevated awareness of and connection with his surroundings. He felt exaltation, perfect satisfaction, profound meaning in the connection.

He stood as in a waking dream. His senses registered the beginning of a fresh chase break out on the far side of the creek, perhaps a mile and a half above him. As the chase proceeded over its first few minutes it was as though something within the vastness of his surroundings had turned its focus in his direction. The hounds were still more than half a mile away and on the far side of the creek, yet he felt something was about to happen right in front of him. He felt he had never been more aware of his surroundings, more intent upon the input of his senses. He raised his rifle to the ready position.

The form of the deer seemed to coalesce before him, already several steps out into the open area of his view and continuing toward his position in absolute silence. Its coat shone as a gray, blue-gray light, its nose contrasting in sharp black, its horns bursting from the background in pure and striking white. Very slowly he raised his rifle to bear upon the neck and shoulder as the deer flowed forward in graceful steps. Hern observed that his own movement was smooth; nevertheless, it felt jerky. He looked down the barrel of the gun and saw it steady, yet the muscles of his arms seemed to him at the last extreme of quietude, at the nearest edge to the onset of shaking. He took in a full breath in conscious effort to remain calm. The buck turned slightly to the side toward the sound of the approaching hounds.

Hern saw the sights of the rifle line up on the animal's left shoulder and began squeezing the trigger as smoothly as he could manage, trying to hold absolutely steady and to have no expectation of when the discharge would come. Then it did come, and the deer went down sharply to its far side, all weight swept from its feet by the force of the arriving bullet.

The deer lay unmoving where it had landed as Hern set about reloading his rifle with shaking hands. He stood for a few more seconds, reloaded rifle at the ready, though unsure he retained the ability to hold it steady for another shot. Then he began to reclaim a sense of calm, began to believe a further shot would be unneeded. He walked up slowly to the spot where the deer lay unmoving, watched it closely for long seconds from a few feet away. He kicked noisily at the leaves at his feet, finally stepped carefully up to the body and nudged it on the left shoulder with the toe of his boot. The deer was dead, and he saw he had shot it through the neck, just forward of the shoulder that had been his aiming point.

He heard the dogs cross the creek two hundred feet above him, working rapidly down the trail of the buck's approach to where it now lay. Push appeared out of the woods to his right and came to his side.

"Looks like an eight-point," he said.

Everyone was back in camp by noon. The dogs had been gathered and fed and now lay drowsing at their tethers in the shade. The three deer from the day's hunt hung by the heels from nearby trees. Besides Hern's eight-point buck there were six-pointers killed by George and by Dave Wilson. Oakley, Mitchell, and Bob had passed up several shots at does, as was the common practice of the group. Bob maintained he'd seen a buck slip past his post at long range. He might have made a try for it despite the range but had been unable to get a clear shot through the trees and brush.

Most of the hunters were satisfied with the morning's production, but Bob and Zak wanted more action. Push suggested they explore the area above camp where he had hunted the previous afternoon to see if they could obtain enough squirrels for tonight's supper. He said he would prepare flour dumplings to go with the squirrels he was sure they would provide. They returned in late afternoon with fourteen squirrels. Together with the remains of yesterday's deer meat, the squirrels made a flavorful stew to accompany Push's dumplings.

Next morning before daylight, the hunters breakfasted on fried bacon, grits, biscuits, and coffee, and set off for the day's hunt down the east fork of the creek. Bob made the first kill on a four-point buck, Mitchell and Oakley each killed six-pointers, and Wilson brought in an eight-pointer. Zak killed a fat four-pointer that was slipping back up into the hills behind the dogs. Push passed up an easy shot at a young spike, and Hern saw nothing that morning but a single doe.

Rain poured off the tarpaulins in the night before the final hunt, but the weather broke after midnight and morning came in clear and cold with the passing of a front. Hern and Push again positioned themselves as the last tier of hunters, this time with their backs to the Coldwater River on either side of its confluence with the creek.

The dogs started drives down both sides of the creek. Three separate shots rang out from the hunters upstream. After a half-hour's silence, another chase broke out on the east side of the creek toward Push's location. Hern remained in position until he heard the crack of Push's rifle, then crossed over to Push's side of the creek. When he was halfway to where Push had shot, he heard a second chorusing of dogs on a hot trail from the west. He heard shots and men whooping, and the chase crossed the creek and was driving toward him. Again he felt the impact of some vast focus of attention and stood against a tree, trying to quiet his breathing, in a state of hyper-awareness.

As he watched, a great cat—a panther—materialized from the forest before him and stood looking in his direction. Its massive head stretched more than five inches between its two uplifted ears. The separate hairs of its tawny coat seemed to stand as individual centers of life, and its visage seemed the coalescence of all the light in the forest. Hern's memory flashed to his extraordinary experience with the rabbits years before. Again he felt the utter stoppage of his verbal thinking—the onset of a striking awareness beyond words. The lion turned side-on to him and snuffled at the ground with its muzzle, raised its massive head once more and looked straight toward him, took two steps forward and stood there. Hern was aware of the gun in his hands but knew he would make no effort to raise it.

The cat stood looking at him for long moments, then turned casually and moved away toward the river. Turning his head to follow his final view of the animal, Hern found himself looking directly at Push, who, he was amazed to realize, must have been standing behind him and almost at his side the entire time. Push's gun was held in one hand, in easy position at the end of his relaxed arm and beside his leg. He had made no offer to take a shot at the cat. Their eyes met for a moment. Each recognized the other's feelings fully, for they were the same feelings.

A slight sound came from the woods in front of them as a six-point buck stepped out into the clear. It lifted its head quickly in confusion at the scent of the cat. Without hesitation Push raised his gun smoothly and shot the animal through the heart. They walked over and began to field-dress the carcass.

"What will we say about the other?" Hern said. "We didn't even try to get him."

"Maybe we won't say anything," Push said. "We have a nice deer right here. And the other I shot a little earlier."

"But they're liable to ask about the cat. They may have shot at him. I heard somebody whooping. They're likely to have seen his tracks."

"Then we'll say the truth. We couldn't get a good shot at him. That's true enough, isn't it? Only you and I need know why we couldn't."

Chapter Five. December, 1856.

"Hold the fort out here for a while, will you Moot?" Red Jameson called to his assistant. "Mr. Henshaw and I have some business in my office." It was ten o'clock of a morning a few days before Christmas in Mr. Jameson's hardware store in Olive Branch. Mitchell handed Mr. Jameson a package of presents for the Jameson family, then took a comfortable seat before Red's office desk.

"I've got some fresh coffee here, Mitch," Red said, booming it out as though in celebration of something significant, at the same time pulling out two coffee cups, "and a good supply of flavoring to make it fresher, yet." He reached below the desk for a jug of whiskey.

"Alright, Red, if you're sure it's not too early in the day," Mitchell replied with a grin.

"Too early!" Red roared with a laugh, apparently hilariously amused, "Why, don't be crazy, man! Of course it's not too early."

The two settled into easy conversation about their families and households. Mitchell raised his cup to his lips for the third time. "Well I will freely admit it, Red," he said, "you make mighty refreshing coffee."

"Refreshing?" Red boomed out, "Ha, ha, ha, why of course it is, Mitch. Of course it's refreshing.

"Looks like there's a big problem building up in the Kansas Territory, Mitch," Red said after a moment. "Have you heard about it?"

"I don't believe I have, Red. What's going on?" Mitchell said.

"There was a piece in the Memphis paper yesterday," Red said. "Seems there's a fight shaping up over the 'Local Sovereignty' position on slavery."

" 'Local Sovereignty,' " Mitchell repeated. "The people of Kansas have to decide for themselves whether they'll have slavery in the territory."

"That's right, Mitch. And it looks like Kansas is about to split down the middle. Neither side is showing signs they'll accept a majority decision if it goes against them."

"If they stick to that course, they could end up with civil war in the territory," Mitchell said.

"That's the way it looks to me, Mitch. That's what I'm talking about."

"There's a fellow named Buford–calls himself Colonel Buford–he's organized a bunch of armed men he calls the Kickapoo Rangers. There's an opposing group led by an abolitionist named John Brown. Neither man appears open to a reasonable solution–not unless it's one that goes his way. Looks like a passel of hotheads on both sides."

"I was hoping the Clay Compromise would hold a lid on it for a good while," Mitchell said. "I guess it was too much to hope for."

"Damn it all, Mitchell," Red said, "You may not like hearing this, but slavery's been an abomination in this country from the beginning. It's a problem that won't go away. We can put it off and put it off, but it keeps coming back. It will keep coming back until we stop it at the point where it started."

"No, Red, I don't like hearing it–probably not any more than you like saying it," Mitchell said. "I'd like to argue with you but I can't–I've thought the same thing too often, myself. I wish to God they'd stopped it at the beginning," Mitchell said. "I know they wanted to; many of them tried hard to do it."

"They tried," Red said, "but they couldn't succeed. In the end it was a choice of having a country with slavery or having no country at all."

"God help us, Red, we may come to the same choice again," Mitchell said. "The talk keeps boiling up. It's been boiling up every few years all my life."

"That's right, Mitch, that's right. But somehow we've held it together this far. Maybe we can keep on holding it together," Red said.

The friends sat on this conclusion for a while. Red refilled their cups, drawing upon his full range of supply.

"I've heard people trying to explain slavery all my life," Mitchell said, finally. "I've even tried to explain it to myself. I never heard a decent explanation–mine or anybody else's. I've tried to accept it as the way things have always been. Maybe I've been a little too successful about accepting it."

"Maybe we all have, Mitch," Red said. "Maybe we all have. But that doesn't really satisfy the question, does it? It doesn't leave us with something we can be proud of."

"It let's us muddle through, Red. That's about the best you can say for it."

They sat for a minute, drank from their cups. Then Red spoke again.

"What about a man like you, Mitch? With your operation? How could you get along without slaves?"

"Well, I can't get along without the help of people like George and Price–not and run the same operation. But the operation supports all of us as it is now. It could support all of us whether I *owned* George and Price or not, just so long as they worked for me the same way."

"I've thought the same thing, Mitch," Red said, "but you'd be going against the accepted practice of the country around you. And it wouldn't be just you and your family. George and Price have to live here too. We both know people that wouldn't take kindly to free Negroes living among them. I doubt they'd move against *you*, but what they might do to George and Price could be mighty ugly."

"Still, the fact is, economically at least, we could do it. That is, a man with a middling operation like me could do it. I'm not so sure about the big operators. I expect it looks to them like a harder proposition. They see the situation as it is as the foundation of their success. I doubt they'd welcome seeing it challenged. I doubt they'd give it up easily."

"No, no, they may never be ready to give it up," Red said. "But, damn it, Mitch, some time and somehow we're going to have to turn loose of it. It's got a hard hold on us. It won't be easy to break free of it."

"Maybe it's true we have to, Red," Mitchell answered, "but I don't know how we can."

"Well, we won't be able to solve that one this morning, Mitch. But I am glad to say we've earned another drink."

"Let me tell you a story, Mitch," Red Jameson said, after a while. "It's a true story, and you might say it's a Christmas story. Yes," he laughed with great content. "Yes, by God, it *is* a Christmas story!

"I was in here late a couple of nights ago, getting my books up to date, and along about one o'clock in the morning I heard this loud knocking at the back door, there. Well, I thought immediately something might have gone wrong at home and I hurried over there and opened it straight up.

"And there stood a tall man with a black shawl thrown over his shoulders and a dark handkerchief drawn over his nose across his face. And he was holding a big single-barrel shotgun, and it was pointed at me. He didn't say anything, but just motioned me to step back, which I did, and he stepped in after me and closed the door.

"He sort of backed me over to the desk, here, and he started motioning with that gun to the bottom drawer where I keep my cash. Now, I hated to see him do that, because I knew I had more than six hundred dollars in there—more than I almost ever keep in here, and for just this reason. But there it was. The money didn't mean so much to me that I wanted him to shoot me over it—besides, if he knew where it was, he could have just knocked me in the head and taken it anyway.

"So I went ahead and opened it up for him. He looked down in there, and he could see all that money just sitting there, and he motioned at me with the gun and held up one finger. Like this.

"Well, this is quite a particular, gunman, I thought. Not only does he want my money, apparently he wants me to count it out for him, too. I looked back at him, and he held up that finger again. One. And he pointed at the palm of his hand. One.

"So I counted out one hundred dollars for him and put it in his hand. I went to bend down and get him another hundred, but he stuck the gun across and waved me away. I looked back at the rest of that money and then back at the gunman, and he shook his head at me. And he held up his finger again. One. Then he stuck my hundred dollars in a pocket of his jacket and motioned me over to my chair, here, and sat me down.

"Now, by this time, I had got to thinking I might recognize this robber, and I got to thinking that as well as I could make him out, he looked and acted exactly like Wiley Johns. Well, he sat me down in my chair, and he started backing his way to the door. When he got there, he stood for a second and looked to see whether I was watching, then he opened the breech of that gun and held it out toward me, and I could see he hadn't had it loaded to begin with. Then he opened the door, backed out, and closed it behind him.

"After a minute or two I got up and locked the doors and went on home. I knew Wiley had been having a mighty hard time lately, but I thought he was still in jail over at Hernando for fighting off that debt-agent that came to take possession of his mules.

"So the next morning, I took a ride over to Hernando to see Gene McBarttle about it. He checked with his deputy and came back and told me they knew Wiley was in his cell the previous night for supper, and that he'd been there again when they brought breakfast that morning. I knew he was supposed to have been locked in there in the meantime, but Gene didn't stress that, and I decided not to make an issue out of it either.

"I told McBarttle thanks and said I guessed I'd be getting on back to Olive Branch."

"'You don't want to press charges, Red'?" he said. "'I don't guess anybody would blame you if you did.'

"No, Gene," I said, "I guess I'll just let it ride. It seems like Wiley's got a pretty good alibi. And I guess he's had about enough trouble lately as it is.

"'Well, I guess there's something to be said for that, too,' Gene said."

"So you just let it go, then?" Mitchell asked.

"Yes. I let it go," Red answered. "But that ain't the end of the story.

"A day later, Wiley's wife came into the store. Far as I could tell, she was acting like she always does. I mean, she didn't seem shy or guilty or anything like that. The only thing different about her was that she seemed a lot happier than I had seen her in a long time. Well, old Wiley must have visited a few more of his friends that night than just me, because Mrs. Johns bought more goods in my store that morning than the hundred dollars' worth Wiley had hit me up for.

"'It's so good to be able to buy a few things again, Mr. Jameson,' she told me. Then she said, 'We've been scraping by hard for such a long time.'

"Yes ma'am, I told her, I sure appreciate your business. And I'm glad things are going better for you and Wiley."

"That's quite a story, Red. I must say I admire how you handled it," Mitchell said.

"Well, I can't take much credit," Red said. "I can't say I admire how Wiley handled his problems. I'd like to think you or I would have handled them better. But how do we know if we would have or not. We've never been where Wiley's been, and I'm mighty glad we haven't.

"Anyway, I guess he needed that hundred dollars a lot worse than I did."

Chapter Six. December, 1856.

Hern was seated before the fire in the McCall living room with Madelyn, her young sister Janie, her mother and her father. He had distributed two Christmas gifts from the Henshaw family to the McCall family. He reached further into his Christmas bag and drew out a slim, gift-wrapped volume. "And here is something especially for you, Miss Madelyn. I took the liberty of selecting it for you myself. I dare hope it will be pleasing to you."

"Oh, my, Mr. Henshaw," Madelyn protested, "you shouldn't have gone to so much trouble for me! But I'm so glad you did! Thank you so much. I can't wait to see what it is."

Madelyn quickly unwrapped the package, taking care to avoid tearing the decorative paper and to preserve the gift tag, which read, in Hern's hand, "To Miss Madelyn McCall, with the love and esteem of the Henshaw family."

"It is Byron!" she exclaimed. "Mr. Henshaw, how did you choose so wisely? I am sure he is my favorite poet. I shall treasure this always." She opened the book and read, to herself, the inscription Hern had written on the inside cover.

"To Miss Madelyn McCall, from one who hopes to be found a true and loyal friend, and your servant always, Herndon Henshaw, Christmas, 1856."

Madelyn blushed beautifully. "What a lovely inscription!" she said.

"It makes the gift all the more perfect. The friendship it proclaims is so welcome to me. Please know, Mr. Henshaw, that you will always have mine in return."

Hern could not have been more pleased. He sat basking and bemused at the success of his gift, happy to observe that Maddie's parents appeared almost as pleased as he was at its reception.

"Hern, you know your parents have always been among the closest friends of our family," Mr. McCall said. "I'm sure it must be gratifying to them, as it is to Martha and me, to see the growth of friendship between you and Maddie."

"Yes, sir, I'm sure that is true," Hern said. He knew his parents had been both pleased and amused at his eagerness to deliver the gifts to the McCall family. Pa had been quick to suggest he might take the buggy for his errand. "It may be you and Miss Madelyn will want to go out for a buggy ride," Pa had said.

And that is exactly what they did. With the ready blessing of her parents, Maddie and Hern ventured into the bright afternoon in the Henshaw buggy. Maddie's cheeks glowed with the excitement of the day and the stimulating effects of the cool air. They drove past Mr. McCall's big barn at the base of the ridge on which stood the McCall home. Through an open end of the barn, beneath the wide spread of the tin roof, they could see big hay racks bulging with hay. The sweet and homey smell of the hay wafted to them through the snapping air.

They passed one of Mr. McCall's clover fields where hay was stacked high around upright poles sunk into the ground throughout the field. Most of the stacks were fenced-off against the approach of stock turned into the field, but the fences stood open at two stacks to allow the animals to feed at will. "I love to see the hay stacked against the winter," Maddie said. "It always gives me a feeling of home and security."

"It always makes me feel that way, too," Hern said, certain she had uttered a subtle and profound truth.

They left the McCall fields behind and went out onto the roadway leading to Robertson's Crossroads, climbed the ridge out of the broad floodplain and passed the lane leading to the McCall home. A little way past the top of the ridge, they came to the meeting house of the Baptist Church.

"That is where we go to church," Maddie said.

"My folks are Baptists, too," Hern said. "Of course, I'm one, myself.

I joined up with them when I was eight years old. I like the Bible stories in the Old Testament and all of the teachings of Jesus. Sometimes I get a little tired of hearing the preaching."

"I think everybody does, if they'd tell the truth," Maddie said with a delightful smile.

They turned to the right past the church onto the roadway leading north across the distance toward the Horn Lake Road and came, after a while, to a broad pasture where cows, horses, and many mules were feeding on grass that rippled in the sunlight. "Mr. Janey has a nice place there," Hern said. "Mrs. Janey and my mama were good friends as girls. They still exchange letters every few months."

"The Janeys go to our church," Madelyn said. "Their daughter is one of my little sister's best friends. Sometimes she visits overnight at our house."

"Isn't it just a perfect day, Miss Madelyn?" Hern said.

"That it is, Henshaw, that it surely is," Maddie replied.

"What do you say, Henshaw, shall we take some bread and feed the ducks?" Maddie said, as they arrived back at the McCall home.

"Why of course, Miss Madelyn. Let us feed the ducks, by all means," Hern replied.

Maddie's ducks, though quite tame, were of exactly the same plumage as wild mallards, the males with striking green heads and boldly contrasting body colors of dark brown and gray. The females, on the other hand, were entirely attired in subtle tones of brown.

"It has always been a little irritating to me that the males of so many birds are so much prettier than the females," Maddie said. "It hardly seems fair."

"It seems strange they should be so different from us," Hern said. "Our females are so much prettier than the males."

"Of course it seems that way to you, being a male yourself," Maddie said with a smile that bordered on the verge of laughter. "But I assure you the males of our species seem attractive enough to their own females."

"Well I'm thrown, Miss Madelyn!" Hern said. "I can see that makes sense, but I confess I never before thought it so."

"But that is entirely to your credit, Henshaw, entirely to your credit, I'm sure."

"Push-pun-tubby–he's a full-blood Chickasaw who's a good friend of mine–Push says the female birds have soft coloration because it blends in with the background and keeps them safe from the sight of predators as they go about their nest-keeping. The males don't often sit on the nest, so they can afford a bold plumage to attract females and intimidate rival males."

"Push sounds like a wise person," Maddie said. "He doesn't sound at all like a wild Indian."

"No, he's quite a civilized person, unusually so, in fact. But when you see what he can do in the woods, you know he's fully an Indian, as well."

"Push sounds like a very interesting man," Maddie said "I expect you are fortunate to have him as a friend."

As they had continued talking and feeding the ducks, Hern and Maddie had taken seats on the grass at the edge of the pond. Each leaned a little toward the other with an outstretched hand for support. At a certain moment their outstretched hands touched. Each of them was amazed at the shock of excitement afforded by such slight contact, and though the the feelings of each were separate and private, a look passed between them that conveyed the feelings completely.

Emboldened by the look they had shared, Hern slid his hand entirely over Maddie's. She turned hers slightly so that their fingers could entwine.

Hern's throat felt so peculiar that it seemed a poor time to attempt speaking. He attempted it, nevertheless, and was gratified to find he retained the ability to talk.

"Miss Maddie," he said, "there is a particular poem of Byron's that I love above all others. I learned it by heart so that sometime I could recite it for you."

"Please recite it now, Henshaw. I would love to hear it."

Hern began, relieved to hear that his voice sounded almost normal.

> She walks in beauty, like the night
> Of cloudless climes and starry skies;
> And all that's best of dark and bright
> Meet in her aspect and her eyes:
> Thus mellow'd to that tender light
> Which heaven to gaudy day denies.
>
> One shade the more, one ray the less,
> Had half impair'd the nameless grace,
> Which waves in every raven tress,

Or softly lightens o'er her face;
Where thoughts serenely sweet express,
How pure, how dear their dwelling place.

And on that cheek, and o'er that brow,
So soft, so calm, yet eloquent,
The smiles that win, the tints that glow,
But tell of days in goodness spent,
A mind at peace with all below,
A heart whose love is innocent!

"That is so beautiful, Hern," she said, after a moment. "I'm so happy you learned it for me—that you apply it to me at all."

"I do apply it to you, Maddie," he said. "I apply it entirely to you. As far as I'm concerned it was written for you."

Hern had said goodby to Mr. And Mrs. McCall, receiving their best wishes to his family, and Maddie had seen him to the door, where he stood now, holding both of her hands in his.

"I hope I can come to see you again soon, Miss Madelyn," he said, "however short the time between, I know it will seem too long to me."

"Please come again soon, Hern," she said. "Please come whenever you can."

Chapter Seven. December, 1856.

There was a party on Christmas Eve at the Henshaw farm for their immediate neighbors and for Push-pun-tubby. The guests arrived in late afternoon, the men in jackets and ties and the ladies in their brightest and finest dresses. Push appeared for the occasion in a black broadcloth suit complete with vest and black tie and black boots of a glossy sheen. The young ladies of the families were especially excited and pleased by the formality of the occasion and the glory of their finery.

Most of the furniture in the great room of the house had been drawn back to the walls to create a broad, open expanse at the center. The floor of close-fitted, wide planks of heart pine had been scrubbed and polished until it shone like a smooth sheet of water. In the dining area at one end of the room, the top of the buffet was covered with pecan pies, a huge caramel cake, and a large bowl of boiled custard surrounded by crystal cups for serving egg nog. Ed Oakley brought forth a jug of whiskey that Mrs. Oakley had dressed in a cloth of bright red for the evening. This was placed on a side table nearby, and a decanter was filled and placed beside the boiled custard, at hand for charging separate servings of eggnog according to individual recipe. A large bowl of Virginia wassail with serving cups already sat on the side table for guests who preferred a lighter beverage. There was a decanter of wine, as well, which was appreciated particularly by the ladies.

The dining table was covered with a festive red cloth and a center piece of fresh pine boughs, pine cones, magnolia, and holly. It also displayed plates of roasted pecans, fudge, and divinity candy with pecans and walnuts. Dave Wilson had brought a large baked ham in a serving dish, and Mitchell Henshaw placed this, under direction from Elise, at one end of the table.

Earlier in the day, Hern and Bob, with the questionable assistance of Ben, had brought in a freshly cut cedar tree from the woods and set it up in a corner across from the dining table. Elise, Lisa, and Ben had decorated it with white satin ribbons and carved and painted ornaments of little angels and birds.

A game table was set up before the fireplace at the far end of the room, and the young people gathered around it for a game of caroms. This was played on a square board something like a billiard table with cloth-net pockets at each corner and at the center of each side. Play was carried out by thumping a flat, wooden ring a quarter-inch tall across the smooth surface of the board so as to hit other rings on the playing surface and drive them sliding into one of the pockets at the corners and mid sides of the table. A player could continue shooting for as long as his shots succeeded in driving one of the rings in play into a pocket. As soon as a player missed a shot, however, the turn passed to the player on his left.

The game was lively, if a bit crowded by the presence of seven players. Hern and Bob dominated as the two oldest and the only male players. They had a definite advantage in the power of their thumps. But success depended more upon accuracy of direction than upon power, and the girls displayed an admirable competence at that aspect of the game. They ranged in age from Lisa Henshaw and Peggy Wilson, at thirteen, to Sophie Oakley, at ten. They gasped and cooed at brilliant shots by Hern and Bob–especially those of Bob, who was much nearer their age. They cheered and clapped hands at each successful shot by one of themselves. Ben Henshaw and Jody Wilson crowded in and cajoled to be given a shot on the first few turns around the table. They were accommodated generously but were too young to manage successful shots and soon lost interest in the game and wandered off.

Hern won the first two games, each time under strong challenge from Bob, then declared he would step aside to allow other players a better chance to win. Bob tried to do the same, but intense protests from the girls–especially from Peggy Wilson–caused him cheerfully to remain for the start of another game.

Hern walked over by the tree where the ladies stood in conversation.

Seeing their wine glasses almost empty, he stepped to the sideboard and returned with the decanter. "May I pour some more wine for you ladies?" He asked.

"Why thank you, Hern," Mrs. Oakley said. "I declare, you've become such a fine young gentleman."

"Thank you, ma'am," Hern said, pouring the wine.

"I'm sure your parents must be very proud of you, Hern," Mrs. Wilson said.

"Thank you, Mrs. Wilson," he said, "I hope they are, at least most of the time. I know I am very proud of them."

Elise Henshaw beamed. Mrs. Wilson exclaimed "Well said, Hern, well said, indeed!"

"Now, Hern, I expect it's about time a fine young man like you has started taking an interest in the young ladies," Mrs. Oakley said. "Tell us truly, have you found a special young lady in particular to be thinking of?"

"Yes, ma'am, I expect it is about time," Hern answered. "I wouldn't be surprised if someone around here hasn't been doing some talking about that very thing."

"Why Hern," his mother said, smiling at him, "you needn't be looking so knowingly at me. You know that's a perfectly natural thing for Mrs. Oakley to ask."

Hern excused himself and walked over to where the men were gathered near the side board and the whiskey decanter.

"Come on in here and join the talk, Hern," Dave Wilson said. "Why don't you pour Hern a drink of whiskey on Christmas Eve, Mitch, if you don't think it would hurt?"

"No, Dave, on the contrary, I think it's a good idea," Mitchell said. "Maybe his mother won't holler too much about it."

"Especially if she don't know it ever happened," Ed Oakley said.

"Just look at that bunch of men, now–or I should say, don't look at them," Jeanie Oakley said. "There they go slipping Hern a drink of whiskey. They think nobody can see what they're doing."

"Yes, I saw them," Elise said. "I don't suppose it will hurt anything. Hern is almost grown now."

"No, it won't hurt Hern a bit," Mrs. Oakley said, "he's a fine young man. It's time he had a drink of whiskey with his father."

"If those men were half as clever as they think they are they'd be dangerous," Mrs. Wilson said.

Aunt Lucy came in from the kitchen with a large platter of fried chicken and arranged it on the dining table, then returned to the kitchen and brought a bowl of mashed potatoes and gravy, then a plate of rolls. She was attired brightly in a green dress with a starched white apron about her waist. Uncle Bud came in wearing a jacket and tie and began to carve the ham. "I believe it's all ready to serve, Miss Elise," Aunt Lucy said.

"Let's all gather at the table," Mitchell called to the room, and once they had gathered, said "let's have the blessing.

"Our father in heaven, we thank you for the bounty of this table and this home. We thank you for the bounty of these friends, and we ask you to bless all here. In Jesus' name we pray. Amen."

"Amen," repeated several of the audience, all of whom appreciated the succinctness of Mitchell's address to the Deity.

"You children go first," Elise told the group. "Take a plate and Aunt Lucy and Uncle Bud will serve you what you want. Lisa, why don't you lead the way. Ben and Jody, and any of you other children who wish, can pull chairs up to the game table and eat there. The rest of us will take our plates and eat at the chairs along the wall."

Aunt Lucy and Uncle Bud waited at the table to serve seconds to anyone who wanted them.

"Aunt Lucy," Ed Oakley called across the room, "I swear I believe you make the best fried chicken in the South."

"You sure do, Aunt Lucy," Hern said.

"I's just glad y'all likes it," Aunt Lucy said, smiling and pleased at the compliments.

"This ham is special, too, Dave," Mitchell said. "It's a real treat."

"Thank you, Mitch, I do think it came from a particularly fine hog," Dave Wilson said.

As the diners finished their plates, they returned them to the table and Aunt Lucy served pieces of pecan pie and caramel cake. Then she and Uncle Bud removed the dinner courses from the table and retired to the kitchen to eat, themselves. Elise and Mitchell served eggnog and wassail as the guests finished their desserts.

Then Aunt Lucy and Uncle Bud returned from the kitchen. Uncle Bud had his banjo, with which he was known as a local expert. He took a chair between the dining table and the Christmas tree and began to play the melody of Charles Wesley's classic carol, "Hark the Herald, Angels Sing." As he finished going through the song the first time, Mitchell said

"That's mighty fine, Uncle Bud. Keep playing, if you will, and some of us will join in with you."

Mitchell and Elise, then Hern and Bob and Lisa, then everyone in the entire group, including Push and Aunt Lucy, began to sing along with the strains of Uncle Bud's banjo. They sang it through twice, and by the time they had finished, everyone was smiling, and a fine feeling of friendliness and well being–the very feeling of Christmas, itself–glowed warmly in every heart in the room.

Uncle Bud started in on "Silent Night," and everyone joined in spontaneously and with high spirit. They sang three verses and ended with laughter and congratulations all around. Pats on the back and small hugs were exchanged among the friends, now joined almost into a single family by the warm feelings that permeated the room.

"Uncle Bud," Mitchell said, "you know that old song, 'Lorena.' If you'll do that one at something like a waltz tempo, I think Elise and I might be able to dance to it."

Uncle Bud started it out, and Mitchell and Elise moved to the center of the room and stepped off together in the stately and majestic movement of the waltz. They moved perfectly together, as on a single impulse, and their twirls about the room soared above ordinary human grace. Hern watched them with fondness and pride. An image of Maddie came unbidden to his mind, and he ached with wishing she were here. How delightful to take her in his arms, for the two of them to twirl together about the room as his parents were doing so effortlessly.

Peggy Wilson tried to get Bob to go out onto the floor with her, but he explained he didn't know anything about doing the waltz, or any other dance, and excused himself.

"I'll dance it with you, Peggy," Lisa Henshaw said, and they moved off in emulation of Mitchell and Elise. After a few turns, they were joined by the Oakley girls, Mary Pat and Sophie. Hern watched the dancers wistfully, and it seemed to him that Bob was looking a little wistful, himself. He seemed to be looking at Peggy Wilson a little differently than Hern had ever seen him look at a girl before.

It was obvious that Bob was growing up, and Hern thought of the time, just three years ago, when Bob had made out a contract worthy of a lawyer to ensure that neither he nor his two younger siblings would slip first to the living room on Christmas morning without the company of the other two. They weren't worried about Hern. His age had by that time lessened his interest in the leavings of 'Santa Claus' to the point that Bob and the others knew they could beat him to the Christmas tree without contest. The contract Bob had drawn up read as follows:

> I, being of sound mind and body, do hereby solemnly
> swear that under no circumstance will I enter the living
> room or approach the Christmas tree on Christmas
> morning, 1852, or at any other time between bedtime
> on Christmas Eve and daylight of that Christmas
> morning, unless I be in the company of the other two
> signatories to this agreement.

> _____

> _____

> _____

Bob had signed his name on the first line beneath the statement, entered the date, and had Lisa and Ben sign their names on the next two lines, although they excused Ben with signing only his initials, which was all he could manage at the time.

Hern knew Bob had executed the contract almost entirely to enhance the pleasure of Christmas for his little sister and brother. After all, it was Bob everyone had to be worried about. No one could beat Bob to the living room on Christmas morning. It was Bob who, for years, had made it a habit of locating everyone's presents, no matter how well hidden, and opening them carefully, inspecting the contents, then re-wrapping them, good as new, and replacing them. Then, just as someone would begin to open a gift on Christmas morning, but before they could manage to get it open, he would call out, delightedly, "Oh, I know what that is! It's a red shirt!"

Snow began to fall in the afternoon on the second day after Christmas, and it continued falling heavily all night. By morning a blanket four inches deep covered the fields and hills.

Not only the children, but everyone in the Henshaw house was in a high mood, overjoyed with the snow. It gave a fresh look to the whole world, made everything look new, different, breathtakingly beautiful. They got two or three good snows most winters but never enough to make it a routine occurrence. Usually it only lasted a few days before melting away, seldom stayed long enough for anyone to wish it gone. It made all chores involving the outside more difficult, but it also made them fresh and new as the landscape. Even George and Price were happy to see it. This particular snow was early by at least a week or two, and it was a Christmas snow. That made it all the more special.

Hern and Bob and Zak went out early and tracked three rabbits across the otherwise unblemished white carpet of snow all the way to the forms where they lay hidden. They could have killed any of the three easily with the clubs they carried, but they found, today, that the successful tracking was enough. Somehow none of the three felt like taking a swing at the first rabbit, even though each one thought the other two would do so. As it hopped laboriously away, Zak said, "I didn't feel like killing that old rabbit, either. I'm glad none of us took a swipe at it."

"I'm glad too," said Hern. "It was enough to know we could have if we'd wanted to."

"Let's see how many we can track down anyway," Bob said. "We don't have to kill 'em."

When they got back to the house, Aunt Lucy was stirring a rich soup of milk, butter, ham, potatoes, and corn. It was one of her traditional dishes for a snowy day. She had a big pan of biscuits ready for the oven to go with it.

"When will that soup be ready, Aunt Lucy?" Hern said. "We've been out hunting rabbits in the snow and we're hungry as bears."

"That ain't nothing new for you two boys," she said. "If you been out huntin', where your rabbits? I don't see nary one."

"We could have got three if we wanted 'em," Bob said. "We felt like lettin' 'em hop on."

"I don't know whether to believe you boys or not," she said, looking at each, "but I reckon I believes you. You look like you tellin' the truth this time."

"We always tell the truth, Aunt Lucy, at least mostly we do," Bob said.

"Mostly is right!" Aunt Lucy said. "Well this soup ain't ready and hit ain't gon' be ready for a good while yet. You boys better get out of here and let me do my work. If you'll let me alone I'll make some puddin' cake for dessert."

"That's the way to talk, Aunt Lucy. We're gone already," said Bob.

Toward the last hour of the forenoon, the sound of jingle bells came from outside the house. Hern and Bob went to the front door and were amazed to see a horse-drawn sleigh pulling into the yard. Matthew McCall had had the wheels on his carriage replaced with a snow-runner rig and had taken his entire family afield for a ride through the snow. And as long as they wanted to go for a long ride, they had come visit the Henshaws. Hern's heart rate jumped to high speed, for right there in the back seat behind her parents, fairly glowing with the crisp air and the excitement, sat the beautiful Madelyn McCall.

Mitchell and Elise, and then the rest of the family, followed Hern onto the porch to greet their visitors. "Howdy, Mitchell, Elise," called Matthew McCall, "hello, Hern. Hello to everybody. Hern was so nice to pay us a visit the other day that I got to thinking it's been far too long since I saw your place. We all wanted to go for a good snow-ride, so I brought the whole family."

"Well I'm sure glad you did, Matthew," Mitchell answered. "We're mighty glad to see you. Hello, Martha. Here, let me help you down. I'm sure Hern and Bob will want to help the girls."

"Hello, Miss Maddie," Hern said, "I'm so happy to see you. This is just a fine surprise!"

"Hello, Henshaw, I am very glad to see you, too. I've been looking forward all morning, just hoping you'd be at home."

"I'm so glad I am," Hern said, "why, I wouldn't be anywhere else for a pocketful of gold.

"How come you all to be here at Center Hill, Miss Maddie? Are you out just for fun?" Hern asked.

"Entirely for fun, Henshaw," she answered, "for fun and for visiting Henshaws. Papa is worse than a child about loving the snow. He started plotting this last evening. He knew it would please me, and I'll admit I freely encouraged him. All night I kept hoping there would be enough snowfall for a sleigh ride, and my hopes were realized."

"Well, this is just the best thing that ever was," Hern said.

"Here, Miss Maddie, I want you to meet my brother Bob—or at least to introduce him to you in modern times. Bob, this is Miss Madelyn McCall. Please say hello to her. She is a special friend."

"Very pleased to meet you again, Miss Madelyn," Bob said. "I hope you will be my friend, too."

"That would give me great pleasure, Mr. Bob Henshaw," she said, reaching out to shake his hand warmly.

"My goodness, Maddie," said Elise Henshaw, "I had half forgotten what a beautiful girl you are–and you've grown far beyond even what I remembered. I'm so happy to see you again."

"Thank you, ma'am. I am sure you are too generous, but I thank you for it," said Maddie. "It's truly good to see you again, too."

They feasted on Aunt Lucy's ham soup and biscuits for dinner. Aunt Lucy always seemed to have plenty of food on hand for whatever was needed–so much so that Elise never even bothered to wonder what she would serve her unexpected guests. Aunt Lucy would take care of it as usual, and she did.

After dinner, Matthew and Mitchell went down to inspect Mitchell's barn and animals. Hern and Maddie went off for a walk across the snow-covered hills beneath a brilliant sun.

The trees stood darkly, bare branches and trunks in stark rendering against the snow. Already, the slanting rays of early afternoon cast knife-edged shadows down the top of the slope of the north ridge.

"Look at the shadows are along the ridge top," Maddie said. "They're so deep and dark they seem to show a tint of blue–or maybe I just imagine they do."

"No, I see it, too," Hern said. But he found himself gazing with even more appreciation into the dark and deep pools of Maddie's eyes–felt he was half lost in the warm aura of that glow. The splendor of this girl imbued the entire scene about them, and his own life, with a marvelous sense of meaning and purpose.

They walked on along the edge of the ridge above the snow-smoothed plain of the fields, through which the flowing stream cut its dark, clean, and winding course.

"Oh, see the redbirds against the snow!" Maddie exclaimed. "Even the female looks brilliantly colored today."

"I love the soft coral and orange color of her bill," Hern said. "I think it must be fetching, indeed, to her male. Did you know they often keep to the same mate the whole year round, breeding season or not?"

"No, I didn't. I must say that seems an excellent arrangement," Maddie said.

As they came to the edge of the woods above an open hillside, they saw two female deer in the marsh below them. They watched the graceful and mincing steps of the deer as they moved across the marsh and into the woods on the far side.

"The deer are so beautiful," Maddie said, "so full of grace."

"Yes, the deer are very beautiful, Maddie," Hern said softly. "They are almost as beautiful as you."

"No, Hern, they are almost as beautiful as you," Maddie said, looking into his eyes. "But why so serious, Henshaw?" she asked with a teasing smile, and reaching out quickly, she gave him a playful push. "Why do you stumble in the snow?"

"We'll see who stumbles in the snow, Miss Smarty Pants," Hern said with a playful grin, returning her push with a shove that imparted more force than he had intended. Maddie's downhill foot slipped its step, and to his horror, Hern saw she was teetering above the plunge of the slope. He leaned far out to catch hold of her with both hands. She grasped him tightly. They hovered over the slope for a moment, almost defying gravity, then fell to their sides and began to roll, twirling over and over each other down the open face of the hill.

"I swear, Henshaw, you've rolled me down the entire side of a hill," Maddie said a little breathlessly.

They lay still wrapped tightly in each others' arms at the bottom of the slope, their faces close together. They looked into each others' eyes. Both moved almost imperceptibly closer and their lips brushed together for a prolonged moment.

It was not quite a kiss. Hern knew Maddie had been raised, as he had, to believe that a kiss between a couple such as themselves should signify an engagement of marriage.

"I didn't intend to cause such a tumble, Maddie," he said, "but now that it's happened, I'm awfully glad it did."

"Yes, I'm awfully glad too," she said.

"I think I've taken quite a fall, Maddie, in more ways than one."

"I know, Hern, I know. I made the same fall, all the way down."

Chapter Nine. December, 1856.

Sitting alone before a smoldering fire on one of the last evenings of the year, Hern reflected that he was growing into a man. It seemed such a short time ago that he was far away manhood. He recalled an adventure he had shared with Bob a couple of years before. They had made a camping trip with their friends in the woods a few miles east of the community of Center Hill. They took a shotgun along with the hope of shooting a rabbit or two and maybe a couple of squirrels for supper. If that failed, they figured they could get by on robins.

"This blackbird meat ain't worth a damn. It's mighty near rank," Hern said.

"I think it tastes good," Bob said. They were seated around a campfire in the woods with three other boys about Hern's age.

"This meat won't hurt us none," Billy Carson said. "Pa says folks down in Louisiana eat all kinds of critters. Sometimes they even eat owls. Been doing it for years. Don't hurt 'em none."

"I think it taste' like chicken," Zak said. Officially, Zak was one of the Henshaw slaves, and he did his share of farm work. But he had also grown up as a playmate to Hern and Bob, and he often accompanied them on local adventures. "Hit is kind o' stringy, though," he admitted.

"It don't taste like any chicken Aunt Lucy ever cooked," Hern said. "Maybe your mama can't cook chicken."

"Yes she can too," Zak said. "She make good chicken."

"Thank God we've got salt," Grey Thompson said.

"We should have got us some robins," Billy said. "Push said they eat better than blackbirds."

"We only saw one robin," Grey said, "and it flew off and we couldn't find it again."

"Maybe we should have tried harder," Billy said.

"Maybe we didn't cook these things right," Hern said. "I don't think they got done good on these sticks."

"I couldn't cook mine anymore. My stick was about burnt in two," Billy said.

"I think it tastes good," Bob said.

"May as well eat it either way," Hern said, "we got nothing else."

"Thank God we've got salt," Grey said.

The boys had finished eating the blackbirds and it was coming on to full dark in the woods. A big moon was just coming up in the east. "Boys, I've got a treat for us as a surprise," Grey Thompson said. He walked over near the horses to where his saddle was slung over a log and reached into the saddle bags. Then he walked back to the fire with two quart-sized canteens in his hands. "This here is persimmon beer, boys," he said. "Pa had a right good amount of it made up and I just borrowed a little for us. We can have it for dessert."

They started the canteens around the circle in two directions, crossing over each other in the middle and continuing on around, the boys each taking a swallow or two as they received a canteen. One or two of the boys leaned back against trees and the rest leaned against a couple of big logs they'd dragged up earlier. Later they might roll these up to the fire so it would burn on into the night. Their bedrolls were still piled with their saddles and tack over near the horses.

"This stuff is mighty good, Grey," Hern said. "I'm real glad you brought it. It sets off the night just fine, don't it boys." There were murmurs of approval from around the circle.

"It's tastes a little sour at first," Grey said, "but the more you drink of it the better it gets."

"It's damned good to me already," Billy said, "fact is, it's god-damned good."

"Sho' it's good," Zak said," hit's mighty god-damned good."

"God-damned right it's god-damned good," Hern said.

"Son-of-a-bitch. God-damn." said Bob.

"Keep it coming this way, Bob. Don't sit there holding it all night," Hern said.

"Sum-bitch, god-damn," Bob said.

"Hell, god-damn, let's put some more sum-bitchin' wood on the sum-bitchin' fire. Shit!" Grey said.

Push-pun-tubby and his dog Rube sat back in the dark woods near the edge of the light from the fire, and Push observed the beer-drinking and cussing with deep amusement. The boys at the campfire were his friends. He had known of their camping trip and had even gone so far as to consult them on their plans. But, of course, much of their pleasure in the trip was to be out on their own, and they had no idea Push was in the vicinity this evening.

"Hell boys, let's tell some stories," Hern said. "Anybody know a good ghost story?"

"I know one that's pretty good," Billy Carson said. "Pa told it to me. It was told as the truth where he used to live over in Tennessee."

"Well let's hear it, then," Hern said. Billy started his story.

"There was an old man living up there around Finger, Tennessee went out huntin' possums on a night like this when the moon was almost full and the woods was lit-up with kind of a soft, pale light like it is now. He got to enjoying wanderin' around in the woods and the moonlight so much that after a while he realized he didn't know where he was anymore or how far he was from home.

"Well, he got uneasy and he started walking faster and faster, and the faster he walked the more he knew he was lost and the more uneasy he got. Pretty soon he got downright panicky. He got the feeling something was following him through the woods. Then he *knew* something was following him. Something was after him. He could hear it now and then stepping in the leaves and swishing through the brush just behind him. He went into a real panic. He called out 'Oh, ooh,' and he started in to running. He slanted off in one direction and then another and wherever he went he kept hearing that thing behind him, swishing through the bushes. He tried to run faster and faster but the thing kept coming behind him, getting closer and closer all the time. He started to get tired from running and he knew he couldn't go on much farther. And the thing kept coming and coming behind him.

"At last he broke out into a small clearing and he stopped in the middle of it. His breath was heaving and he felt like he couldn't go another step. Just then a horrible scream rang out from the trail behind him. It sounded like a woman in high pain and rage. It was the horriblest scream the old man had ever heard. He started to shaking so bad he like to dropped his gun.

"And then the bushes parted where he'd run out of the woods and all at once there was this *ghost* cat standin' there just a-staring at him."

"A *ghost* cat?" Bob burst out.

"It was a ghost cat," Billy said. "Its eyes glowed a sickly yellow and it was tall and long. It looked like a panther, but it was 'way too thin, like it was nothing but skin and bone or maybe nothing but spirit. And its hair was 'way too pale and it glowed like foxfire.

"Then that cat looked him right in the face and grinned at him like a crazy man. Then it gave off a soft, crazy laugh.

"Then it charged him fast, swerving to this side and that and boring in on him so fast he couldn't think. He tried to raise his gun, but it fired-off into the ground at his feet and the thing was on him. It leaped up for his throat and its paw struck him in the middle of the chin. He fell hard straight backwards and his head hit down on a big rock and everything went black.

"When he came to he was lying on his back, scared and confused. He rolled over and got to his hands and knees and he saw his gun where it had been thrown behind him when he was knocked over. The gun was propped up on a rock and he saw he was back in his own front yard and that the barrel of the gun was pointing straight at the door of his cabin, which was standing open.

"He went in the cabin holding his gun ready to fight off the cat, but the cabin was empty and he latched and barred the door. When he went to look in his mirror he found he had two deep claw marks, one on each side of the middle of his chin, and around each claw mark the hair of his beard had turned from dark to snow white. And it stayed that way for the rest of his life."

"What do you think it means?" Bob said. "You think it really *was* a ghost cat?"

"I think it was," Billy said, "and if there was a ghost cat at Finger, Tennessee, there might be one around here. They might be anywhere."

Bob and Zak had started to tremble a little despite themselves and their eyes were big like they were about to jump out of their heads.

"Take it easy, boys," Hern said. "I never heard of any ghost cats being around here. I don't know as I believe in ghost cats, anyway."

"Me neither," Grey said.

"It was a ghost cat, alright," Billy said. "They could be anywhere."

Just then Push, who had been listening from the woods nearby, gave out with the call of a barred owl, delivered at high volume.

"What was that?" Bob shouted. "Was that a panther?"

"Hold on, hold on," said Hern, "that was just an old barred owl."

"It was too hollow-sounding for a regular owl," said Billy. "Maybe it's a ghost owl."

Just then Push screamed out the high, piercing wail of a panther, then again. The horses stirred their feet back and forth, rapidly flirting one way, then another; they pulled back against their tethers. The boys leapt to their feet.

"It's a panther!" Grey shouted. "It's a panther right here on us."

"It's a ghost panther!" Billy screamed.

"Let's get out of here," shouted Bob.

The boys milled about, looking all around for a direction in which to flee. "Wait boys, wait," Hern shouted. "What about the horses? We got to get the horses."

"Hold on boys. Hold on now," Push said in a clear voice as he stepped out of the forest and into the firelight. "Hold on boys, I'm here to help you. I won't let that old ghost cat get anybody." Then Push couldn't keep his face serious any longer. He began to laugh, softly at first, then louder and louder and the boys began to realize they had been tricked, that Push was the panther. Most of them began to laugh, too.

"Dang you Push, you old dog. How come you to tease us like that?" Hern said.

"I'm sorry boys, I'm sorry," Push answered. "I just couldn't resist the chance. Now, tell the truth, I think you enjoyed it as much as I did."

"Why, I guess we did at that, Push," Hern said. "Boys, I don't guess there's much of anything more fun than getting a little scared. Ain't that right?"

"Yeah, you're right, Hern. Yeah," Billy and Grey said. "We forgive you Push. We're just glad it was you, after all."

"I ain't sure I forgive you, Push," Bob said. "I was getting almighty scared."

"We all were, Bob, we all were." said Hern.

"Is ya'll sure there ain't no panther?" said Zak.

Push and Rube sat around the fire with the boys for a while until some of them began to get sleepy, and he watched them unfurl their bedrolls and fix up their fire for the night. He said his goodnights and he and Rube walked off in the direction of his cabin.

Hern learned later that after Push appeared to leave, he and Rube had circled around and slipped back near edge of the firelight. Then Push sat down against a tree in the dark, and Rube lay down at his side. The two of them stayed on watch at the edge of the camp through most of the night. A little before dawn they got up and quietly headed away toward home.

Chapter Ten. January–February, 1857.

Push rode into the Henshaw yard at mid morning on the first mild day of the New Year, as he and Hern had agreed. Hern was watching and stepped out the front door of the house to greet him. The two went down to the barn. Hern saddled a horse, then put a halter on the young mule, Gabe, and led him out of his stall. They rode off down the lane toward the east end of the Henshaw place, Hern leading Gabe behind his horse. They came to a place where an old tree stump remained standing near the corner of one of last year's clover fields. The stump was three feet in diameter and a little over waist high. Looking at the stump, Push turned his horse into the field, and Hern followed him down to the area where it stood.

"We'll get down here," Push said. "You can tie-off your horse and Gabe to the fence over there."

Push stripped the saddle and bridle from his horse, yet the horse followed him as he walked to the fence. He slung the saddle across the top rail, lay his bridle across it. "I want to show you something now, Hern," Push said. "I want you to see what you can accomplish by working with a horse—or with a mule, either, I reckon. What I'm going to show you is a little extravagant, beyond most anything you'd do for practical importance. I learned to do this mainly just to see if I *could* learn it, still, it does have value in establishing trust between yourself and an animal. I'm showing it to you just for a demonstration—to give you some inspiration, you might say."

"I'm all eyes, Push," Hern replied.

Push's horse stood nearby, entirely bare of saddle, bridle, halter–absent all the usual equipage upon which human control was based. He took hold of a hank of mane near the horse's withers and leapt from the ground onto its back. With his right hand holding the mane and his left held casually at his side, Push rode the horse out into the field and put it into an easy lope. He described a wide half-circle below Hern and the stump, then made a straight line toward Hern from the far edge of the half-circle. As the horse began the straight run, Hern saw it change its lead foot from right to left. Then as it neared Hern, it changed back to a right-foot lead. The lead-changes were impressive, especially when obtained, as here, in a horse that wore no bridle. Hern noticed that subtle adjustments of Push's attitude on its back anticipated each lead-change perfectly. He wasn't sure what cues Push used to initiate the lead-changes, but he knew it was happening at Push's direction.

Push rode twice more around the half-circle, continuing the lead-changes with each straight run toward Hern. Then, from the point of the arc farthest from the old tree stump, Push spun the horse from the circular path and took it in rapid acceleration across the center of the circle directly toward the stump.

As horse and rider closed rapidly with the stump, in direct collision course, Hern felt a quick rise of anxiety as to what must happen next. Then horse and rider rose smoothly in a high jump and sailed above the stump in splendid coordination. They landed smoothly on the other side, then came up to an easy stop directly in front of the spot where Hern stood amazed.

Just as Hern was about to recover his power of speech, Push made a slight sweeping gesture toward him with his left hand and started the horse back out to the lower point of the circle. Again he spun the horse and accelerated toward the stump, but this time, instead of jumping the horse, Push put it into a sliding stop directly in front of it. Horse and rider remained motionless before the stump for a few seconds, then the horse spun rapidly to the left, turning tightly on its own axis. It spun two times around, then came to an abrupt stop with its head directly toward the stump.

It stood motionless for five seconds, then abruptly began a tight spin to its right, this time spinning only through a single revolution and again stopping smartly, head directly toward the stump. It stood for five seconds, ten seconds, then in a swift and sudden series of movements, made sixteen steps rapidly backward, directly away from the stump.

Again the horse stood motionless, Push as still as a statue, sitting upright on its back. Suddenly, in rapid acceleration from a standing start, the horse drove directly at the stump, made a smooth leap high above it, made an easy landing, and came to a sliding stop as its front feet struck the earth for the third time on the other side.

Horse and rider remained motionless for five seconds. Then Push rode easily over to where Hern stood, threw his right foot across over the horse's neck, and sprang to the ground.

"My God, Push!" Hern said after a few seconds. "My God, that was incredible! I never dreamed of seeing such a thing. It's hard to believe it's possible, even though I know I just saw it. A demonstration? A demonstration? It was a demonstration, alright!"

"I'm glad you liked it," Push said.

"Liked it? Yes, I liked it. I won't ever forget it."

"Well, no particular reason to keep it a secret, I guess," Push said. "On the other hand, there's no need to say much about it, either.

"You can start working with Gabe now," Push said. "Now you got a better idea of what can be done. You can't be in too much of a hurry. It takes time to build an animal's trust, and this is your first time to try it. You won't have any trouble, but it may be hard at first to realize you're getting anywhere. You got to stay patient and just keep doing the things I tell you. Take your time, and once you get the right confidence established, things can go a lot quicker.

"Now here's what I want you to do first. Just put him on a short lead with his halter rope and walk around with him. Go anywhere you want. Every now and then, take an abrupt right or an abrupt left. Every now and then stop short and stand for a while, then start off again straight-away, at normal walking speed. When he misses following you, try to go on with what you were doing without a pause, so he'll have to catch up. It's alright to pause slightly for him if he needs it, but mainly you want him to follow right along with whatever you're doing.

"Once he's following you pretty good on stopping-and-starting, and on your turns, you can start backing up on him. Just take one or two steps back at first. You might have to back right into him a few times. If you do, don't pay it any mind. You just go ahead and do what you started out to do and he'll adjust to it. After he gets used to backing up whenever you do, you can begin backing a little further and further each time. I don't guess there's much need to back him more than five or six steps for now.

"Every so often, walk down to some water he's used to and let him sniff it or take a drink. Every so often, lead him over to some good grass and tell him he can eat a few bites. Then move on somewhere else whenever you're ready. As you're walking around, try to find something he might be scared of, like a smooth sheet of water where he doesn't expect it, or the end of a limb that's jumping funny in the wind or waving around in the current of a stream. Walk him well around those things, like you're kind of wary of them, yourself. Like you got enough sense not to lead him into trouble. Keep going by those scary things now and again. After you've been by the same thing a few times, start showing more confidence and go by it a little closer, then a little closer the next time. If you take your time about it, after a while he'll walk right by something that would have spooked him earlier and never be concerned.

"Now, you'll notice after a while–it won't take long–he'll be following along behind you close and smooth, just taking his lead from what you do. Start lengthening his lead rope until he has six or eight feet and just keep walking him around like you been doing. Then start giving him a spoken cue a step before you do something different each time. Say 'hup' when you start off from a stop. Say 'gee' before you make a sharp right and 'haw' before you take a left. Say 'whoa' before you stop. Say 'back' before you back up on him. No need to speak in a loud voice. In fact, a soft voice is better. He'll pick up on it soon enough.

"Once you think he's started to take notice of your spoken cues, start making what you might call an 'intention' move just before you give the spoken cue each time. Your intention move can be anything you like. It don't matter what it is, but try to make it the same one each time–just something you might naturally do before making the change you have in mind. After a while, you'll notice he's anticipating your spoken cue before you can give it. It don't matter what intention moves you choose because once he's learned to pick up those cues from you, he'll pick up the same kind of cues from anybody else, even somebody that don't know he's giving any cues. To somebody that don't know any better, it might seem like Gabe's reading his mind.

"Take Gabe out every day you can and work with him like that for a couple of weeks or so. You can start right now. I'll head on back to my place. I'll come back in a couple of weeks and see how you're coming along. I expect then we can go on to doing some other things."

"Alright, Push. I'll be seeing you in a couple of weeks," Hern said. "I sure do thank you."

"You bet, Hern," Push said, "it's nothing but fun for me."

Push returned in the second week of February to check for the first time on Hern's progress. They entered an open clover field, and Hern put Gabe through the paces. Hup, gee, haw, whoa, back. As Gabe performed instantly and smoothly throughout, Push could see that his lead rope hung slack the entire time. This was what Push had both hoped for and expected.

"Good work Hern, good work Gabe!" Push called.

"Now let's try something just a little different, Hern. I hope it will show you've accomplished more than you realize. I want you to slip Gabe's the halter off him and hand it to me. Then step up to his head and run through your drill again."

"Gosh, I don't know, Push," Hern said. He looked doubtful.

"Just step up there with confidence and we'll see what happens," Push said.

Hern stepped up in front of Gabe, stood for a moment, said "hup," and started out. Gabe immediately stepped out behind him, as before. "Whoa," said Hern, and Gabe stopped right behind him, maintaining his usual distance. "Hup," Hern started out once more; "gee," said Hern, and turned sharply to the right. Gabe made the same turn as Hern, followed along behind him exactly as before. "Whoa." Hern stopped smartly. Gabe did the same. "Back," Hern called. He made five steps directly backward. Gabe stepped back just as quickly behind him, maintaining the same distance to which both were accustomed.

"Good boy, Gabe! Good boy," Hern said with pleasure. He turned and patted Gabe beside the jaw, rubbed his ears. "Good boy, Gabe. What a smart, old boy. Good boy.

"Great goodness, Push, I guess I should have expected this, but I never thought of it. Gosh, this is great." Hern said.

"Old Gabe is already more 'trained' than you thought," Push said, grinning. "Good. Now let's see how well he'll follow your intentions without the spoken cues.

Hern again took position in front of Gabe, said "Alright, Gabe," stood for a moment, and started walking smartly ahead. Gabe followed as before. At a certain moment, Hern stopped suddenly and so did Gabe. They started off again, Hern first, then immediately, Gabe. Hern reached a spot he had picked out and made a sharp left, followed by Gabe. Hern stopped. Gabe stopped behind him. Hern began stepping backward. So did Gabe, and when Hern stopped again, Gabe did the same.

"Good boy," Hern said again, turning to Gabe. "Good old Gabe."

"That's good, Hern," said Push. "That's as good as I'd hoped.

"Now there's one other thing to check on this morning. A mule has to do most of his work with a man behind him rather than in front of him. Now, it's natural for a lead horse to sometimes be in a position behind one of the horses that accepts his leadership. So that should be natural to a mule, too. If Gabe ain't ready for this yet, there's some things we can do to get him used to it, so we don't need to be worried about it. But I think you may have laid enough groundwork already. I want you to take a position behind Gabe, just like he was about to pull a plow for you, and see if the two of you can 'gee' and 'haw' around this field."

Hern stepped up to Gabe's left side, rubbed his ears a little, ran his hand down Gabe's back as he moved to a position directly behind him. He stood quiet for a moment, took a breath, said "hup," and started walking straight for Gabe's rear end. Gabe only hesitated a split-second before he began walking straight ahead at their usual pace. "Good boy, Gabe," Hern called from behind.

Hern let them make more that a dozen steps. Gabe turned his head once to see if Hern was with him but kept walking ahead in a straight line. "Whoa," Hern said. Gabe stopped in front of him and stood. "Hup;" they started again. "Gee," and Gabe immediately turned right and kept walking. "Haw;" Gabe made a quick left. "Whoa;" Gabe stopped. "Back;" Gabe came straight backward until Hern again said whoa.

"Good boy, Gabe," Hern said excitedly, rubbing Gabe's ears once more. Then he turned and walked casually back to where Push was standing, saying "Come on Gabe." Gabe walked quietly behind him.

"That's mighty fine," Push said. "It's everything we wanted."

"Well it's a lot more than I was hoping for," Hern said with a big smile. "I'm just amazed."

"There's just a few more things we need to do," Push said, "and Gabe will be ready to go to work. We need to get him accustomed to wearing his work harness, then to pulling a load with it. I want you to introduce his working gear one piece at the time, starting with the first thing you'd put on him if he was going out to work.

"The first time you put it on him, just let it set there for a second or two, then take it off. You can do a lot of this right up at the barn. Be sure you act confident all the time. Show him you ain't afraid of the stuff and there's nothing for him to be afraid of, either. Take your time. If there's something he don't like, don't crowd him. Just keep showing it to him and fooling with him until he loses his concern. It's better to take too much time than it is to crowd him. You want him to get used this stuff without ever getting spooked the first time. You want him to accept it just like he does his food and water.

"After he's had plenty of time to get used to all the equipment, moving around in it, working with you while he's wearing it, you can introduce him to pulling things with it. Start off by putting a little back pressure on his tow lines as you walk along behind him. Then hook to something like a short pole that's just heavy enough to pull the lines back behind him. Show it to him first and let him see you hook it up behind him. Stay back there with it, like it's part of you, not something that's chasing him across the field.

"Gradually you can introduce heavier and bigger things for him to pull, finally a plow. Hold it on its side so it just slides across the ground at first. Then let it barely dig in, a little deeper each time you work. After a while, you can introduce him to different plows, harrows, whatever you want.

"You'll also want him to get used to you riding him. That should be easy, 'cause he's used to working with you and he already likes doing it. Just introduce it to him gradually, like the rest, and let him get used to everything you want him to do at a slow pace. You can get him used to pulling a wagon the same way. Just take your time.

"Let him walk along on a lead behind a wagon, with you driving. Then tie him alongside the mule that's pulling it and let him walk there a good bit. After a while, you can hitch him up to it and let him pull it, himself.

"You and Gabe are coming along fine, Hern. It won't be long before folks will be calling you a *mule-trainer*."

Chapter Eleven. March, 1857.

Hern rode astride Gabe on a trail through upland woods of oak, hickory, and maple; gum, ash, and many smaller trees like dogwood, snowbell, and hop-hornbeam. Many of the trees were giants six feet in diameter and one-hundred-twenty feet tall. There were huge short-leafed pines, located mostly on the upper slopes of the ridges. In the hollows, the forest floor was rich in ferns, and the low, umbrella-like leaves of May-apple stalks climbed the slopes toward the ridges. The air was sweet with the respiration of life in the season of nature's renewal.

He reached Push's cabin after a ride of less than an hour. Push's place was built on a gently rolling section of ridge top near the drop-off of the west bluff above the Coldwater River Bottom. The cabin was of log construction, somewhat in the style of the homes of many of the early white settlers in the country. It was a single room fourteen feet wide and eighteen feet long, with an eight foot deep porch under roof across the front end. There was a plank floor and a big fireplace across the back and two large windows that opened outward along each side. The inside walls of the cabin were lined with hickory withes woven into mats and whitewashed with clay in the old style of the Chickasaw. Push had gone to the trouble of covering the low gable roof with cedar shakes for durability and weather tightness.

To the front on the right side of the cabin, Push had also constructed a summer house in the Chickasaw fashion. It was of pole construction with walls of loosely woven hickory withes, calculated to admit the flow of air. Long strands of dried grass had been worked in among the openings to discourage the entry of insects. The slightly pitched gable roof was shingled with strips of hickory bark. The summer house was divided into two rooms, one for sleeping and one for cooking and sitting at the fire. The cooking room had a dirt floor with a stone-ringed fire pit in one corner, where a crude tin chimney opened at roof level to admit the outflow of smoke. The sleeping room had a raised puncheon floor built on a low stone foundation and contained Push's raised bed slatted with strong sticks and covered with soft-tanned deerskins. As with the cabin, a wide porch under roof extended across the front end of the summerhouse.

Push's vegetable garden was already laid out beside his cabin, and beyond that was a sizable corn patch for his own corn and meal and from which he could store a supply in his corn house for feeding his two horses through the winter. Push was sitting in a chair of his own make in the shade of the porch of his summer house. Rube reclined at his side. Rube glanced up with interest as Hern and Gabe rode up but remained seated and quiet.

"Morning Hern, welcome. I'm glad you made it. We'll have some fun, and I expect some good fishing tomorrow," Push said. "Set your gear over on the porch of the cabin and we'll unsaddle Gabe and put him up in my horse shed.

"Take some of this bear grease and rub it on your face and neck and hands before we go down into the bottom," Push said. "It'll keep most of the mosquitoes off. They ain't too bad anyway, this time of year, but there's always a few around down there except in cold weather. Wipe a little on the sleeves of your shirt, too."

Push led the way down a steep trail off the bluff and into the flat, alluvial land that surrounded the river across a distance of more than a mile. The forest changed as they entered the bottom. The upland versions of oak were replaced by lowland varieties—water oak, willow oak, cow oak and over-cup oak. Green ash replaced white ash and swamp hickories replaced the upland types. There were still plenty of towering gums. Broad stands of huge cypress trees lined sloughs and swampy areas across the bottom and stood in profusion along the river. Some of these were ten and twelve feet in diameter and one-hundred-fifty feet tall. Only a few stood in the waters of the river, itself; the general flow of its current was far too swift.

Push led the way to a shallow and narrow pond of water in a small slough well back from the river. The water in many of the sloughs throughout the bottom was nearly permanent. They were prone to become shallow in long stretches when there was no rain, and some dried up entirely, but they were replenished to full depth each time the river flooded.

Push pulled out a seine-net from his pack and spread it on the bare ground at the edge of the slough. "We need a couple of stout poles as framework for the seine," he said. "They need to be long enough to keep the net spread from top to bottom. Then we need a couple of feet left over at the top for a handle."

They cut two poles and Push began to attach one of them to the narrow end of one side of the seine. Hern watched what he was doing for a moment then went to work on the other side.

"Just hold the bottom of the pole to the bottom of the pond as we go, Hern, and follow my lead." They waded out into the pool, spread the seine almost to its full width between them, and thrust it down into the water until they held the low end against the bottom. Then they took off wading at a brisk pace down the center of the pool, bending low enough as they waded to keep the lower end of the net running along the bottom.

When they reached the far end of the pool, Push kept them moving straight on up onto the shore. They stepped out of the pond, running the seine all the way to the bank, and when they spread it 'face' up, they found they had caught more than a dozen each of river perch and crawfish of various sizes from very small to several inches long.

"Looks like we found a good hole, Hern!" Push exclaimed. "Look at all this bait."

The dog Rube walked calmly up to the net, where the small fish were flopping furiously, and took a good look. But he made no move to go after them.

"Let's fill the bucket about two-thirds full of some of that pond water," Push said. "We'll pour in these fish and then make another run or two with the seine."

Within a few minutes, they had all the bait they needed and more. "We'll pick up some fishing poles on the way back," Push said. They walked back toward the cabin and stopped off at a canebrake near the edge of the bluff. "Anything over eight feet long is good enough," Push said. "Let's cut four poles each. If we want any more we can always get 'em tomorrow."

They got their poles and started back for Push's cabin. When they reached the place where the trail started out of the bottom and back up the bluff, they stashed them in a pile at the side of the trail. "We can pick 'em up there when we come down in the morning," he said. "Unfortunately, we better haul the bait all the way back to the cabin. Otherwise a coon is liable to get into them."

It was a comfortably cool evening and Push and Hern slept with the cabin's windows thrown open. Hern heard barred owls calling through the night from the bottomland woods beneath the ridge. Then, far too quickly, Push was waking him from his sleep just when it seemed he was most enjoying it. "Time to be waking up, Hern. It'll be daylight in a half hour and we want to be heading for the river as soon as we can see to walk. Come on out and get limbered up for the day. I got us a pan of biscuits just about ready."

The light was streaming up over the hills across the river as they reached the edge of the ridge and started down the bluff. They descended into the distinctive aroma of the river bottom, accentuated now in the heavy air of dawn–an odor compounded of willows and water and long-wet sandy earth. By the time they reached the flat land, the light was strong enough for them to see deeply into the woods on either side of the trail. They spooked a doe with two fawns that bounded and ran away into the woods with exquisite grace, making hardly a sound in their passage. They stood in silence for a moment, watching until the deer were gone from view. Neither of them spoke of it. When Push turned back to the trail, Rube immediately fell in line beside him.

They continued winding deeper into the woods and toward the river. At a certain point, Push turned out of the trail and proceeded northward through the unmarked woods. He was heading for a wide curve of the river where there was a deep pool that was one of his favorite fishing holes.

A pair of wood ducks jumped up from the surface of a nearby slough and flew away side by side in the pearly light, making the alarm calls that sounded a little like a pig's squeal but were much purer and more musical, beautiful and evocative of wild nature, herself. Their music faded away in the soft air of dawn. The fishermen walked on. They were nearing the river now. They could hear the smooth gurgle of its current running past the banks and around logs and stobs that protruded from its depths to break the smoothness of the surface. They stepped to the edge of the trees and there it was.

The river shone with a subdued glow of copper in the strong twilight before sunrise. They were at a wide bend that brought the flow of the current hard into the bank on the side they were to fish but where a greater depth and width than usual reduced the speed of the current, making it easier to fish there. "The fishing is good anywhere along this bend," Push said. "I wouldn't know just which place is better than another. I've caught 'em all through here.

"Rig up about ten feet of line on each pole and put your lead on a foot-and-a-half above your hook so when your lead hits bottom your bait will drift in the current just a few inches above. Once you get one rig fishing, stob the pole in the bank good and rig up another. We'll use a perch on some and crawfish on the others and we'll see what they're biting. We can vary the size up from rig to rig, too. We'll find something they want."

Not five minutes passed before Hern pulled in the first fish. It was a sleek, silver-gray channel cat of about two pounds. Hern strung him up quickly. Before he could get settled in good, he had a hard strike on another of his poles and had another fish flopping on the bank.

"When are you going to catch one, Push?" he called out. "Maybe you better check your hooks. I think you forgot to put on any bait." Hern was vastly pleased with the morning.

"No, I'm satisfied my bait's alright," Push said. "Maybe I'll catch one in a minute. But don't wait on me. You go ahead and catch as many as you want."

They caught fish steadily for the next half-hour. Already they had almost more than they could use.

Suddenly an eerie bird call pierced the early morning air. It was pure and musical, like someone blowing on a hunting horn, but it was high-pitched and nasal-sounding. It bore the same wildness as a wolf's howl or a panther's scream. It came three times in quick succession, ringing through the forest.

"Let's be quiet, now Hern," Push said softly. "Let's be quiet and be as still as we can."

Push was obviously in a state of intense alertness. His nostrils were flared. His eyes covered the trees on the far bank of the river, his head turning in smooth, slow movements to one side, then the other. Observing his behavior, Hern followed suit.

After a few moments, a magnificent bird flew in from the depths of the forest and landed in full view on a cypress limb that stretched over the river on the opposite bank, not one-hundred feet from where the fishermen sat motionless and mesmerized.

The bird gave voice to its piercing cry again, then again, and a second bird emerged from the forest and landed beside the first. The birds were obviously woodpeckers, but their tremendous size and implicit power made them seem almost supernatural. They were far bigger than a crow. Bigger even than a red-shouldered hawk. Their plumage was black overall, with a bold white stripe running in a curve down the length of the neck and across the back to merge with a large patch of white on the back of the folded wing. The male bird had a tall, upturned crest of brilliant red; the female's crest was slightly smaller and was black. But the most outstanding feature of each bird was its bill. The bills were long and strongly built and shaped like a narrow, sharp-pointed wedge, and they were white as bleached bone.

The birds looked toward each other, inclined their heads, and lightly touched their bills together twice. As they turned back toward their surroundings they must have sensed something strange about the objects sitting in the open on the opposite side of the river. Both birds lifted from the branch, seemingly upon the same impulse, flew upstream over the river for fifty feet, then swerved back into the forest. In flight, their heads were held back so that their long, ivory bills led the direction of movement like a straight-line continuation of the head and extended neck.

Hern said nothing, but looked to Push, who appeared almost as if in a trance. At length, he assumed his usual visage and spoke.

"That's maybe the finest bird in all this wilderness, Hern. You can't find them often, even out here. We've seen something special today. Something to remember. We've seen the ivory-billed woodpecker—the Great God Almighty, himself."

Chapter Twelve. February, 1834.

When Push-pun-tubby was twenty-five years old an infectious fever struck his village. His wife and young son were stricken and were dead within two days. After their burial he went off to himself and stayed for three months alone in the wild country at the headwaters of Little Coldwater Creek north of it's juncture with the Coldwater River. When he went back to his village, he knew there was no longer a life for him there, at least not one that he cared to live. He longed instead to roam the wild country again, to live in the old way, to be alone in the realm of the forest.

In the villages, the old life of the Chickasaw was deteriorating. The Mixed Bloods had assumed most of the old power of the Council and had infused the ways of the white man's government into the management of tribal affairs. Chickasaws had become full-time farmers, and many, emulating the whites, had acquired slaves to do their farming for them. Others sold the skins from their hunting and trapping to white traders to buy whiskey. There was much drunkenness and slovenliness. In many cases, the old ways of morality in relations between men and women were breaking down. There was increasing pressure from the White Government for the Chickasaw to cede their ancestral lands and emigrate west of the Big River. Push-pun-tubby wanted no part of it.

He sat in the lodge of his uncle. The two men were alone. A small fire burned between them. They passed a pipe back and forth and smoked. Long silences passed between their comments, and when they spoke, they did so with deliberation. In the silences between, they glanced at each other, looked at the design of the pipe, watched the smoke drift up to the ceiling and out the smoke hole.

Lush-pun-tubby, his uncle, was also his clan chief. As the elder brother of his mother, Lush-pun-tubby had been his primary male guide in his journey to manhood, as was the Chickasaw way.

"I understand what you want to do, Nephew. I might wish to do the same if I were a young man." Lush-pun-tubby paused. "The way ahead is not clear for the Chickasaw. I fear it will not be to my liking. But I will follow the path that opens before me. You must find your own path."

Push-pun-tubby sat in silence for a time, considering his uncle's words. "Yes, Uncle. That is what I feel, myself. I have no way to know where my path will lead. But for now I feel it takes me deep into the woods and wild country, to be much by myself, alone with the spirits. Alone with He Who Lives in the Clear Sky."

Again there followed a period of silence between the two men. Then Lush-pun-tubby spoke once more. "I can feel the wisdom of that path for you. But will you have no company at all? A man might be very lonely."

"Maybe I will take a young dog with me," Push-pun-tubby answered at length. "One I can teach to sit quietly and to keep from movement or chase unless I send it. One who can get his own food if set on his own. Such a dog would be a good companion, and I will have plenty of time for working with a dog."

"A dog is good," Lush-pun-tubby said next. "What of a woman?"

The pause between them stretched more than a minute. "Maybe I will want a woman's company again, Uncle. For now I don't wish for another woman. I don't wish the responsibility of a woman. I don't know if I ever will again."

After a while, the uncle spoke again. "Your path is a lonely one, Push-pun-tubby," he said. "But it is a good path. Follow it in peace."

Chapter Thirteen. March, 1857.

Hern and Maddie sat in proper order on the sofa in the McCall living room–not touching, not too close together, but not far apart, either. Martha McCall hovered in the background from time to time, seemingly intent on business of her own.

"I'm awfully glad you came to see me this morning, Henshaw. It's about time you did, too," she said. "It seems like an age since I saw you last."

"I've thought about you every day, Maddie–many times every day. I've been busy with Gabe. I've been working with him a lot the past few weeks."

"I've thought of you often as well, Henshaw," she said. *More often than you need to know about*, she thought. "But thinking is not the same as seeing you," she said.

"I know, Maddie. It's not the same for me, either–not nearly the same."

"And how are you doing with Gabe? How is he coming along?" Maddie said.

"He's doing great things, Maddie. It's going a lot faster than I thought it would. Gabe is learning as much as I am.

"I rode him over here today, and you should have seen how he handled!" Hern said. "I hardly had to touch him with the reins at all."

"But if you don't use the reins, how do you control where he goes and what he does?" Maddie asked, genuinely surprised. She had done a good deal of riding, herself, but had not taken a great interest in horsemanship.

"Well, if I wanted to, I could tell him what to do—he takes spoken commands very well. But my knees are in contact with him all the time. He responds to pressure from my knees so well I don't have to tell him what I want. Lately I don't even have to think about giving a signal with my knees. It's enough if I just think about what we're going to do next and imagine he's about to do his part of it, and he does it—does whatever it is I thought of him doing."

"Why, that's marvelous, Hern! I had no idea!" Maddie said.

"Well, neither did I until Push showed me—and told me how to go about doing it, myself," Hern said.

"And you did all that in just a few weeks—I never would have believed it," Maddie said.

"But the most important part of it all is that Gabe handles just as well with all sorts of working rigs as he does with a man on his back. You can work in front of him or behind him. It doesn't matter. He'll do anything you want him to do. It doesn't matter whether he's got the reins on or not. He works as well without reins as with them."

"But that is amazing!" Maddie said. "I've never heard of anything like it. Why, that is wonderful!"

"The most wonderful thing about it is that it gives me a start—it gives me a start on a big dream," Hern said.

"Why, I'm intrigued, Henshaw," Maddie said. "Tell me about this dream."

"I want to start my own business—a mule-breeding business. I want two or three big Jacks—male donkeys, the bigger the better—and a good number of big brood mares. I want to breed mules and then work with them the way I've worked with Gabe.

"Then I want to place them on farms all around this county, Maddie, then all around this part of the country. I want to turn out animals so well bred and so well trained they'll attract attention and talk. I want people asking where they came from and who trained them. I want people all around the country clamoring to get mules like those for themselves. I want them to know where they can get those kinds of mules. They can get them from me. They can get them from Henshaw Mule Breeders, Center Hill, Mississippi."

"My goodness, Hern! That is a big dream. A huge dream! A wonderful dream!" Maddie exclaimed.

"I know it will take time," Hern said, "I need to get more experience somewhere, first. I need to earn some real money and save it. Pa can help some, but I'll need to come up with a good deal more on my own. But one day–maybe a day not so very long from now–I hope I can do it. Gabe has shown me it is possible. Gabe has given me a start."

"Henshaw Mule Breeders!" Maddie said, her eyes bright. She was seeing Hern's dream; it was becoming her own dream, as well. "Known across DeSoto County. Known from Natchez to Nashville. Known across Mississippi, in Arkansas and Alabama. Oh, Hern, it is a beautiful dream!"

"But the farm is just the first part of the dream, and it isn't the most beautiful part–not by a mile," Hern said softly. "Maddie McCall is the most beautiful part of the dream. It is you, Maddie. It is having you on that farm with me."

As Hern was speaking, Maddie's hand had started to drift slowly across the space between them. Hern reached out to take it in his.

Maddie looked into his eyes. "Then it will be my dream, too, Hern. It is my dream already," she said. They sat for a moment, Hern squeezing her hand, feeling corresponding pressure as she squeezed his. "Oh, I wish it could be now," she said. "I am too impatient. I do not want to wait."

"I don't want to wait either, Maddie. But I think we have to, for a while, at least. Until I can make a start on my own. Maybe it won't take all that long. We don't have to start out fashionable to begin with, we just have to have a place to start from."

They continued to hold hands. Sat quietly for a minute.

"Well, Henshaw," Maddie said brightly, "we can't sit here being serious all day. Would you like to go out for a while and feed the ducks?"

"Why, Miss Maddie, of course I would," Hern said. "You know it is one of my favorite occupations."

Chapter Fourteen. April, 1857.

Hern left home before daylight and headed Gabe across the north side of the place toward the wilderness north of Push's cabin. He had no clear idea of what he sought there, but he wanted to spend the day on his own in wild country, where the world remained as it had been from the first.

Gabe wore only a halter. Its rope lay slack as Hern guided him with slight changes in the tension of his legs at Gabe's sides–often, it seemed, with only the movement of his mind. It was cold in the early dawn of mid April, and Hern wished he had brought along a jacket or an extra shirt. *But it will warm soon enough once the sun is up,* he thought.

They wound their way uphill through a long hollow past newly opened white flowers of dogwoods that seemed to glow with their own light along both sides of the hollow. The explosive gobble of a Tom turkey rang out from somewhere over the ridge to their right, not far away. From the middle distance, they heard the answering yelps of a hen that sounded like she might be ready for courting.

"Turkeys have it easier than we do, Gabe–than people do, I mean. As a fact, the whole issue don't concern you. Could be you're just as lucky it don't," Hern said.

"But as I was saying, a Tom turkey just has to grow up to where he's accepted as a full male. Once he's done that he can go out and court any female that acts like she's ready to start a family–like that one we just heard. He can go right into strutting and breeding.

" 'Course, to get to be grown in the first place he's had to outsmart every fox and wolf and bobcat in the country that would like to kill him for supper. Then he has to be bold enough to dominate most all the other males in his section, or it ain't likely he'll be allowed a decent chance for a single courtship. On second thought, Gabe, I guess that old Tom don't have it so easy after all."

Hern and Gabe topped out at the head of the hollow and continued across the gentle roll of the ridge top through an open forest of mature hardwoods. They heard the high-pitched calls of a big, crested flycatcher from the top of a tree nearby, "Wheep, wheep," it said.

"That's the first flycatcher I've heard this spring, Gabe," Hern said. "I bet he just got in here last night or this morning from somewhere down south. He's carving out a place for himself already. Soon he'll have a female move in there with him. Then he can go about getting his family started. All he has to do is to keep catching insects, keep rivals out of his space, and keep out of the clutches of a hawk, and he can have a successful season. I guess he's got his work cut out for him, at that, Gabe. I guess things ain't all that easy for anybody."

They crossed the ridge top and started down another hollow. When they came to where a small stream started out of the hillside, Hern guided Gabe over and let him take a good drink, then rode him out onto a level bench and hopped down. "I'm going to leave you here, Gabe, and wander around for a while by myself."

He led Gabe over to a tree with a convenient limb and wrapped the lead rope around it a couple of times. Gabe would stay put if Hern told him to, even without the rope, but this was not an exercise. There was no reason to leave Gabe under the mental strain of following an order in Hern's absence. With his lead rope looped over the limb as a token restraint, Gabe could relax his mind entirely. "You just take it easy for a while, Gabe. I'll be back before long." Hern patted Gabe's neck a couple of times and walked off.

Hern walked until he came to the edge of a cut-bank that dropped fifteen feet or so to the edge of a creek. He sat down with his back to a tree trunk and looked out across the creek into the forest beyond. He was alone now in the strangeness of the forest. The wilderness loomed and strengthened about him. He felt a great power and energy, almost an alien force in its utter separation from himself. The stark awareness of his own apart-ness was discomforting. He tried to quiet the busy-ness of his mind—the constant flow of mundane and pointless comment that enforced his separation, that imposed a barrier that separated him from the life all around him. He accomplished a few moments of quietness. The words started to flow again, unbidden, but he stopped them, cut them off in mid comment, was quiet. He experienced a unique, tingling sensation in the area of the solar plexus. The separation between himself and the world of things faded and was gone. It was as though he were now but a single aspect of a vast consciousness that included everything. He experienced a fine sense of perfection in all the things around him. He knew their full satisfaction with existence just as it was. Eternity was here, now, fully present in the immediate moment.

A red-shouldered hawk flew upstream above the creek, flared out in a quick turn in front of Hern, came to a brisk landing on a branch above the opposite bank. He screamed his hunting cry. It rang clear and loud again and again. A second hawk sailed into a tree just downstream from the first. *His mate*, Hern thought.

Hern climbed onto a log at the edge of the bank, took a step to his right to gain a view of the female hawk. The bank crumbled and fell away at his end of the log, the log dipped and turned beneath his feet, and Hern was thrown in a somersault over the edge of the bank. He landed hard on his left side; his head slammed against the sandy mud beside the creek. Above him, the log teetered; more of the bank crumbled away beneath it. Slowly, majestically, it gave up its purchase, succumbed to gravity, bounced once on the bank-side, rolled, and came to rest atop Hern's left knee.

Hern came awake in a sea of sickness and raw sensation. He was unable to focus his eyes and his head felt shattered. Something was terribly wrong in his left side. It screamed at every breath. His knee was crushed and pounding beneath a heavy weight. He moved his head slightly to get a look at where he was, and was rocked by a shocking wave of dizziness and nausea. His mind faltered. He was slipping away. *Is this what it feels like to die?* he thought. But the pain continued in blinding intensity, and he knew he was still alive

Hern realized he was lying on his back in the sandy mud of the creek bank. A good deal of time had passed. His right leg lay in the water of the creek and had started to get very cold. His left leg was buried in the mud beneath a big log. *The log rolled out from under me when the bank caved,* he thought. *It threw me down and it must have come down behind me. I should have looked at that log before I climbed on it. Dumb! That was dumb!*

Okay, so it was dumb. So what? Get up off your back. You got to drag yourself out of here.

He took a good breath against the stabbing in his side. Steeled himself for more, sat up, waited for his head to settle, reached back with his hands against the flat sand, worked his right foot up against the log and pushed back as hard as he could. A flood of pain washed through him and he fell again to his back. He lay there. Maybe he had lost consciousness again for a while. He didn't know. What he did know was that he had not moved his leg an inch beneath the log.

I'm in a fix, here, a hell of a fix. I'm caught good. I can't move my leg at all. He felt the beginnings of panic.

Be calm! Panic some other time, if you have to. You got work to do here. You got to do something to help yourself.

He struggled to a sitting position again and looked at the ground around him. There was a stick not far away. He could reach it if he stretched a little. He got the stick, leaned forward and began to dig at the sandy mud beside his knee beneath the log. He dug at one side, then the other. It was very slow going. One side and then the other.

The stick broke. Hern sobbed twice in his frustration and pain.

No crying! No acting like a crying baby! Now ain't the time. Look around and find another stick, you got more digging to do.

He found another stick, stronger and longer than the first, at the edge of the creek to his right. He couldn't reach it with his hand but managed to catch hold of it by using the longer half of his first stick. *Now get back to work. Take it slow. Be careful. Don't break this one. If you break this one you may not get another.*

He worked slowly and steadily. He lay back and rested from time to time, when he had to, then went back to his digging. After a long time–he had no way to judge how long, but it seemed a very long time–he had dug out on both sides and well under his knee for as far forward as he could reach with his stick beneath the log. Night was coming on. His strength was beginning to fail. There was nothing more he could do with the stick, anyway. He lay back and rested for a time. Prepared himself for one more big effort.

He sat up, positioned himself carefully, both hands flat behind him, right foot braced against the log. Drew his breath slowly, pushed away from the log with all his strength, drove himself harder and harder, until he fell back, shaking and exhausted. He had gained nothing–not a fraction of an inch.

He lay there on his back, panting for breath. Felt the wetness in his eyes. Didn't chastise himself this time. There was nothing more he could do.

Maybe they will come and find me, he thought. *I will just have to wait until they come. I'll wait as long as I can.*

Death held no terror for him. It was a loss of time, an onset of eternity. But neither did it hold an attraction. He wanted time. He wanted to be in time with Maddie. There were so many things he wanted to do, so many experiences he wanted to have. Maddie would be here, and he wanted to be here with her. *Maybe I can last the night*, he thought. *They will get Push. When daylight comes, he can track Gabe to where I left him—*

"Gabe!," he said aloud. "Gabe! Yes, Gabe."

He thought, *If I could get Gabe down here, he could help me pull free. He could pull me right out of here. He's not tied down. He can pull loose. Maybe he can find me.*

Hern struggled to a sitting position, took in his breath. "Gabe, Gabe," he called. His voice sounded frail to his own ears. Frail and pathetic. He tried harder, yelled with all his strength. "Gabe. Back, Gabe, back. Back, back. Come get me, Gabe. Come on, old Gabe." He fell back to the sand, exhausted, panting, drifting, drifting away. Something like a dream possessed his mind, and he was once again with the rabbits of his youth, in the chamber of shrubs. The rabbits were very near. Somehow he knew he could touch them, now. They would not run away this time. But he did not want to touch them; he knew if he did he might never leave the chamber.

He felt warm breath, calling him back from the dream, then the nuzzling of Gabe's lips on his cheek. "Old Gabe, Gabe. You found me, Gabe! Good old Gabe. How'd you get down here, boy? I'm mighty glad to see you, old Gabe."

Hern took Gabe's lead rope and wrapped it tightly around his right forearm. He braced his right leg against the log and set his left hand flat behind him. "Alright, Gabe. Back."

Gabe started backward, the rope tightened. Gabe pulled against the weight and Hern pushed away from the log with all his might. "Back. Back, Gabe," he called again. Nothing gave for a moment, then there was a slight movement, a slight gain. Then his knee came loose from beneath the log, his leg pulled free, and Gabe was dragging him backward across the sand of the creek bank.

"Whoa, Gabe. Whoa, old fellow. Good old Gabe! What a good old Gabe!"

Hern caught his breath, worked his way up under Gabe's head, pulled himself to his feet with the lead rope. He hobbled along, leaning on Gabe, until they came to a low bank. Hern dragged himself up the bank, got Gabe to step up alongside it, was able to work his left leg across Gabe's back and get himself into something resembling a riding position. He leaned forward and slipped the halter from Gabe's head and wrapped the halter and lead rope around his own waist. Then he lay his chest on Gabe's neck, locked his hands beneath the neck, said "Let's go home, Gabe. Let's go home, boy."

Doc Mallory left Hern's sickroom and was met almost in the doorway by his anxious parents. "He should make a good recovery from this Mitch, Elise," Doc said. "It's his leg I'm most concerned about. His other injuries don't seem life-threatening and are getting better already. Aside from the leg, the head injury is still of some concern. He sustained a pretty serious concussion. It seems to be clearing up alright, but it could still be a problem. We're not quite out of the woods on it, but I feel good about it. Still, it needs watching. His ribs are painful, but they're nothing to worry about. He seems to have broken two and severely bruised several others. They should heal routinely."

"His leg is another matter. There's so much swelling I can't be sure of how severely the knee is damaged. So far he has good circulation to the lower leg and foot, and that's a good sign. If it stays that way he's in no danger of losing the leg."–Elise's hand flew to her mouth.– "Now don't jump to conclusions, Elise. It will probably be alright. But I want you to check that circulation every now and then. As long as the foot stays warm and keeps good color, we're okay. If you find it staying cold to the touch or losing its normal color, I want you to send for me directly, no matter the time of day or night.

"It's not possible to say yet how much use he'll get out of that knee once he recovers. He may have to show us that, himself. But you know these youngsters are tough, and they heal fast. If Hern will work that knee hard–and I know he will–there's a good chance he can regain full use of it. But we'll just have to wait and see.

"So everything looks pretty good, considering what he's been through. All in all, we're lucky to have him still with us. If he'd lain out there in the cold all night, I don't know what would have happened."

"Thank God, Doc," Mitchell said, "that sounds like the answer to a prayer. We're lucky you were able to get out here so quickly. Elise and I appreciate it more than you know. I know we still have some problems, but you've taken a load of worry off our minds. I don't know what we would have done without you."

"Well, Mitch, to tell the truth that's about all I did—relieve your minds some, and Hern's. A patient's attitude toward his illness is important, so I may have done some good, there. As far as what I could do for Hern, physically, it didn't amount to much. Rest is what he needs, and for us to keep a close watch on the circulation in that lower leg and foot.

"If something changes and you need me, you just send word. Otherwise, I'll be back in a couple of days and see how's he's coming along. Things may look a good deal better by then."

"Thanks, Doc, you're a good citizen to have around. We're mighty lucky to have you."

A half-hour after Doc left, Matthew McCall's buggy pulled fast into the yard. Maddie jumped out before the wheels came to rest, ran up the steps to the door and opened it without knocking, although Mitchell was standing there, just about to open it, when she did.

"How is he, Mr. Henshaw? How is Hern?" Maddie cried. "Please tell me he'll be alright."

"He is alright for now, Maddie," Mitchell said. "Doc says there's every reason to think he can make a full recovery, in time. He was banged up pretty bad. He has a concussion and two broken ribs. The big problem is his knee. It was badly mashed by a falling log. That's the main thing we have to worry about."

"Is he awake, Mr. Henshaw? Can I see him?"

"Of course you can see him, Maddie. If he's not awake, he soon will be. Seeing you is likely the best medicine we can give him."

"Come with me, Maddie," Elise said. "I'll take you to him."

Hern opened his eyes, and there was Maddie, leaning over his bed. He wondered if he was dreaming, then saw he was not. She was really here. The look of tenderness and concern on her face was something he might well have dreamed about, if he'd had the imagination to dream up such an expression.

"Hern. Oh, thank God you are alright," she said quietly. "I was so worried about you."

"Maddie, it's so good to see you," Hern said. "I admit I was some worried about me, too. I'm not sure I would have made it through if I hadn't thought about you, Maddie. It helped me a lot. I didn't want to leave you."

"What happened, Hern?" she said. "How did you end up in such a mess?"

"I just did something foolish, Maddie. I just took a step without a care for where I was stepping. It was the wrong step, and I paid for it. I tipped over a big log and got thrown down a bank. Then that old log came down after me, and it got me good. Finally I dug myself out, and old Gabe pulled me out from under it. I never would have made it without Gabe."

"God bless Gabe!" Maddie said, "good old Gabe."

"My knee is awfully messed up, Maddie. Nobody knows yet how bad it will be. I hope I can get it back. I'm going to try hard to get it back. But there's a chance it will stay stiff. I may not be able to get use of it again. Maddie, I may have ruined myself."

"No, Hern, no. You haven't ruined yourself. You never could. I know someday you will die. Everybody does. But you will never be ruined."

Chapter Fifteen. April, 1857.

There was a knock at the door of Hern's sickroom, it opened, and a black man somewhat above middle height came in. "How you feeling, Hern?" he said. "Is you feeling any better?"

"Yes, I'm a lot better today, Price. Thanks for coming to see me," Hern said. "My head ain't hurting much now, and it seems to be working a lot better. My ribs feel a lot better, too. But my knee...I don't know about my knee."

"You afraid it might end up like mine," Price said. "But maybe it won't." Price had been in a logging accident as a young man. It happened that a log had rolled over his leg, too. The circumstances had been different, but the result had been similar to what had happened to Hern. Price had ended up trapped beneath a heavy log and his knee had been ruined. It had never recovered its ability to flex. Price had done his walking by swinging his leg forward from the hip ever since.

"Maybe I'll be lucky if I can get around as well as you do, Price. I've always admired the way you handle it," Hern said.

"I gets around alright. You can do it, too, Hern, if that's what you have to do. But that ain't what you wants to do. I didn't want it, neither, but it was all I had. I had to get used to it. You can get used to whatever you have to if you got no choice. Hit's with you every day. If you keep on living, you get used to it after a while. But it hurt me, Hern. Hit hurt me in my manhood. I got used to that, too, after a while. Hit don't hurt me that way anymore. But I remember when it did. I remember when it hurt me bad.

"We don't want that for you, Hern," Price said. "You don't want to settle for that. Chances are you won't have to. Maybe your leg ain't hurt as bad as mine was. Maybe you can work with it. Maybe you can make it as good as it used to be."

"I'm sure going to try, Price. I'm going to try my hardest," Hern said. "Would you take a look at my leg, Price? I'd like to see what you think of it," Hern said.

"Sho', I'll give it a look, Hern. I don't know if I'll be able to tell you anything, but I'll try," Price said.

Hern pulled the bedclothes away. Price drew a chair up close to his side and examined the knee carefully. "Hit look pretty bad, Hern, but it ain't nowhere near as bad as mine was. Hit's all swelled up and purple, but that'll go away soon enough. Then you can see what you can do with it," Price said.

"I want to know something now, if I can, Price. I want to get a better idea of what I'm faced with," Hern said. "Take a hold of it for me, Price. See if you can bend it a little."

"We got to be careful with it, Hern. We might make it bleed some more and swell up worse."

"We don't have to move it much, Price. But it would mean a lot to me if we can make it move at all," Hern said.

"Alright, then. I'll give it a try. Hit's likely to hurt some."

"I don't care if it hurts, Price. I want it to move," Hern said.

Price took hold of Hern's lower leg with both hands well down on the calf below the knee.

"Alright, Hern, you clasp your hands behind the thigh and pull against me," Price said. "You ready?"

"I'm ready, Price. Let's do it."

Hern gasped at the pain, but he was sure the knee had moved. "I think it moved, Price. I think it moved!" Hern almost shouted.

"Hit moved, alright, Hern. I seen it bend."

"It moved! Great God Almighty, it moved!" Hern was almost laughing, and Price too, almost laughing with him.

"See can you move it by yourself, Hern," Price said.

Hern turned onto his right side, let the left leg rest on the bed. "Watch it for me, Price. I'm going to move it now." Hern strained, gasped, but the leg moved again. The knee bent. Only a little, but it bent.

"You done it, Hern! You sho' done it!" Price said happily. "Praise the Lord, boy. You's still got you a knee."

Hern lay back exhausted. Exhausted and very happy.

"That's enough for now, Hern," Price said. "But from now on you can start working on it, time to time. You can do it even there in the bed. You can work it a little more and a little longer every day. I'll bet it won't be long, you'll be running up a hill!"

"Thanks, Price," Hern said. "I thank you a lot. You're a good friend."

"You a good friend to me, Hern. I feel mighty good about your leg," Price said.

"Would it be alright if George come in here for a minute?" Price asked. "He come up to the house with me. I know he'd like to see you."

"Well, it would make me feel good to see George. I'm glad he came. Please bring him on back here, Price. I'd love to see him."

By the time Hern was again able to stay out of the bed most of the day, he was walking around the house and yard, albeit with a pronounced limp. It was a limp, alright, but it wasn't a drag. Nor was he swinging his leg forward from the hip the way Price had to do. His knee was flexing at every step; he just couldn't take it too far; he couldn't rest too much weight on it, or for too long at a time. He extended his range and distance of travel each day. Each day he tried to bend the knee more than he had the day before. He worked at flexing the knee constantly through the day when he was sitting and as he lay in bed at night before sleeping

His head was entirely well now. It was working better than ever, he said, such as it was. His ribs only pained him now when he bumped them on something or made a quick move he wasn't used to. He spent a good deal of time reading during his convalescence, and each time he came across a passage he wanted to think about for a while, he worked at flexing the knee while he thought. This happened often as he was reading Walter Scott's *Ivanhoe*. Sometimes Scott's writing seemed unnecessarily convoluted as it twined its way through ten or twelve phrases in a single sentence. Scott had a good story to tell, but Hern sometimes wished he would get on with it.

He reread Chapman's translation of Homer's *The Iliad* with great enjoyment. He liked the majestic flow of poetic language, the violent acts of the participants and the detail with which they were described. He liked the way the gods were constantly making mischief in the affairs of the godlike but struggling mortals. *Mortals always have to struggle,* he thought, *godlike or not.*

As his leg strengthened and the tightness in his knee gradually loosened, Hern walked in the sun among the freshly planted fields of cotton, corn, and clover. He walked the length of the main field road along the creek through the middle of the place—the cultivated fields lying on either side; three-quarters of a mile from the barn to the farthest field, three-quarters of a mile back.

He began climbing the slope up the ridge on the north side of the barn. On his fourth climb, he made it all the way to the top. As the days passed, he climbed it faster and faster. He experimented with running—only a few steps, at first, then a little faster, a little farther each day.

A day came when he thought he was ready for a run up the hill to the ridge top. He rested his leg through the afternoon and walked out late in the day as the sun was about to go down. Started into a jogging run on the flat before the hill, continued it straight up the slope. On he went, dodging among the trees and bushes, keeping up his jogging run till he reached the top of the hill.

In his concentration on the task before him, Hern had failed to notice George and Price, returned from the day's work, standing in the lot below the barn. They watched with increasing tension as he began his run and headed with determination straight up the slope. His intention was obvious. "Do it, Hern, you can do it, boy," George said, almost to himself. "Go ahead, Hern. Go ahead all the way," Price said.

Hern heard a disturbance below him as he reached the top of the ridge, looked down, saw George and Price standing there, clapping their hands, recognized the noise he had heard as the shouts of their cheering. He turned and faced them directly, raised his hands in the air and waved them like a political winner at a victory rally, grinning back at the grinning faces below.

Chapter Sixteen. May, 1857.

Mitchell Henshaw walked down to the barn and into the milking parlor, where George was finishing the morning's milking. "Morning, George. Everything going okay?"

"Yassuh, Mr. Mitch, everything goin' just fine," George said.

"George, I want you to knock off work at noon today," Mitchell said, "I want you to go over to Olive Branch this afternoon and pick up three new hay mows from Mr. Jameson's hardware. Then you can go over to Mr. West's store and pick up 50 pounds of flour before we run out of biscuits around here. The clover in a couple of those patches is getting pretty near ready to cut. If we get some new hay mows I might have some success in getting those boys to cut us some hay over the next few days."

"Yassuh, that'd be a good success indeed, Mr. Mitch. I'd like to see that myself," George said.

"Take the small wagon, George. Everything ought to fit in it alright. You can take Laura in with you if you want to, if she ain't too busy."

"Why, thank you Mr. Mitch. I 'spect she like that, alright. I'll make sho' she get her business done early."

"Alright, George. Just tell the gentlemen at the stores the stuff is for me. They'll write it down. Have you a good trip, now."

George and Laura left in the wagon about 1:30 that afternoon. When they got to town a little over an hour later, George parked the wagon in the square, unhitched the horse, and led it over to the big well in the center of the square. He drew up some water for the trough and let the horse drink. Then he took it back over to the wagon and tied it off short to the hand rail on the passenger side of the wagon. He and Laura walked across the square and went into Mr. Jameson's store.

"Afternoon, George," said Mr. Jameson, " how's that old boss man of yours? Wouldn't come to town for himself, eh? Had to take a man out of the field where he could be getting good work done and send him to town, eh?"

"Good afternoon, Mr. Red," said George. "Aw, you know Mr. Mitch, Mr. Red. I 'spect he got some business to tend to out to the place this evenin' hisself. Anyway, he tol' me to come in here for him and what to get. I 's just happy for the change of scenery."

"Why, certainly you are, George," Mr. Jameson gave his big, friendly laugh, "of course you are. Who's that you've got with you this evening?"

"Oh, Mr. Red, you know that's my wife, Laura. She like to just look at some of them bolts of cloth while I take care of Mr. Mitch's business, if that be alright, suh."

"Of course it's alright, George," Mr. Jameson boomed, laughing again. "Of course it is. Look all she likes. Now what can I do for you and Mr. Henshaw today?"

George and Laura were driving back toward Center Hill in the late afternoon, the flour and the hay mows stowed in the wagon box behind them. Laura was talking about the bolts of cloth she had seen in the store, which colors she liked best, and what dresses she could make if she had the cloth. She needed a new dress or two, she said, if she was to keep herself dressed good enough to be working in the Henshaw house without embarrassing Miss Elise for having her there. George said he'd ask Mr. Mitch about maybe buying some cloth when he got a chance. There was little traffic. They were well out in the middle of a long, lonesome stretch when they came upon a white man in the trees beside the road. He seemed to be having some trouble with his horse. He looked up from the horse's hoof he'd been studying to see George and Laura in the wagon. "Say, boy," he called out, "would you mind getting down off that wagon a minute and seeing if you can help me with my horse? He seems to have some problem with his foot."

"No suh, I'll be glad to help if I can." George climbed down from the seat and walked over to where the man and the horse waited in the trees. "Would you like me to take a look at the foot, suh?" George asked politely.

"Yes, I'd appreciate it if you would," the man said. "I can't seem to make out what's wrong with it."

George took hold of the horse's hoof with both hands, turned it bottom up and took a good look at it. He examined the frog, or sole of the foot, felt around the edges of the hoof and looked at the back. He checked the lower leg in front and in back. He saw nothing wrong anywhere and couldn't feel anything wrong in the ankle or find any spots that seemed tender to the horse. Finally he said, "I'm sorry, Boss, I can't see as there's anything wrong with that foot."

"Maybe that's because there is nothing wrong with it, George. You see, I just wanted a chance to talk with you a minute," the man said.

"'Scuse me suh, you knows me by name?" George said.

"I know who you are, alright. I know who owns you and I know where you live. I just want to ask you one question, George. I want to know if you'd like to be a free man?"

George looked at the man in confusion. He didn't answer. He didn't dare make an answer to such a question.

"Because that's what I want to offer you, George. I want to offer you your freedom."

"I 'preciate it, Boss, I sho' does, but I ain't thinking of no such thing as freedom. I feels satisfied just like I is. I can't be study'n no freedom."

"That sounds loyal, George, and that's good. But I'm serious about making you free. Just listen a minute and I'll tell you how we'll work it.

"I'll write out a paper says you belong to me. Says I bought you over east of Nashville. I'll come by the Henshaw place and pick you up in a night or two. You and your family, too, if you want to bring them. I can make papers on all of you. Then we'll clear out of here.

"We'll go somewhere where I can sell you. Then after I sell you, I'll come back and pick you up and we'll take off somewhere else. I'll give you half the money on the sale. We'll work our way north and we'll sell you again. You'll get half the money every time. Then after I sell you two or three times, you'll have enough money to set yourself up in life and I'll take you to a free state and I'll set you free. Write you out a good set of freedom papers, too, you and your family both. You'll all be free and set up in life.

"How does that strike you, George? What do you say to that? Free and set up in life."

"I don't know, suh. I thanks you kindly, suh, but I don't think of such stuff as that. I prob'ly be better to just stay like I is. I got no complaints. I been with Mr. Henshaw a long time. Hit's all I know."

"I know it might take a minute to get used to the idea, George, you just take a minute, now. Just take your time. I'm not rushing you. But you won't get a chance like this every day. You'll never get another chance like this in your life, George."

"I thank you kindly for your consideration, suh, but I don't need no mo' time. I just wants to go on home where I belongs. Please, suh, just let me go on home. And thank you, suh. Thank you."

"Now look here, boy. I've taken enough time on your foolishness. You're coming with me whether you like it or not. You'll like it well enough, once you get used to it. You're coming with me, you hear?" The man had drawn a pistol out of his waistband, and George thought he was about to get shot. He was worried about Laura, still sitting in the wagon.

"Please, Boss, just let me go on home now. I needs to get on home."

The man drew back the pistol and struck George hard in the face. George fell back and sat on the ground. In the wagon, Laura gasped and clapped her hand over her mouth. She didn't know what to do.

George struggled quickly back to his feet. "Laura, you just stay where you is, you just stay right there," he shouted.

"She'll be alright for now, boy, but you've got no more choice. You are coming with me tomorrow night. I know where you live. I know where your family is. You don't come with me I'll kill them all, George. All of 'em, even the little girl. You're coming with me boy, coming tomorrow night. There's a place where the Henshaws make their wood, a wood lot at the end of a little field road running south from the big house. You know what place I mean, boy?"

"Yassuh. I knows the place," George said.

"Well I'll be there at the end of that field road tomorrow night an hour after sundown. You show up within fifteen minutes or you'll be sorry, boy, mighty sorry, you and your whole family. You understand me?"

"Yassuh, yassuh, I understands you. I'll be there. Just don't hurt my family, please, suh. Just don't hurt my family."

"Alright. We understand each other. You better be there tomorrow night. Now get on out of here."

Chapter Seventeen. May, 1857.

George came up to the kitchen door at the Henshaw house just after supper and knocked. Aunt Lucy was still cleaning up the supper dishes. She came and opened the door and looked out.

"Laws a mercy!" she cried. "What done happened George? What done run into yo' face?"

"I got to see Mr. Mitchell, Aunt Lucy. Tell him I think it be better if he see me out here in the kitchen, please, ma'am. Ask him please come when he can."

"My God, George, what's happened? What happened to your face," Mitchell exclaimed.

"Hit ain't so bad, suh," George said, "hit look wuse than it feel. I had some bad trouble, suh. I didn't know what to do about it. I knew I better come ask you what to do."

"Alright, George. You did the right thing. Now tell me everything that happened."

George told the whole story. "Now what can I do Mr. Mitch? Oh Lawd, what can I do now?"

Mitchell thought for a moment. "I'll tell you what we're going to do George. You're going to meet that man tomorrow, and I'm going to be with you. But I'm going to be there ahead of you and hiding in the trees. And unless I miss my guess, Mr. Oakley and Mr. Wilson are going to be there with me. We'll settle this fellow's hash, George. I don't want you to worry about it any further. Tell Laura not to worry, either, and to keep this business to herself–not just tonight and tomorrow, but from now on. You did right coming to me, George. I don't won't you to worry about it anymore. Anybody asks you about that face, tell 'em you run into a fence post in the dark.

"Now, what did this man look like, George?"

"Well, he a fair-looking man but have a kind of a wolfish look to his face. He got black hair and big sweeping mustaches, kind o' slicked up mustaches. He about yo' size, Mr. Mitch, and he look like he can move some better than average."

"We'll be ready for him, George. You go on home and you and Laura get you some sleep. We're going to take care of this and it won't trouble you any more after tomorrow. Be up at the barn at mid afternoon tomorrow and I'll tell you just what to do. Now go on home and take it easy."

Just after breakfast the next day Mitchell rode over to the house of his nearest neighbor on the south side. Dave Wilson was just stepping out of his house when Mitchell rode into the yard. Wilson walked over to greet him, a big grin on his face. "Howdy, Mitch, how you doing today, old rascal?"

"I'm not doing so bad, Dave, but I do have a problem," Mitchell answered. "It appears we got a slave robber in the neighborhood, and he's already approached George."

"A slave robber!" Dave exclaimed. "That is a problem, a serious problem."

"Dave, I'd appreciate it if you'd saddle up and ride over to Ed's place with me right now. I'd like the three of us to talk about this," Mitchell said.

"I'll be with you in a minute, Mitch," Dave said immediately.

Ed Oakley saw his two friends riding up and walked out from his barn to meet them. "Morning, boys, you fellas had anything to eat today?" he said.

"Howdy, Ed. We've eaten plenty, I reckon. Let's walk over to your feed room where we can talk. Something serious is in the air." Mitchell said.

"We've got us a slave robber in the neighborhood, Ed," Mitchell said, after the three men had entered Oakley's feed room and closed the door behind them. Oakley looked from Mitchell to Wilson and back, raised his hands to his hips. "Tell me about it, Mitch," he said.

Mitchell told them George's story in detail. They listened with thoughtful expressions. Neither man interrupted until Mitchell finished his story.

"I heard about a scheme some of these outlaws have been running," Oakley said. "They lure off a slave to go with them on a promise of freeing him. They sell him three or four times, then when things start to get hot and the slave starts suspecting he'll never be freed, they kill him, maybe him and his whole family. This slave robber ain't just your problem, Mitch, it's *our* problem," Oakley said.

"I feel the same way," said Wilson. "What do you want to do about it, Mitch?"

"I was hoping you'd see it that way," Mitch said, "and I sure thank you. Here's what I propose to do.

"You fellows drift over toward my place just past mid afternoon this evening. Bring a pistol or two with you. We'll meet at the head of the field road that runs up to my wood lot. I'll have George there with me. We'll all go up to the spot he's to meet the slave robber, but we'll go early and the three of us will hide in the woods near the spot. We'll leave George a little ways down the road toward the house, but within sight of the meeting place. When the robber shows up, George will walk up toward him, but just before George closes with the him, I'll step out and confront him, myself. You boys will have me covered from the woods."

"We'll likely have to shoot him, Mitch," Oakley said. "Think we ought to send for the Sheriff, instead?"

"No. I thought about that. We've got nothing but a slave's word against a white man. Besides, I doubt there's time now to get McBarttle over here from Hernando before the meeting. We'll have to handle it ourselves. If the man will be taken, we can just escort him down to the railroad around the Coldwater Bridge and start him walking for Holly Springs, absent his money and his weapons and his horse. If not, we may have to kill him."

"That's alright by me," Wilson said. "If he shows up for that meeting, then he's nothing but a varmint, anyway ."

"I agree," Oakley said. "I'll see you boys over at Mitchell's place this afternoon. And we might as well keep this among ourselves till then."

"My idea exactly," Mitch said. "We'll see you this evening, Ed. And thanks."

They left Ed's feed room, Mitchell and Wilson walked over to their horses, mounted, and rode away.

After dinner that afternoon, Mitchell told Hern that he'd be out of the house for a while that evening. "I told Mr. Wilson I'd look around with him and see if we could find a hydrophobic skunk that's been hanging around the neighborhood. I might be out for a good while and I want you to help your mother keep things quiet around here tonight. Don't let anybody go out wandering around, now," he said, "we might do some shooting nearby."

The twilight was running long now, and the three men stood hidden in the woods, Oakley and Mitchell on the right side of the field road and Wilson on the left. Wilson had a single-shot pistol and a lean walking stick five feet long. Mitchell had a Colt revolver that could shoot six times without reloading. Oakley carried two single-shot pistols and a rifle. George waited beside the road fifty feet away toward the direction of the house.

Just as darkness was falling, a man with a sharp face and a long black mustache came riding slowly through the south woods, stopped his horse at the end of the field road, stood down, and tied the horse to a tree limb. George started down the road toward the robber. The robber started forward to meet George. When George came up even with where he stood in the trees, Mitchell stepped out of the shadows into the road beside him. They were within twenty feet of the robber. Wilson, on the other side of the road, was even closer.

"Hold it right there, Mister," Mitchell said in a loud voice. "I think you're a damned skunk on my property, and you got a heap of explaining to do."

"Now hold on, Mister Dirt Farmer. Of course I can explain. I *will* explain. I'll explain right now." The robber reached for a revolver, and as he brought it up to center on Mitchell's chest, Dave Wilson flung his walking stick hard at the gunman's arm. The stick struck the robber's wrist a split second before he fired and the shot went wild. Mitchell Henshaw and Ed Oakley fired together a heartbeat later. The robber caught one bullet at the base of the throat, just below the chin, and the other near the center of his forehead just above the level of the eyes. He was driven straight back with the back of his head leading the fall, his feet clearing the ground and trailing. He hit flat on his back, bounced slightly, and was utterly still. Neither Henshaw nor Oakley nor Wilson ever asked or said who fired which of the two fatal shots.

The men walked up to the body and stared at it for a long moment. Finally Ed Oakley said, "Well, we've sure accounted for him, Mitch, what do we want to do with him now?"

"I expect we'd better get rid of him, Ed," Mitchell said.

"We could send for the Sheriff, turn the body over to him. I wouldn't be surprised if they had a long sheet on this hombre. Besides, he drew his gun on *us*, and it was him shot first."

"No, I can't risk George on it, Ed. There's folks in this county would take less of an opportunity than this to string up a slave involved in a white man's killing. We can't be sure the man will be recognized or that he'll be known as an outlaw. We better get rid of him, ourselves," said Mitchell.

"I tell you what. George, ease down to the barn and bring us back a big cotton sack and a good length of plow line. Ed, you can go on home and keep things quiet at your place. Dave and I will wrap the body in the cotton sack and pack it on his horse.

"Then we'll take it through the woods down to the Coldwater Bridge and we'll leave it in the open along the railroad where it'll be found early tomorrow. We'll throw the saddle in the brush somewhere, drive the horse off a little ways, and come on back home. We'll bring the sack and the plow line back with us and Dave can take 'em over to his place and burn them tomorrow, if he don't mind. It's further away from where the shooting took place. We ought to be done with it and back before midnight. Nobody's likely to see us except maybe Push, and if he does he won't ever say anything about it, not to us or to anybody else."

"Sounds as good as anything else," Ed Oakley said.

"Okay by me," said Dave Wilson.

"Good. Then that's what we'll do."

Two days later Sheriff Gene McBarttle and a deputy rode into the yard at the Henshaw house and got down from their horses. Mitchell Henshaw met them at the front steps of the house.

"Howdy, Mitch, how've you been?" the Sheriff said. "I been checking with some of the folks hereabout and figured I ought to stop in and check with you, too. Seems a man was killed, shot to death, a couple of nights ago and left down beside the tracks near the River Bridge. We don't know if he was killed there or killed somewhere else and carried there. There wasn't much blood there where he was found. I was wondering if you might know something about what happened. I'd appreciate anything you could tell me."

"Well Gene, I'm sorry to disappoint you, but I'm afraid I can't tell you anything about it at all," Mitchell said.

"Hmm, so you can't tell me anything. Well, dang it, Mitch, I was hoping you'd be some help," Gene McBarttle said.

"I'd like to help you if I could, Gene, but I can't," Mitchell said.

"Uh huh," McBarttle said, "well it would be a good thing for somebody if I could find out who killed that polecat. Turns out he was recognized as Will Starke. He was a horse thief and a murderer. There was a reward posted on him. A thousand dollars, dead or alive."

"My Lord," said Mitchell, "I'd surely like to have that reward, Gene, but I just can't tell you a thing about this Will Starke or his killing."

"Well, thanks all the same, Mitch. It's good to see you. You be sure to stop in and see us next time you get a chance," McBarttle said. Then, turning to his deputy, "Come on, Luke, we may as well get on back to Hernando."

The lawmen rode out past the edge of the dooryard and entered the woods. Luke turned to his boss and said "I think maybe he knew something, Gene. Didn't he know something?"

"Well, I can't say what he knew or what he didn't know," McBarttle answered. "But I do know Mitchell Henshaw, and he never did a dishonorable thing in his life. I was raised-up with him back there in Limestone County.

"Let me tell you something, Luke. If Mitch Henshaw and I had fifty-one dollars between us, and I gave it to him to divide behind a dark barn at midnight and he handed me my share, I'd just put it in my pocket without counting and go on down the road. And I'd know I had twenty-six dollars."

Chapter Eighteen. May, 1857.

"What is it that's out here, Push?" Hern said. "It's like a force–like some strange kind of energy. It seems like I notice it out here, particularly."

"It is not only here," Push said quietly, "it is other places, too. In fact, there is nowhere that it is not. It is within us and without us. It is with us at all times. But to notice it, we have to stop doing other things."

Push and Hern sat beside each other on a log in the wilderness along Little Coldwater Creek.

"Yes," Hern said after a while, "but I find it especially here, in this wilderness."

"Yet you have found it in other places, too," Push said. He gazed directly at Hern.

"Yes–yes you're right! But how could you know about that, Push?"

"Don't be alarmed, Hern. I can't see into your past–not directly, anyway. But I *can* see you have long familiarity with this thing we are speaking of. Maybe you had no words for it before, but it is not new to your experience.

"But you are right about this wilderness," Push continued. "The thing we are speaking of is very strong here. Here it is harder to ignore."

They sat in silence on the log. Time passed, stretched away from their last comments.

"It is here now," Hern said. "It is with us now."

"Yes," Push said.

They sat.

"What can we call it?" Hern asked. "What can we say about it?"

"You can feel it, see it, as well as I," Push said. "What would you say about it?"

"It is bigger than everything," Hern said. "It takes in everything, but nothing takes it in. It has no bounds."

"Yes," Push said. "What else?"

"It is good, kind; it is familiar—you might say intimate—yet there is an indifference, at least an indifference to human wishes. It is merely and exactly what it is, regardless of what we say."

"Good," Push said. "Say more. I think you can say more."

"There is happiness, or better, there is pure satisfaction with things and with itself."

"Good," Push said. "How long has it been here, would you say?"

"Looking back, I see no end. I see that everything that was ever here is still here—still represented. Looking forward I see potential, stretching forever."

"Yes," Push said. "Well, for one who asked what we could say, you had quite a lot to say, yourself."

"I surprised myself, Push," Hern said. "It's not so much that I already knew those things, although I suppose I knew some of them. It's more like I just looked at what was here and said what I was seeing. When I said something that was true, I *knew* it was true. I felt agreement and confirmation all around me."

They sat quietly for a time.

"Would you call it God?" Hern asked.

"I might call it God," Push said after a moment. "But it is different from the God envisioned by most men. I would want to recognize that difference. I might call it the God-in-Itself." Push paused, then continued.

"A problem happens when people try to make a vision of God that is bound in words. The problem comes from the nature of words—from the idea we can pin something down with words. Whenever we try to do that, the thing becomes limited by the words we use. Words bring limitations—that is just one of the things they do, whether we like it or not. Words fail, in this case, because the thing we are speaking of this morning is without limits."

"Yes," Hern said.

"The problem is made worse by a tendency to let the words become as important as the thing we are trying to address with them. We end up with our focus on the words, not on the thing, itself.

"Many words have been spoken about God, different words in different traditions. Traditions wrapped in words have been handed across generations. The words have brought their limitations. There's nothing anyone can do about that. Yet the thing we are speaking of exists as it is, beyond limitation. It is beyond words, no matter how carefully chosen, how reverentially preserved.

"It is the same in Chickasaw tradition. Our ideas of Deity are beautiful. They have many similarities in Christian tradition. But they, too, suffer from the limitation of words, of accepted and time-honored interpretation.

"This thing we are speaking of is simply what it is. We can say true things about it, but we can not catch what it is in words. It is not to be captured.

"The best thing I know in Christian theology for what we have here is what God said to Moses at the burning bush: *'I AM THAT AM.'*"

"Yes," Hern said. "Yes, that fits the situation, doesn't it?" He paused for several moments. "Push, that is what this wilderness says to us!"

"Yes," Push said.

"I'm new at this, Push. It is obvious you are not."

They sat quietly for a while.

"How did you come to know so much about Christian theology, Push?" Hern asked.

"The missionaries taught it to me in their schools," Push said. "They taught Christianity and they taught English language. Lush-pun-tubby, my uncle, insisted I must learn both.

"In the missionaries' vision, God was portrayed as our Father, as though he were like a wise, old man. They always referred to him as *he*," Push said.

"But that is the way everyone refers to him," Hern said quickly. "Even Jesus did it. He told us to pray to our Father in heaven."

"Yes. That gives people an easy way to think of God, to feel a relationship to God. No doubt it is a comfort to many," Push said.

"And the Bible says we are made in God's image," Hern said. "What about that?"

"Yes, so we are," Push said. "And what of the trees? What of the birds?"

"Yes," Hern said. "Yes, I see."

"The words have been helpful in many ways," Push said. "Maybe people cannot get along without them. But look at the limitation they impose. This thing we are speaking of, Hern, do you find that it is masculine? Is it actually a *he*?"

Hern considered this for a moment. "It has a strong sexual element," he said, "plenty strong. But, of itself, it is neither male nor female. It is both—and it is far more than either."

"Yes," Push said. "But to many people, words have made God not only a human-like being, but a *male* being, at that."

After a while, Hern spoke again. "This thing we have here, Push, you said you might call it the God-in-Itself. Is there another name you might call it—one you like better?"

"Whatever name we may give it. You and I will understand that the name is only a convenience for ourselves. The thing we are speaking of remains just what it is, unaffected by our name for it."

"Of course," Hern said.

"Then it doesn't matter so much what we call it. Even so, if we are going to use a name, we will be as accurate as we can," Push said. "I call it the Source—the Source of all things."

"Let's walk up the creek a way, Hern," Push said. "It could be we'll see something."

They came to a place where a feeder stream running into the creek had been dammed-up by beavers, creating a small pond in the woods. A pair of wood ducks swam furtively away to the far side of the pond as they approached.

"This seems like a good place," Push said. "Let's just stand here for a few minutes and see what happens."

They stood beside the pond without speaking further. Both were still and alert. Then Push spoke softly. "Look up, Hern. Watch the sky above the pond."

Hern saw the form of a vulture emerge from above the screen of trees into the visible part of the sky above the pond. It glided across the space at a high angle, never using a wing-beat.

"Why, it's a black, Push—it's a black buzzard," Hern said. Black vultures were by no means rare, but they were far less common in this country than turkey vultures.

"No—not the buzzard alone. Keep looking," Push said. And at that instant a swift-flying hawk—a red-shouldered hawk—appeared high above the woods a quarter of the way around the pond from where the buzzard had emerged. It continued across the sky above the pond in a fast glide, high above the flight path of the buzzard, cutting directly across the buzzard's trail.

"There," Push said, "there it is!"

Hern stood in silence, wrapped in the power of the Source.

"Just a little longer," Push almost whispered... "Now!"

Hern saw the emergence of a second black vulture from the same spot above the pond as the first had come, looked to the place a quarter-way around the pond at which the first hawk had appeared. Then he saw what he must see, what he knew he would see–streaking across the high sky, slicing through the buzzard's trail–the awesome flight of the second red-shouldered hawk.

Chapter Nineteen. May, 1857.

"That slave-robber man, George...I keeps thinking 'bout him," Laura said. "He upsot my mind."

"He gone now, honey. He gone and he ain't coming back. Mr. Mitch, Mr. Oakley, Mr Wilson–they done took care of that man. You won't have to worry with him no further," George said.

George and Laura were talking softly, lying in bed at the end of the day, their children asleep in the loft above.

"I knows they got rid of him. I's glad they did. I didn't want no part of that man. He got what he deserved. I ain't scared of that man no more. That ain't what I been thinking 'bout," Laura said.

"Hit's his talk. All that talk of freedom, being free. I keeps thinking of it. He got me thinking and I can't seem to stop."

"Ain't no need you worrying with such stuff as that, girl," George said. "You ain't never worried over such stuff before. How come you wants to start doing it now?"

"Hit ain't what I wants," Laura said, "hit's just what I doing despite myself."

"That ain't like you, honey. Ain't you happy, Laura?" George asked. "Ain't you happy here with me?"

"I's always been happy with you, George," she said. "That ain't got nothing to do with it."

"Ain't you happy with your family? Ain't we been happy here on Mr. Mitch's place?"

"I happy with my family. I happy with Mr. Mitch and Miss Elise," she said.

"Only it ain't really my family is it–that's the point–hit's really Mr. Mitch's family, ain't it? Mr. Mitch own us all," she said.

"But you don't need to worry 'bout Mr. Mitch," George said. "He don't break up no families. He ain't never done it.

"They's lots of men would have broke up Price and Maybell when they didn't have children for so long. Would have made Price take in another wife. If that don't work, make Maybell take another husband, maybe make Price do without a wife. Mr. Mitch don't do nothing like that," George said.

"One day he told Price, far as he concerned, him and Maybell husband and wife, same as Mr. Mitch and Miss Elise. He say they a family whether they has children or they don't. Mr. Mitch done that 'cause he suspected Price might be worried about it. I know Price felt more easy in his mind after that."

"But it ain't just Mr. Mitch," Laura said. "Mr. Mitch can't live forever."

"Then it'll be Hern," George said. "You don't need to be worrying 'bout Hern. He gwine be a fine man, like Mr. Mitch. So is Bob. You ain't got to worry over them, not neither of 'em."

"Even if Mr. Mitch don't die, he may not always be rich," Laura said. "And if he do die, Hern and them may not can stay rich. They may not can stay rich enough to keep slaves no more."

"You looking out 'way too far, girl. We got no call looking out so far. Ain't no use doing it," George said.

"But what we got to look forward to, George? What we ever got to look forward to? What gwine become of us when we gets old?" Laura said.

"Why, ain't you just said a minute ago you been happy, Laura? Ain't you just said we been happy here on this place? How come we can't look forward to that? Look forward to being happy, just like we been?" George said.

"Look at Uncle Bud and Aunt Lucy," George said. "They old. They been with the Henshaws all they life. Ain't nothing never happen to them. They still here. If they ever did worry what gwine happen to them, then they was wasting they time, warn't they?"

Laura was quiet for a time, but she wasn't finished. There was something else she hadn't mentioned, something that troubled her more than the rest of it.

"What about Zak, George?" she said. "What gwine become of Zak when he grown? He almost grown now."

"Mr. Mitch won't let nothing bad happen to Zak," George said. "Neither will Hern. Hern and Zak was raised together. They friends. Hern won't let nothing happen to his friend."

"What about Baby Girl, George?" Laura said. "What happen to Baby Girl when she grow up some more?"

"Why you doing this, baby?" George said. "You know I can't look out forever. I can't tell you just what gwine be the outcome of this and the outcome of that. You pushing me too far out. Can't nobody say what coming that far off."

"Oh, I know you can't, George," Laura said. "I just been worrying lately. That man's talk set me to worrying."

"Can't you just feel like everything might be alright? Can't you wait on your worrying till something come up you got to worry with? You was a baby girl once, yourself. Remember that," George said. "Didn't nothing so bad happen to you, did it?"

"No, George, nothing bad didn't happen. Didn't nothing happen to me but good things," she said.

"You a good man, George. I's always been proud of you. I know I lucky to be with you. I sorry to be a trial."

Laura's hand moved beneath the coverlet. Her fingers slid smoothly across the flat of George's belly. His body stiffened slightly, settled more deeply into the bed.

"Hit's alright," he said. "You ain't no trial. Everything be alright. Hush, now, baby. Let's don't talk no more."

Chapter Twenty. June, 1857.

"Let's go out for a walk, Miss Maddie. I want to show off my knee," Hern said.

"Are you sure that's wise, Henshaw?" she said. "I don't want to see you hurt it again."

"Don't you worry about that," Hern said. "I intend to show it off–not hurt it."

"Alright, Henshaw. But you had better be right about not hurting it," she said. "I'm not sure I'm strong enough to carry you back here by myself."

"Well," Hern said, "we'll just have to see who gets carried and who does the carrying, Miss Prissy."

"Mighty big talk for a man who was flat on his back last time I saw him," she said. "Alright, let's just see what you can do with that knee you're so proud of. I'll be the judge of whether it shows well or doesn't."

They walked down the lane from the house to the road across Camp Creek.

"Let's walk down the hill and out to the creek," Hern said.

"Very well," Maddie said, "but just remember, everybody that walks down the hill will have to walk back up it later."

"That's right, Missy–at least everybody that doesn't get carried back up it," Hern said.

Maddie had been paying close attention to Hern's walking since they had first stepped into the lane. She was unable to discern any sign of his injury. He seemed just the same as before.

"Kidding aside, Hern," she said softly, "your knee is working wonderfully well. You were right to want to show it off. It shows beautifully."

"Wait until you see how it carries you back up that hill," he said, smiling.

"Well, seeing how well it operates, I'm beginning to think you could do it," she said. "But you'll not be doing it today. No need to be foolish."

"Alright, Maddie, but it'll be a let-down for me. I was sure looking forward to carrying you. I bet you would have enjoyed it, too," Hern said.

"No doubt I would," she said. "But I'll have to enjoy that pleasure another time."

"Sometime soon, then," Hern said. "One day soon I am going to pick you up and carry you. I'm going to carry you away and never bring you back."

"Then I hope it will be one day very soon," she said. "And if you can't carry me, I am perfectly capable of walking or riding–just so I'm doing it with you."

They walked on down the hill in silence. They were holding hands now, each relishing the returning pressure of the other's grip. It seemed a fine afternoon, indeed.

A great blue heron rose from the edge of Camp Creek with a raucous squawk and went off up the stream in a lumbering flight, squawking a new protest with every few beats of its wings.

"He objects to us messing up his fishing," Hern said, "but he's afraid we may be tougher than he is. I'm not so sure we are, but he can't afford to take the chance."

"He might be tough enough to scare me away if I were alone," Maddie said. "But I'm not so easy to scare with you here. Besides, I might have to be tough and protect your new leg if he attacked us."

"A heron ain't going to attack anybody–not a person, anyway," Hern laughed. "But I do feel better knowing I'm under your protection."

"Yes, we are both under the other's protection," Maddie said. "I think that is a very good way for us to be."

Hern slowly turned Maddie around to face him, reached out to take her other hand in his. "You are very dear to me, Maddie," he said. "I want to protect you always, and always to have your protection in return."

"You do have it, Hern," she said. "You have it now, and you will have it always."

After a while they walked away from the edge of the creek and started down a field road beside one of Matthew McCall's corn plots. The young corn plants shone bright green in the sunlight. They rippled in the light breeze across the field.

"How long must we wait, Hern?" Maddie said.

"Not so very long," Hern said. "A year, maybe two years. I hope not three years."

"Oh, but even a year seems a very long time to me," Maddie said.

"I am a woman who has made up her mind, Hern. I am a woman who is ready to act on her decision."

"My mind is made up, too, Maddie. Believe me, it is. But I must make a start first. There are things I must do. I must establish my prospects. You are accustomed to a life of security and comfort. I must prepare myself to offer you those things. I must make a future for us before I ask you to hitch your star to mine. I must know it is a star that will rise."

"But I know that already," she said. "Everyone who knows you can see it."

"But it is I who must do it, Maddie," he said, "I who must make it happen. No one else can do it for me, even if they wished to."

"But Hern, half the young couples who marry in this county move in with one of their parents' families to start with," Maddie said. "You know that. I know we could do it, too. It wouldn't matter to me.

"I know your Pa would be glad to add a room at his house for us."

"He'd do it, alright, but it wouldn't be fair to him and Mama. It wouldn't be fair to Bob and the kids. Pa's operation ain't big enough for them and another new family, too, and it shouldn't have to be.

"That ain't the kind of start I want for us. I want us to start out with our own place, and I know we can. I just have to get to work and make it happen."

"And then there's my Papa," Maddie said. "He's very fond of you, Hern, and he admires you a lot. I know he'd like it if you came in to work with him. He'd make you a partner, in time. He'd even help you get started with your mule business. I know he would," she said. *I know he'd do it if I asked him*, she thought.

"No, Maddie, it won't do," Hern said. "Raising mules is *my* dream. I won't impose it on your Papa. He has his own dreams, and he has a right to follow them in his own way, without having to clear a path for me to walk.

"I have to clear my own path. That's just the way it is."

"Then your mind is made up. I can see you've thought about all this before now," she said. *Just as I have*, she thought.

"I had to think about it, Maddie," he said. "It was my responsibility to think about it."

"Yes, I know it was," she said. "I want you for what you are, Herndon Henshaw. I won't go trying to make you something you're not.

"But I'm afraid of time, Hern," she said. "Too many things can change with time. You can't ever know what changes it will bring. I know we are ready now, and I am afraid of time."

"Time won't change us, Maddie—not about each other. I know it won't. You have to try to know it, too," he said.

"Yes," Maddie said. "I will try to know it, too.

"But I already know one thing, Henshaw," she said. "You are about as stubborn as one of your damned old mules."

"But Maddie, that is just a myth," Hern said. "Mules ain't really stubborn."

Chapter Twenty-One. June, 1857.

Aunt Lucy came up to the house an hour before daylight, well before her usual time. She went straight through the kitchen and on through the house to Mitchell's and Elise's bedroom and knocked firmly on the door.

"Mr. Mitch, Mr. Mitch," she called. "I needs you, Mr. Mitch. Something done happened to Bud. Something bad wrong with him."

Mitchell appeared in the doorway in his nightshirt. "Just let me pull on some trousers, Aunt Lucy. I'll be right with you."

"What is it, Aunt Lucy? What's wrong with Uncle Bud?"

"He just laying there with his eyes open. He moaning a little, but he can't say nothing. He moving a little on his left side. His right side don't move at all. I think he par'lyzed, Mr. Mitch," she said.

"It sounds like he's had a stroke, Aunt Lucy. We'll go right out and see what we can do for him," he said.

Elise came out of the bedroom in a housecoat, put her arm around Aunt Lucy's broad back, gave her a hug and a pat. "We'll do everything we can for him, Aunt Lucy," she said.

"Just let me get Hern up," Mitchell said. "I'm going to send him to town for Doc Mallory. Then we'll go out and see Uncle Bud."

"It's a stroke, alright, Mitch," Doc Mallory said. "Looks like a bad one, but we can't be sure yet. Not much we can do but watch him and make sure his airway stays open. Likely he'll get a little better over the next few hours—or maybe a lot worse. If he's had a brain hemorrhage, it may still be bleeding. If it is, it will keep increasing the pressure on his brain. There's nothing we can do about it. If that's not happening, maybe he'll start to get better soon.

"He can't talk—in fact, I don't believe he can make a sound at all now. But he's still alert, and we should be able to communicate with him. Come on in here and I'll show you."

They moved from Uncle Bud's and Aunt Lucy's porch into the house, itself. Aunt Lucy sat at the bedside, holding Uncle Bud's left hand in both of hers. Not even the left hand was moving now.

"Uncle Bud, I think you can hear me alright," Doc Mallory said. "I'm going to ask you some questions. You can answer by 'yes' or 'no.' If the answer is yes, I want you to blink your eyes once. If the answer is no, I want you to blink twice. Can you do that, Uncle Bud?"

Uncle Bud made one deliberate blink of his eyes.

"Good, Uncle Bud. That's very good," Doc said. Aunt Lucy was watching closely.

"Now, are you in pain, Uncle Bud?" Doc asked.

Two blinks. "No."

"So, are you fairly comfortable?"

One blink. "Yes." Aunt Lucy looked much relieved, patted Uncle Bud's hand between both of her own.

"Do you want to tell us anything, Uncle Bud?" Doc asked.

One blink. Uncle Bud cut his eyes to Aunt Lucy.

"You want to tell Aunt Lucy something," Doc said.

One blink.

"Do you want to tell Lucy you love her, Bud?"

One blink. Uncle Bud's eyes filled with tears. Aunt Lucy wiped his eyes gently with a damp cloth.

"I loves you, Bud," she said. "We's had a good life together."

Uncle Bud blinked, one blink.

Elise, standing behind Aunt Lucy's chair, put her hand to her mouth, held it there tightly.

"We'll have a good life again, Bud. You be getting better again soon," Aunt Lucy said.

Uncle Bud's eyes brimmed again as he looked for a long time at Aunt Lucy, then he blinked deliberately again. Two blinks.

Aunt Lucy wiped his eyes. "Oh, you don't know nothing, Bud. You be alright. You'll see," she said.

"Uncle Bud, I can get a preacher here for you if you want one," Mitchell said. "Would you like me to get you a preacher?"

Two blinks–but Uncle Bud held Mitchell's eyes. There was something he wanted, here.

Mitchell thought for a moment. "Would you like me to read you something from the Bible?"

One blink.

Aunt Lucy reached to her side and got Uncle Bud's bible.

"Do you know what passage he wants, Aunt Lucy?" Mitchell asked.

"He like the opening passage in the first chapter of Saint John," she said. "That prob'bly what he want."

Uncle Bud blinked once.

"Alright, Uncle Bud," Mitchell said. He found his place and began to read.

> In the beginning was the Word,
> and the Word was with God,
> And the Word was God.
> The same was in the beginning with God.
> All things were made by him;
> and without him was not any thing made that was made.
> In him was life; and the life was the light of men.
> And the light shineth in darkness;
> and the darkness comprehended it not.

Mitchell paused in his reading.

"That was it, Mr. Mitch," Aunt Lucy said. "He also like that first part of the fourteenth chapter." Mitchell turned a few pages, read again.

> Let not your heart be troubled;
> ye believe in God,
> believe also in me.
> In my father's house are many mansions:
> if it were not so,
> I would have told you.
> I go to prepare a place for you.
> And if I go and prepare a place for you,
> I will come again,
> and receive you unto myself;

that where I am,
there ye may be also.

By the time Mitchell had finished reading, Uncle Bud's eyelids had started to flutter. They closed, and he slept. A few minutes later, they realized he had slipped into a coma.

That evening just at sundown, Aunt Lucy came out of her house and sat down heavily in a chair on her porch. Mitchell saw her come out and walked down from the big house.

"How is he, Aunt Lucy? How is he doing?" he asked.

"He gone, Mr. Mitch," she said. "He done gone on home."

"Uncle Bud didn't need a preacher when he died," Mitchell Henshaw said, "and Aunt Lucy says he doesn't need one now."

He spoke to the gathered members of his own family and those of George and Price. They stood beside Aunt Lucy before the freshly dug grave on the bench to the side of the big house, above the quarters and the barn.

"Uncle Bud was a good man and a good friend to all of us. We will miss him. As Aunt Lucy said, he has gone on home. We know what he wanted in his hour of need, so we know what to read now."

Mitchell opened his bible to the marker he had placed in the book of Saint John.

Hern heard a noise from the kitchen in the middle of the night about three weeks later. He went to see what had made the noise and found Aunt Lucy trying to pick up the shattered pieces of a glass she had dropped on the floor. She was having trouble because her hands were shaking badly. She looked like she had seen a ghost but, in fact, she had heard one.

"Aunt Lucy, what's wrong? What are you doing in here this time of night?" Hern said.

"I had to get out of there," she said. "I had to get out of that house. Hit's Bud. He done come back! His ghost done come back! He out there now."

"My goodness, Aunt Lucy, what happened? What makes you think Uncle Bud has come back?"

"He out there," she said. "He out there right now, playing his banjo."

"You just stay here a while and try to calm down, Aunt Lucy. I'll go down to your house and see what I can find out," Hern said.

"You be careful, Hern," she said. "Don't you be going in that house, neither."

Hern walked down and took a seat on Aunt Lucy's porch. He sat for a few minutes in the silence, then he heard the pluck of a banjo string—the sound of Uncle Bud's banjo. A minute or two later, he heard it again. He got up and returned to Aunt Lucy in the kitchen of the big house.

"I heard it, too, Aunt Lucy," he said. "We'll investigate tomorrow and find out what it is. Meanwhile, you'd better stay up here tonight. Let's get some blankets and we can make you a pallet in the living room or here in the kitchen. You'll be safe. Uncle Bud's ghost won't be coming up here to bother you."

The next morning Hern, Bob, and Mitchell went down to Aunt Lucy's house. They looked in the loft, where Aunt Lucy had said she had stored Bud's banjo, and found that a family of mice had moved into it.

"Well I'll be damned!" Mitchell said. "I guess that explains it. Looks like we got us some banjo-playing mice here."

But it didn't explain it to Aunt Lucy.

"Them warn't no mice I heard, Mr. Mitch," she declared. "That were Bud, hisself. I know his playing when I hears it, and that's what I heard—his playing."

They stood in the yard before Aunt Lucy's porch. It was as close as Mitchell could get her to the house. George and Price were there, too. They had come over from the barn to see what was going on.

"I can't go back in that house," Aunt Lucy said. "Please don't tell me to go back in there, 'cause I can't do it."

"But even if it was Bud in there last night, and not just those mice, I still don't see why you need to be so afraid," Mitchell said. "Uncle Bud would never hurt you. You know he wouldn't."

"That ain't his good side in there," she said, "hit's his bad side. His good side is safe in heaven. Hit wouldn't come back to scare me. That his bad side, sont here to get me by the Devil hisself," she said.

Mitchell placed his hands on his hips, looked at Aunt Lucy for a moment, looked around the rest of the group. He shook his head slowly.

"Bob," he said, "you and George and Price start moving Aunt Lucy's stuff out of there. You can put it over on George's porch for now. Take Uncle Bud's banjo up to our house and ask Elise to store it in our bedroom. We'll keep it there for a while.

"When you get the house emptied out you can start pulling it down. Carry whatever material is still useful down to the barn and store it away.

"Hern and I will go down to Tom Pullins' woodyard and get some new lumber.

"We'll build Aunt Lucy a new house down at the other end of the row."

Chapter Twenty-Two. June, 1857.

"I have to go away for a while, Maddie," Hern said. "Just for a while, not so very long."

"How long is 'not so very long'?" she said.

"I hope to be back by Christmas."

"By Christmas! But that is six months, Hern. It is half a year. I will not see you for half a year!" Maddie tried not to show how upsetting she found this unexpected news, but with little success, she knew.

I am ready to marry, she thought, *and Hern is ready to go off across the country for half a year.*

"I have to get some experience, Maddie," he said. "I need to go where I can earn good money and save it. I want to establish a future for myself and for you."

"I think we have a future right now," Maddie said.

"We need money to make a start," Hern said. "And if I can get the right kind of experience, I'll have more to offer potential partners in my business. I'll need partners to get together enough money to make it work.

"I need experience and I need money of my own, and this is the best way I can think of to get both."

Maddie was silent. She hoped she didn't look as upset as she felt.

"There is a big breeding farm at Jackson, Tennessee. They should have lots of young mules to train. I'm hoping they'll hire me as a mule trainer."

"Jackson, Tennessee! Why, that is half way to Nashville," Maddie said. *I wonder if the mule breeder will have daughters?* she thought. Her own Papa would be glad to hire Hern, but here he was leaving her so he could go work for another man–be around some other man's daughters. For six months.

"And if there's nothing for me at Jackson, I can go on to Columbia," Hern went on. "It's one of the biggest mule centers in the South."

"Columbia! Why Columbia is as far away as Nashville. Who knows what will happen on such a long trip, Hern. It's too dangerous. It frightens me to think of you going so far."

"Aw, Columbia is not so far away. It won't be too dangerous. Push will ride out with me. He knows how to handle things. Anyway, I have to go to where the opportunities are," Hern said.

"Likely, I won't have to go any farther than Jackson," he went on. "I can write you a letter as soon as I get settled, Maddie, and then you'll know where to write me. Then we can send letters back and forth as often as we like and it'll almost be like seeing each other."

"Letters will help," Maddie said. She smiled for the first time in the conversation. "I hope you'll be good about writing them."

"I will, Maddie. I promise I will. I'll write you often and I'll think about you every day and every night. The time will pass quickly, Maddie. You'll see. And then I'll be back again and it will be like I never left.

"Only then I'll have some money and I'll be an experienced man. I'll be prepared to launch my business and, best of all, you and I can get started making a life together. It's going to be wonderful, Maddie, you'll see. Everything will be fine."

"I hope it will, Hern. I want it to be so more than anything," she said.

"Where will we live, Hern? Do you have land picked out for the mule farm?" Maddie asked.

"There's a fine piece of land just the other side of Mr. Wilson's place at Center Hill. I think I can get it when I'm able to make an offer," he said. "It's only a little over two hundred acres–not nearly as big as Pa's or your Papa's–but it will be plenty for us to start with. A hundred acres of it is already cleared. All we need is enough for pastures, hayfields, and a corn field or two. We can clear more later if we need it. Most of it is fairly level land, but there are some nice wooded ridges. There are three or four branches of water, and some of them run past good sites where we can build our house. Of course, I wouldn't think about trying to pick a house site without you."

"I've always liked the way our house sits along the ridge top and overlooks the fields down in the lowland, but it wouldn't have to be just like that," Maddie said. "I like the way your Pa's house is situated, too, sitting on its bench above the flow of level land in front. Oh, Hern, it will be such fun looking over our new land, picking places for our house, for the barn and the different fields. Of course, the barn and the fields can be wherever you want them. But I want to be there when you pick them out, anyway. I'll feel like I'm helping to choose the landscape of heaven. Oh, I hope we can do it soon."

Maddie could see herself walking across the fields with Hern through the sunshine and the waving grasses as they decided the shape of their future. It was a wonderful picture.

"It will be soon, Maddie, but it must wait until I come back from the trip," he said.

"When must you leave?" she asked. She didn't look forward to the answer, but it was true that the sooner he left, the sooner he would be able to come back.

"Push and I will be setting out early tomorrow. We hope to make twenty miles before we camp. We should be able to make it to Jackson within four or five days," he said.

"Tomorrow—so soon," Maddie said.

They were silent for a time. Maddie was thinking again about mule breeders and their daughters. She reached out to take Hern's hands, looked into his face. "Hern," she said, "do you think we will ever have babies together?"

"Why of course we will, Maddie. We'll have babies. We'll have our own home and our own children in it. We just have to give it a little time. It will all happen. I promise it will all happen," Hern said.

Maddie continued to look into Hern's eyes. She had him pinned good. "Hern, do you remember when we were first together?" she asked. "Do you remember how we went to feed the ducks?"

"Of course I remember it, Maddie," he said. "It's something I'm not ever likely to forget."

"You were a little awkward, then, Hern. But you were bold and full of life," she said.

"Well, I don't doubt I was awkward. Sometimes I still feel pretty awkward, now," he said.

"Do you realize I knew it then, Hern?" she asked. She was still holding him with her eyes. "I knew even then you would become the man I would marry one day."

"But Maddie, how could you know any such thing?" Hern exclaimed. "I think you're imagining that. You're just putting me on, aren't you?"

"Henshaw," she said, "there's a lot you don't know about women."

Chapter Twenty-Three. June, 1857.

Hern and Push left Push's cabin before daylight, rode toward their fall hunting range along Little Coldwater Creek, then cut through the woods to meet the Memphis-to-Jackson road before its crossing of the Wolf River near the community of Moscow, Tennessee.

"There was a big Chickasaw village here until twenty years ago," Push said. "I visited it often when I was a young man. There was good, clear water in the river—even better than it is now—good for drinking, bathing, fishing; good ponds and swamps for hunting ducks in winter and for trapping. Good hunting for deer and turkeys along the ridges down into the flatland. The higher shelves of the bottom seldom flooded and made good corn fields. It was a good place to live.

"The white men saw it, same as we did. It was one of the first areas they moved into when most of the Chickasaw left."

"I can see why they did," Hern said. "They have a good place, here."

"We got no business in Moscow," Push said, after they had crossed the river at the road bridge. "If we cut north, we'll skirt the town and run into some wilder country near the North Fork of the Wolf. We'll find a good place to camp there."

They came to the edge of a wide swamp bordering the North Fork and followed it for three miles as it trended north-easterly in the direction of their eventual destination. They turned at a small stream of clear water entering the swamp, moved upstream for a quarter-mile to where the brook emerged from the hills at the bottom of a ridge, set up their camp with their backs against the slope.

Push made a fireplace and gathered wood while Hern picketed Gabe and Push's two horses on a rich patch of grass near the stream. After observing these activities for a few minutes, Push's dog Rube moved off alone through the trees to obtain his supper.

When Hern returned from the animals with a pot of water from the stream, Push had a fire going and was shaving slices of bacon from a slab into an iron skillet.

"Bacon, biscuits, and grits for supper," he commented, "with a little coffee to keep it company."

He started the coffee and the grits, got out a glob of butter wrapped in oil-paper to add to the grits when they were ready. He could have used the bacon grease for flavoring, but both he and Hern preferred grits with butter, and Hern had brought some along. The bacon was already sputtering in the skillet. Its aroma joined the smells of forest, grass, water, and wood smoke. Flames danced beneath the cooking pans and the coffee pot. By God, it was a camp already!

Dusk came on and chuck-wills-widows started their clear-whistled songs from several directions along the ridge above the camp. Barred owls began to talk over in the swamp. Rube came in from the woods and settled to the ground not far from Push. He didn't say what he'd found for supper, but he looked pleased.

"I expect Rube would like to hear a wolf-howl or two," Push said, "but he ain't likely to get any tonight. Not this far downstream. Too many people around. Wolves don't favor company."

Sure enough, they heard no wolves on the Wolf River this night. But they did hear the squall of a bobcat, and the barred owls talked the night away.

They were on the trail early, the wet forelegs of the animals stepping smartly through the dew-drenched grass. It was still mid morning as they skirted the extensive holdings of the Ames Plantation and re-entered the main road to Jackson a few miles north of Grand Junction, Tennessee. Nearing the town of Bolivar, they left the road and made their nooning on the banks of a creek named Pleasant Run, giving the animals a midday break.

After bypassing the town, they struck the main road north as it began its way across a broad swamp at the headwaters of the Hatchie River. They were almost across the bottom when three riders emerged from the trees, turned their horses into the road and pulled up, apparently awaiting their approach.

"Afternoon, fellas," one of the riders called out. "Looks like we're all heading in the same direction. Thought we might ride along together. It don't hurt to have a large group, what with bandits and such about these days."

Push regarded the rider soberly for a moment, then spoke in a quiet but distinct voice, "No sir, I say it pays to be aware of bandits," he said. "They could show up anywhere on these roads."

As Push was speaking, his horse, apparently nervous at the stop, and without discernible guidance from its rider, flirted its feet here and there a few times and ended facing the center of the roadway, in a side-on position to the riders. Push's rifle, carried across his saddle bows, now covered the riders, without his having moved a muscle, as far as anyone could see. At the same time, Hern's mule had drifted like a fog into a similar position at the other side of the road. Apparently the two men had been riding with their rifle barrels pointed to the outside of the road, because both rifles now pointed directly at the strangers. The dog, Rube, had eased forward along the side of the road until he stood half-crouched beside one of the riders at a flank of the group.

Push and Hern now sat in positions from which they could see up and down the road in both directions, and such that the eyes of each covered the area to the other's back. Meanwhile, the muzzles of their rifles held steady on the riders in the road.

The strangers could see that any chance of a surprise attack from the rear was lost. They noticed that each of the men before them wore a revolving pistol at his belt. They noticed that Push was an Indian. His horse, apparently nervous a moment ago, now stood like a rock, as did the mule before it across the width of the road. They felt the impress of the singular expressions on the faces of both men—expressions of deadly calm and resolve such as men might wear when called to execute a court-ordered death warrant upon a prisoner they didn't know.

The lips of the rider who had spoken earlier thinned down slightly, and he paled a little about the eyes. The heat of the day may have started to bother him, too, because a line of sweat appeared above his upper lip.

"I swear, you fellas don't seem very friendly," he said.

Push looked at him for a slow count of three, "Sorry," he said. "Guess we ain't in a sociable mood."

"Well come to think of it boys," the rider who could talk said to his companions, "I recall some business we need to see to back in Bolivar before we go traipsing off to Jackson. What say we head on down there and see to it?"

They might not talk, but they could hear and nod their heads. One of them may have grunted.

Push's and Hern's animals took a couple of steps directly backward, leaving the full width of the road between them for the riders, who made good use of it.

"See you fellas another time," the talking rider said as they passed.

"Be looking forward to it," Push said.

Push and Hern watched the riders' departure until they were a hundred yards down the road, then turned toward Jackson and proceeded away at a walk. As soon as the riders were out of sight, they put their animals into a lope. When they reached the spot where a trail Push knew headed off the road to the east, they slowed to a walk, eased over into the grass at the edge of the road. Well past the trail, they cut into the woods, made a wide half-circle until they intersected it, and headed down it into the wilderness.

"That worked mighty well, Push. I think we surprised those boys. I think we impressed 'em a little," Hern said.

"Just as well we did," Push said. "We didn't want to kill them fellas, anyway."

They sat at early morning before a small campfire. Push had made coffee and a pan of biscuits. Rube had left camp just at daylight and returned a few minutes later looking satisfied and well fed. His relaxed state through the previous evening and night had lent credence to the belief they had not been followed here.

Their camp sat atop a wooded ridge above a deep hollow running roughly north and south. They had ridden in yesterday from the west and made their way northward around the head of the hollow, then worked back southward along the other side for several hundred yards before selecting a campsite. Anyone following their trail to this place would have been led to pass directly in front of their camp, but on the far side of the hollow. But no one had followed.

"I think we could walk down the hollow a little way," Push said. "The animals will be alright here, and we can leave Rube with them. There's a place down here I want you to see."

They walked southward along the rim of the hollow, then descended into it to a spot half-way down where a rock shelf projected from the slope.

"Let's take a seat on this shelf.," Push said.

They sat looking out over a long stretch of the hollow. The slope was timbered all the way to the bottom with old-growth hardwoods, widely spaced. The effect was as if they were perched at a midpoint along a wall of a great cathedral. The power of the Source emerged in the quiet as though a veil had fallen away or a curtain had drawn back.

"Seeing what we have here, there is a question I would like you to consider," Push said.

"Alright. What is the question?"

"The question is, why is this here?" Push said. "Why should any of this exist at all?"

Hern considered the question as he looked around him, as the power of the Source pulsed and flowed from every object. To his surprise–but not to Push's–he saw how readily the question was answered, as though it had answered itself.

"It is here because it is beautiful," he said. "That is why it exists." He was silent for a time as Push watched, his eyes warm above the slightly flared nostrils.

"It is creation," Hern resumed. "It is a continuing realization of the Source." He paused again, then continued. "It is a continuing realization of the Source. And so are we," he said.

Push said nothing. Confirmation from him was superfluous to what surrounded them at that moment. Silence stretched out between the two men. They sat as companions within the Source.

After a long time had passed, Hern spoke again. "There is something I have often wondered about, Push," he said. "I have hesitated to ask about it. It is a personal question about you."

"You may ask it," Push said. "No matter if it is personal."

"You lost your family as a young man–your wife and your son," Hern said.

"Yes," Push said.

"Maybe I shouldn't ask about it. Maybe it brings sadness."

"No, it is alright," Push said. "It brings no sadness–not for a long time, now. No, it brings only happiness. My wife and my son were beautiful, as what surrounds us now is beautiful."

"I see you have no bitterness," Hern went on, "but didn't you ever have any? Didn't you ever resent their loss?" he asked.

"No, I wasn't bitter, except toward my own life, which continued when I wanted it to stop–when I thought the time for it was over. I felt a sadness that seemed unbearable. I thought perhaps it would kill me, but it didn't. When I saw I would have to live, I went alone far into the wilderness. But there was no solace there, either, at least not at first. I had no connection with it anymore. There was nothing left in me to connect with anything.

"Then one day I slipped on a wet log and plunged into a deep hole of the Coldwater River. The shock of that icy water wiped away all my thoughts and feelings. I was reduced to a wordless animal fighting for its life. I even observed with surprise how intensely and effectively it fought.

"When I climbed out onto the bank, the power of the source was suddenly all around me and within me. I felt its immense satisfaction and perfection, just as before. It had not been changed at all by my tragedy.

"Then I saw that it *had* been changed. It now included my wife and my son. Their personalities were *there*, alive within the Source. Tears of happiness streamed from my eyes as I saw they had not really been lost. I saw that nothing had been wasted, not even their suffering, for it had deepened the character of what they had made here, in this world of things."

As Push said this, Hern saw that tears, even then, were flowing down his cheeks. Then Hern realized they were flowing down his own cheeks, as well. "As I was saying," Push continued after a few moments, "my wife and son had not been lost, but it was still true they had been taken from me, from this world of things. The potential of what they might have become here had been taken away, too. But they had been taken from me in their full beauty, and I saw, now, that they would never again change, never make a slip, never fall from the grace they had achieved. I saw that the Source would not have become what it now was without their contribution, and that they would continue forward with it, ever beautiful, ever fresh, forever young."

Push had spoken almost without pause for several minutes. He paused now, and the two men sat in silence and reflection. After a time, he spoke again. "There is a further point to consider in answering your question about resentment," he said. "In order for there to be resentment, it seems to me there must be some controlling agent, such as God, whose actions we can resent. If we believe God controls the operation of the world, then it might be natural to us, as human beings, to feel resentment when God fails to protect those we love from disaster. If that had been my belief, I might have been unable to withhold my resentment at what happened to my family. But that is not how I see the operation of the world.

"Let me ask you to consider something. What if all that surrounds us here were pre-ordained to the smallest detail? Then how could it have the freshness, the power, the excitement we know it to have? What would be the point? What if God, or the Source, reserved the option of re-arranging the world to protect you, or me, or any thing whatever that is in it? Then your actions and mine, and the existence of every protected thing, would be stripped of meaning, would they not? In that case, what we do no longer matters, for we are protected entities, secured against mistake and mischance. We are then merely actors playing out assigned roles.

"But, on the other hand, what if there is real freedom here–real creation? What if God, or the Source, is fully invested in the reality being made here? –Remember, in Christian tradition God loved this world so much he came here to die with us as a man.– Our lives and actions, in *this* world, are endowed with immense significance. Now, what we do here matters very much. Yes, we are now vulnerable to mistake and mischance, but now our actions contribute to the ongoing creation of the world. What we become here can add to the future of the Source, Itself. At once, we have a world of towering excitement, filled to the brim with meaning. That is the world I find about me at this moment."

Push finished speaking, and the two men sat in silence for most of an hour. Then both rose at the same time and walked back to camp.

Chapter Twenty-Four. June, 1857.

Hern and Push camped outside Jackson on their third night out from Center Hill. At early morning the next day they turned into the property of King Mule Breeders on the Nashville road northeast of town. They rode up to a hitching rail before what looked like the main barn. A wizened man of some fifty years walked over to meet them.

"Morning, gents," he said, reaching out to shake hands, "I'm Mal King. What can I do for you fellas today?"

"Howdy, Mr. King. I'm Hern Henshaw, from over near Memphis. Pleased to meet you. This is my partner, Push-pun-tubby, goes by the name Push. He's been a friend of my family since before I can remember."

The men shook hands, and Hern continued. "The truth is, Mr. King, we're hoping we can do something for you–that is, I hope I can–I'm looking for work as a mule trainer."

"Well, now. Could be you come to the right place, Mr. Henshaw. It's a fact I got plenty of mules on the place right now that need training. Only question is, are you the man to help get the job done," Mr. King said.

"Well, sir, I don't expect you to know that just by looking at me," Hern said, "but I hope I can show you I am that man."

"That's well spoken, young fella," Mr. King said. "What have you got to show me?"

"I got this mule right here," Hern said. "I'd like to show you how he works. I trained him, and I can train more just like him."

"Proud of him are you?" Mr. King said. "Alright, I got a few minutes, Mr. Henshaw. You can show me right now."

Hern stepped over and retrieved Gabe from the hitching rail. King led them into a fenced lot alongside the barn. Hern stripped the gear off Gabe and placed it on the top rail of the fence. As he was doing so, a young woman of fifteen or sixteen years walked up from the direction of King's house, climbed the fence, and sat down on the top rail to watch.

"Would you like some plow lines and gear from the barn, Mr. Henshaw?" Mr. King asked.

"No thank you, sir. I think I'd like to show you what he can do just like he is, if it's alright with you," Hern said. "Then we can put some gear on him if you like."

"Alright, Mr. Henshaw. Nothing wrong with confidence, I guess," King said. "Go ahead whenever you're ready."

"Alright, sir. We're going to start off across the lot, and if you would, please, just holler out whatever you'd like for us to do, and we'll do it," Hern said.

Hern took a position four feet behind Gabe, stood for a couple of seconds, and started walking forward at a brisk pace. Gabe moved away immediately before him, though no noticeable command had been given. They continued in a straight line for eight or ten steps as King's eyes narrowed down in intense interest.

"Stop him there," Mr. King called.

Hern and Gabe immediately stopped.

"Bring him back six steps."

The man and the mule stepped directly backward together and stopped smartly at six steps.

"Go forward, then make a square to the left."

They did so in perfect unison, six steps to each side of the square. As far as anyone could see, Hern had yet to issue a command. He and Gabe were now in a position pointing directly away from the fence where Push and Mr. King stood watching from a dozen steps away.

"That's impressive, son–almighty impressive," Mr. King said. "Can you leave him there and come over here, yourself?"

Hern did so. Gabe stood as he had been.

"Can you bring him in from here?" King asked.

"Gabe, back," Hern called. Gabe started backing toward the fence at an even pace.

"Whoa," Hern said, when Gabe's rear end was two steps away. "Gee around, Gabe," Hern said, and Gabe turned smartly to the right on his own axis and came to a stop with his head facing Hern, where he stood beside Mr. King and Push.

"By the Great Flood, Mr. Henshaw!" King exclaimed. "That beats about all I ever saw. What did you think of it, Becky," he called to the young woman on the fence. "Mr. Henshaw, Mr. Push, my daughter Rebecca," he said. They nodded to each other.

"I don't know much about such stuff, Papa," Rebecca said with eyes wide, "but it looked to me like a miracle."

"Thank you, sir, ma'am," Hern said. "Would you like to see him work with some regular equipment? It's all the same to him."

"No, son, I don't believe that will be necessary," Mr. King said. "After what I've seen, if you say he can do it, that's good enough for me.

"Tell me, Mr. Henshaw, can you bring a green mule along to anywhere near the condition of this one in a reasonable time?" King asked.

"Oh, yes sir," Hern said, "it comes a lot quicker than you might think."

"Then, Mr. Henshaw, I believe we've got all the work you want around here. Training a mule up to the condition of this one will add fifty dollars to the price I can get for him–fact is, they won't have to be as good as this one is. I'm sure we can agree on a reasonable standard. Anyway, I'll give you half of the fifty for each one you train–twenty-five dollars a mule. What do you say?"

"I say that's a good offer, sir," Hern answered. "I'd be pleased to accept it."

"Now, mind you, I'd expect you to train 'em a-lot-at-the-time," King said, "not just go picking here and there for the easiest you can find."

"Of course, sir. That's just what I'd expect to do," Hern said.

"Alright then, Mr. Henshaw, let's call it a done deal," King said. "And how about you, Mr. Push, you a mule trainer, too?"

"If it's alright with you, sir, I'll stay around for a week or two and work as his assistant–help him get a good bunch started to begin with. Then I'll have to be off on some personal business," Push said.

"Fine, fine," Mr. King said. "There's a bunk room in the barn where you fellas can set up. Come on and I'll show you."

"Very nice to meet you, Miss King," Hern called to the young woman before they walked away.

"And very nice to meet you, Mr. Henshaw," she called back. "I think it's wonderful what you've done with that mule."

Hern and Push started to work that same afternoon, selecting twenty-four young mules at random from two different lots and placing them in individual stalls in the barn. From now on, until their training reached an advanced level, the only time these mules would be leaving their stalls was when they explored the world under the guidance of Push or Hern, who also would provide all their feed and water. The men planned to work with each mule for close to an hour each day, sometimes in a single session, sometimes divided into two sessions. Push suggested they alternate the particular mules they worked with occasionally–to give the mules experience working with both of them, Push said. He didn't mention a second reason for the arrangement, which was to ensure Hern would work with every mule, thus broadening his experience as rapidly as possible.

Through the long days of early summer they worked the hours away from daylight to dark, and often worked for more than an hour after dark, to give the mules that variation in experience, as well. Push and Hern came to know each mule, and the mules to know each man. Each mule acquired a name, based usually on a distinctive feature of coloration or behavior. The two trainers conferred upon and shared these names so that each mule was always called by the same name and soon came to respond to it.

It wasn't long before the mules came to recognize, as well, the sounds of Hern's or Push's footsteps as they approached the barn. They would step forward in their stalls and stick their heads out over the stall doors in greeting. They would frisk about in excitement when given a sign it was their turn to go with one of the men, like a bird dog or a coon hound being released from its kennel to accompany its master on a hunt. Each mule anticipated its outing with the trainers with the same enthusiasm it showed when given its feed twice a day. The men were their keys of entrance to a world of experience and to companionship with a lead 'animal' they liked and trusted.

Hern and Push reached their bunk room each night thoroughly tired and ready for sleep, but also with feelings of satisfaction in a long day's work well done. Hern was anxious to get a letter off to Maddie but found the achievement more easily wished for than accomplished.

He began a letter on his first night in Jackson but grew so sleepy he stalled out after a few lines and crawled off to bed. He thought about writing on the second night, as well, but knew he was too exhausted to make progress with it. He managed a few more lines on the third night, and again on the fourth, finished his letter on the fifth night and turned it over to Mr. King the following morning. King posted it two days later at his earliest convenience.

Miss Rebecca King acquired an interest in mule training but seemed more attentive to Hern's activities than to Push's. Perhaps she found the younger man, who was much nearer her own age, more approachable than his elder companion. She was careful to stay out of the way but often sat atop a fence nearby when Hern was working in the vicinity of the barn.

He had little time for visiting but enjoyed the companionship of having her nearby and always acknowledged her presence with a word or a smile. It seemed to him she might be lonely for the company of people her own age. She reminded him of his sister, Lisa. It was likely she looked at him as like an older brother, he thought. Now and then, through the days, when he felt he had a few minutes to spare, he walked over and shared some conversation with her.

"Is Center Hill in Tennessee, Mr. Henshaw?" she asked one day.

"No, ma'am, it's down in North Mississippi, but its only a few miles south of Memphis. We can get there from home easily in less than a day's ride," Hern said.

"I've never been to a city as big as Memphis," she said. "It must be very exciting."

"No, ma'am, it probably ain't as exciting as you might think," Hern said, "at least I didn't find it so when I first went. It's just a town like Jackson, only it's some bigger. And, of course, the River is there under the bluff, and often some steamboats on it. I guess I'd have to say they make an interesting sight."

"I'd love to see the steamboats, Mr. Henshaw. Please tell me about them," she said.

"Well, they're just big old boats—usually two decks high with the pilot house on top of that, and two or three tall smoke stacks. They have big steam boilers fed by a wood-burning furnace and tall paddle wheels across the back that are turned by steam-driven pistons. They can go fast down river and go upriver, too, but at a lot slower speed. But they can go pretty much anywhere they want. They have a shallow draft, so they don't often get stuck against the bottom.

"There's usually lots of cargo, like cotton bales, stacked up on the decks and sometimes a crowd of people on board. Now and then one of those boilers blows up and kills a bunch of folks."

"They sound so dangerous! Aren't people afraid to ride on them?" she asked.

"Sure, there's danger," Hern said. "A few years ago one of the earliest citizens of a town near where I live had to go to New Orleans on business. On his way back up the River, the boiler blew up on his steamboat and he was killed by the explosion. They brought him back home for burial, and he was the first person buried in the Olive Branch Cemetery.

"But the boilers don't blow up all that often, and people just ride on as though there's nothing to worry about. I guess they think the boiler's always going to blow on somebody else's boat—never on the one they're riding."

"I don't believe I would think that," Rebecca said. "I think I would be afraid to ride one of those steamboats."

"Please tell me some more about Memphis, Mr. Henshaw," Rebecca King said a few days later. "I suppose there are lots of stores there."

"Yes, ma'am. There are lots of them and just about every kind you could think of, and several different ones of each kind. There are big hotels and lots of saloons, and in some areas of town there are painted ladies walking around on the streets and stalls where anybody that has the money can walk up and buy beer or whiskey. I never bought any of it, but I've seen 'em sell it to boys that didn't look over ten years old."

"Well, my word," Rebecca said. "I had no idea."

"Well, I should say that Memphis also has some big churches and some fine residential districts," Hern added. "I don't believe there's near as many churches as saloons, though."

"What was the most interesting thing you ever saw in Memphis, Mr. Henshaw?" Rebecca asked. Hern had started to look back at where his mule was waiting, and she liked to keep the conversation going as long as possible.

"Oh, that's easy, Miss Rebecca," he said. "It was something I saw not long ago. I saw a lynching—or, to be more accurate, I saw what was almost a lynching. My brother Bob and I were looking around down by the river docks while Pa did some business over on Front Street. All of a sudden a commotion arose amongst a big crowd of folks down there, and we walked over to see what was happening.

"Folks at the edge of the crowd told us one of the slave traders down there had shot another one for taking one of his slaves and selling him to a man who was leaving town on a river boat. They'd taken the man to jail, but a mob of the dead man's friends gathered up, and they went to the jail and got him out.

"Bob and I looked toward the river and saw they had him down there on a dock with his hands tied and a rope around his neck. It looked like they was about to throw that rope over a cross-timber and string him up."

"Oh, no!" Rebecca gasped. "I'm almost afraid to hear what happened next."

"Well, no ma'am, they didn't hang him after all," Hern said. "About that time a tall man pushed through the crowd and stepped out in front of the mob leaders. He turned around and looked 'em in the eyes. Then he reached over, took the rope from around the man's neck, and said 'Some of you men come up here and help me take this man back to the Sheriff.'

"Some of the crowd started to mumbling this and that, and the tall man spoke up even louder, 'I said some of you men step up here and help me get this man back to the Sheriff,' and he scowled around at the crowd like he was about to bite somebody's head off.

"Well, sure enough, three or four men stepped forward to help him, and that crowd parted like a bunch of cattle and let him pass through, and they took that fella back to the jail."

"My goodness, what a frightening story," Rebecca said. "The tall man certainly did a brave thing."

"Yes, ma'am, I thought so, too," Hern said. "I asked who the tall man was and they told me he was another slave trader. They said his name was Bedford Forrest."

"I think we've got this first bunch coming along pretty well, Hern," Push said one night after they'd been working at the King place for twelve days. "You won't have any trouble finishing them out. And you won't have trouble with the next bunch, either. I think it's about time I left."

"I hate to lose your company, Push," Hern answered, "but I know there's some things you want to do. And I know it will be good for me to have to get along from here by depending only on myself.

"You've been a big help and a good friend to me, Push. I sure thank you a lot."

"No need," Push said. "There's not another thing I could have been doing that would have brought me as much pleasure."

"Of course, you've got money coming, too," Hern said. "I intend for you to have half of what we get for this first bunch."

"No, Hern. You need that money and I don't need any more than I already have. No, I did this without any thought of money except to help you get some.

"But you be mighty careful when you start back home," Push went on. "You slip out of here, and don't be any too clear to anybody about when you're going. Stick to the back trails, like we discussed, and stay shy of people. Keep that money entirely to yourself and don't be trustful of anybody. There's plenty of folks between here and Mississippi would kill you for your mule and your clothes, let alone that money."

"I'll be careful, Push. I'll be alright," Hern said.

"'Course you will," Push said.

Chapter Twenty-Five. July–August, 1857.

"Maddie, Maddie, it's come, it's here!" Matthew McCall shouted as he entered the house. "It's a letter from Hern!"

"I'm coming, I'm coming, Papa," Maddie called from outside the room, then burst through the door almost at a run. "Thank goodness it came. It's finally here. Oh, thank you, Papa."

"I knew it would be coming soon, honey," her father said, "I'm glad it came today."

Maddie took the letter to her bedroom, sat down in a chair beside the window, and carefully tore open the flap.

"My dearest Maddie," she read, "It's my first night in Jackson. I came to the right place. I have a job already! I'm to train mules for Mr. Mal King—for twenty-five dollars per mule, Maddie! Can you believe that? It's even better than I hoped for. At that rate, I should be able to build up some money fast."

Oh, good! Maddie said to herself. *Good, good, good.*

"Mr. King was really impressed with Gabe. I'm sure that's why he made such a good deal to me."

Way to go, Gabe, she thought, *good old Gabe.*

"Push and I made it to Jackson with no trouble, really, and got here at Mr. King's on the fourth morning after we left home."

The fourth morning! Maddie thought, *then why has it taken sixteen days for me to get a letter from you? I was so worried. You could have been lying wounded in a ditch beside the road for all I knew.*

"We did run into three fellas that looked like they might start some trouble on the road out of Bolivar," the letter continued. "But if they had any such idea, they must have thought better of it. I guess Push and I looked too tough for them. Ha!"

I knew it! Thank God he had Push with him.

"The work with the mules is coming along real good. Push is helping me get started and we're working twenty-four mules every day! We work so hard and long we're both dead tired by the time we come to bed at night. This is the third night since I started this letter. I just get so sleepy I can't write more than a few lines at a time, it seems like."

Well, I guess I can understand that, Maddie thought. *Poor baby.*

"Do you realize twenty-four mules is six hundred dollars?" she read. "That's more than half of the thousand I figure I'll need to start in business."

So much. Why do you need so much?

"Of course, that's only a small part of what it will cost to get started," Hern continued, "but that should give me enough to attract partners. I think Pa can come in for two or three thousand–I don't mind taking an investment from him, because I think it will be a good one. Then we'll need maybe one more investor to have enough starting capital."

My goodness, Hern, you are even more ambitious than I realized. I bet Papa would be glad to invest, too, but Hern probably wouldn't want that. At least he is willing to take help from his own family. Just be glad of that.

"Of course, I won't be able to work as many mules at a time once Push leaves in another week or so," Hern continued. "So it will still take me a good while to get the money I need."

Push is leaving? Maddie thought. *Will he be back for the trip home? Surely you're not going to make that ride by yourself.*

"Oh, I almost forgot to tell you, there's a real sweet girl here–"

Almost forgot! Almost forgot?

"–named Rebecca King. She's Mr. King's daughter."

King's daughter! Wouldn't you just know there would be a daughter–a 'real sweet' daughter?

"She's just a young girl," Maddie read on. "I doubt she's much over fifteen years old."

Fifteen years old! Maddie shouted to herself. *Henshaw, are you a complete innocent? Yes! Yes, damn it, that is exactly what you are!*

"I expect she's lonesome for folks her own age, –"

No doubt! No doubt she is. Oh, poor her!

"–because she often comes down to watch me working with the mules."

Of course she does! Oh, Henshaw, have you no idea at all?

"She reminds me of my little sister Lisa. I expect she thinks of me kind of like an older brother," Hern continued.

Henshaw, Henshaw, you helpless innocent! You'd better stay an innocent if you know what's good for you! From now until Christmas! Oh, my! Oh, my!

"I'm so busy all day I don't have much time to talk to her."

Talk to her!–Much time! Maddie shouted silently. *How much time? Well, keep working hard. Work until you're sick with tiredness, until you can hardly crawl into bed at night. Much time, indeed!*

"I miss you a lot, Maddie. I think of you often–"

Not often enough–not as often as I want you to.

"–and I'm only helped by knowing I'll be with you again soon. I can hardly wait for that day to arrive."

Now that's better, Maddie thought, *that's the way to talk.*

"You can write me care of Mr. Mal King, Jackson, Tennessee. I will be waiting every day for a letter," Hern finished up.

"Your loving friend and servant forever," Hern closed.

"Come back to me, Hern," Maddie whispered. "Please, please come back to me soon."

Hern wiped his forehead with a handkerchief and let out a sigh. It was near time for a midday break and the heat of late July was getting to him. He brought the mule he was working back toward the barn and caught a glimpse of Miss Rebecca King walking briskly down from the house. It was obvious she meant to cut him off before he reached the barn, so he took the mule over to the place on the fence where she was set to intersect his path.

"Good morning, Mr. Henshaw," Rebecca said rather breathlessly as she walked up. "My, it's surely warm today."

"Morning, Miss Rebecca. Yes, it's certainly warm, alright, if you don't want to go ahead and call it hot," Hern said.

"Have you been working all morning, Mr. Henshaw?" Rebecca asked.

"Yes, ma'am, ever since before sun-up, and as I judge it, the morning's about gone," Hern answered.

"Oh, Mr. Henshaw," Rebecca said, reaching into a pocket of her skirt–she hated thus to end the conversation, but it didn't seem right to hold it back any further–"I almost forgot this letter. It came to you this morning from Olive Branch."

Hern's face lit up like the sun and he reached out immediately for the letter she held. *My, he is awfully eager for this letter,* she thought. She already had determined the letter had been addressed by a woman's hand. *Well, it could have been his mother or sister.* But the intensity of Hern's action and expression in receiving it went a long way to spoil her hopes that it was a family letter. Almost certainly the letter was from a sweetheart. Rebecca essayed to keep a pleasant expression on her face.

"Thank you so much for bringing the letter, Miss Rebecca. I've been looking for it to come for two weeks, now, and I'm sure glad to get it," Hern said happily.

"You're welcome, Mr. Henshaw," Rebecca said resignedly, "I'm happy to be of service. I suppose I'd better get back to the house. They'll be serving dinner soon." Rebecca beamed a nice smile in Hern's direction, but he had already turned away with his precious letter.

"See you later, Miss Rebecca, thanks again," he called over his shoulder as he walked away.

Hern put the letter in his shirt pocket, took the mule in and put him away in his stall, then took his letter and a jar of cool water over to the shade of a big elm tree at the edge of the barn lot and sat down to read.

"My dearest Hern," Maddie started out. "You wouldn't guess how happy I was to receive your letter, and relieved, too, to learn you are alright and that you found the job you wanted so readily. I had already worked up quite a worry about not hearing from you for so long, imagining you might be injured somewhere and needing help. It is so good to know you are safe.

"I can see why you are happy in the job you found. It sounds like just what you had hoped for, and it will pay so well. I was truly surprised at how much money you are making but surprised, as well, at how much you think you need to make. You have awfully big plans, Hern, and I hope so much you will realize them in just the way you want. But then, I have every confidence that is just what you will do.

"After reading your account of the 'sweet girl' you have found for companionship there, I confess I was happy to have heard how tired you are every night. You see, I don't want you to have the time and energy for much visiting with any 'sweet girls.'

Uh oh, Hern thought. *Maybe I said too much about that. Maybe it would have been better not to mention Miss Rebecca at all. But Maddie must realize she is only a kid.*

"A girl of fifteen is likely to have much more mature interests than I think you suspect, Hern," Maddie continued. "I fear you are all too innocent about such things. I must caution you to keep that in mind in your dealings with her. I feel certain her feelings are tender, and you would not want to do anything to damage them, I know. You may feel like a big brother to her, but you must realize that doesn't mean her feelings toward you are those of a little sister—I doubt very much that is the case. So be careful of her feelings, Hern. And while you are at it, you can keep my feelings in mind, too. I assure you they are as tender as hers, and they are not comforted by talk from you of 'sweet girls.'

You won't have to worry about that any more, Maddie, Hearn thought. *You won't be hearing any more such talk from me. Besides, there won't be anything to hear about, anyway.*

"Much more welcome to me were your words of kind friendship and of how you miss me and look forward to coming back to me soon," Maddie continued. "That is the way I feel about you. Having you come back safe, and as soon as you can, is what I want more than anything. I so much want us to be as we were before you left, and for us to go on to even better things than that, and to be even closer friends than we have ever yet been.

"The time is dragging by at a snail's pace, it seems, and so much of it yet to go before I see you again. I hope time will speed up. I don't know how I will see it through if it doesn't, but I know I will see it through, and I will be here waiting for you when you return.

"I was almost upset to learn that Push was about to leave you—I suppose by now he is gone. Will he be coming back to accompany you on the trip home? Oh, I hope he will. Maybe I am too foolish, but I shudder to think of you making that dangerous journey alone. It just scares me, and I can't help it.

"I'm going to stop writing now so I can get this into the mail to you. I hope you are as glad to get it as I was to get yours. Please write again as soon as you can.

"I long to see you, Hern. You are the dearest friend I have ever found. Please, please, keep yourself safe until I can see you again.

"Your loving and true friend, Maddie."

Chapter Twenty-Six. August, 1857.

Push-pun-tubby traveled slowly down the edge of the old Chickasaw holdings southward through Tennessee and into eastern Alabama. The route he chose took him to the sites of old villages he had visited in his youth. He passed on quickly at places where white men had settled and paused at those that were uninhabited now and returning once more to wildness. In some of these he sensed a residue of energy from generations of his ancestors—or perhaps only the continuing presence of the spiritual power that had drawn the people of the old time to establish homes in those places to begin with—and he remained for a day or for several days. He hunted and fished and sat through the mornings and evenings watching the movement of the day, listening to the sounds of the animals and the water and the wind in the trees. Rube accompanied him in his explorations and hunted alone for his own food or sat in camp with Push, apparently as content with quiet as with adventure. On these days the horses were pastured in ankle-high grasses and ate and rested at their pleasure.

As the days stretched to weeks, Push and his animal companions ambled their way ever nearer to a place that shone in Push's memory with the glow of legend or myth, a country known to him only by reputation. It was the area of the Sipsey River of North Alabama and the deep hollow of the Cove Forest—known as a singular focus of spiritual power, wherein trees existed at twice the size they attained in ordinary circumstances. Push followed the guidance of words heard in his youth before the smoke of campfires whose ashes long ago had returned to the earth. And the words guided him truly, and he found the deep hollow and the Forest.

It was past mid afternoon when he came to the edge of the Cove. The trail led out to a point above the hollow and began a series of switchbacks that descended into its heart. Push tied his horses near the point and started down on foot. He was surrounded by a forest of unprecedented size and power. Many times in the wilderness he had come upon individual trees of tremendous size, but never had he found an entire forest of giants such as those around him now. All about him were tulip poplars, sweet gums, white ashes, oaks, hickories, and big-leaf elms as large or larger than any individual specimens of their type he had seen anywhere. Many were more than eight feet thick at breast height, and Push guessed they must top out at more than two hundred feet—maybe a good deal more than that.

He stood for a long time, unaware of its passage in the power surrounding and emanating from ancient members of the Source. Finally he noticed that Rube had crept near and had rested his head on Push's foot. It was unusual behavior for Rube. Push wondered to what extent Rube sensed the power of the place. Maybe he did sense it. Maybe it made him seek a closer companionship with his friends.

"Come on, Rube. We'll go back to the horses now," he said. He would come here again at dawn. Rube could stay behind and keep the horses company.

Push sat long at his campfire that night in a mood of profound peace he did not wish to interrupt. But the mood stayed with him even after he had gone to his blankets. He was swept away in a dream of huge clouds and flowing mists that slid constantly from icy hills and ridges into a protected place where giant beings in the making moved and expanded across the sway of seasons on end. The illumination of the dream gradually strengthened, and Push awakened in the early dawn and descended alone into the Cove.

He drifted as in a vision among the giants to the heart of the Cove, followed the rill that ran there down the throat of the hollow. He descended gradually, unmindful of time and distance, and came to the place where the rill entered the river.

Here were huge hemlocks, feathery and bright in their plumage. Waterfalls streamed from the edges of pale limestone walls to the floor of the canyon, and their streams wound their courses into the river. He paused beside a grotto formed over ages by the splash of a fall and stood in continual mist amid the perfection of the white flowers it had fostered, their leaves bright green and dewy with droplets from the mist. His vision plumbed the waters of the river that ran a clear and vivid green, like the leaves of April that make tree-flowers of the oaks and sycamores.

He thought of the holy man, Tishomingo, and the country where he had lived among the forests and the great limestone boulders on the hillsides above Bear Creek. The place was in Mississippi. He could stop there on his way home. He thought of the old Chickasaw deities with pleasure and gratitude. Through them, he had opened his eyes to the world of spirit that surrounded him. They remained with him, even now. When he knew it was time, he started to move back toward his camp in a state of elation, as though he had spent the day walking with the grandfathers of his people.

Chapter Twenty-Seven. August–November, 1857.

Midsummer arrived at Robertson's Crossroads and time for Maddie ceased to be a medium of passage and assumed rather the quality of a single continuing point of existence around which events recurred without significance or meaningful differentiation, as in a quiet dream whose only hold on interest is the dreamlike essence, itself. Morning passed into noon and evening. Clothes were donned and removed; meals were eaten, one much like another, the family at the table, talk of the cotton and the corn, of rain or the lack of it; talk of heat and humidity, stillness at dusk or a welcome breeze.

She heard little from Hern. Reread his letters many times long after she had memorized them so fully she could repeat the words as readily whether she held a letter before her or not. "Oh, why cannot he write more often?" she had asked, until that, too, became so often repeated it ceased to be a question and was only a repeated refrain of no consequence. Even as she complained to herself of a lack of communication from Hern, Maddie had to admit that her own production of letters to him had slowed to a trickle, as well. This was not a defensive reaction of tit-for-tat on her part but a natural result of there being little to write about in the malaise of her own life. What there was to say had been said too many times already–how she longed for his return, how she missed seeing him and being with him, how her devotion to him was strong as ever. She sat before her writing paper and stared, meditated on the slow turning of the earth, awaited the appearance of fresh words and new ideas upon which to comment. Often she managed only a sentence or a line or two at a single attempt. Then, reviewing the product of several days of feeble outflow, she often wadded the paper into a ball, resolving to start afresh tomorrow with better result.

Hern's dullness as a writer proceeded from what was nearly an opposite circumstance than Maddie's. His problem was not malaise but exhaustion. Yet the result produced was almost identical. He continued to put in more than twelve hours each day in an all-out effort to finish as many mules as possible before his December departure. The work still held interest for him–kept fresh by the varying personalities of the animals with which he spent his days. But there were too many mules, too many repetitions of the same drills and lessons. He varied his daily procedures in as many ways as he could think of but it was not quite enough, eventually, to overcome the impression of an endless trek across a meagerly featured landscape toward a goal that receded into the distance as he advanced.

August 14, 1857

My dearest Maddie,

My days are filled with thoughts of you, with mules, mules, mules, and with little more. I take Sunday mornings off out of respect for the Sabbath, and that is my best time for writing you, as now. I'm in the field with the mules the rest of the daylight hours and some of the dark hours, too, and only leave for shelter when a thunder storm sends lightning close by. The days flash by, despite the sameness of one to the other, and the weeks pass into months almost without notice. Yet as they do, they bring ever closer the time I will be coming back to you. So I am glad to see them go, and the faster the better.

These days are not wasted, for as they speed past I am making progress in my work apace with their passage. Already I have finished the first two dozen I started with Push and am well along toward finishing a third dozen. If I can hold to this pace–and I believe I can–I'll return on schedule with more than enough money to get my business started.

The work goes routinely with most of the animals, and I won't bore you with telling about them again and again. But there is one I am working with that I would like to tell you about.

This mule seemed deathly afraid of being near a man and couldn't be approached at all, so there wasn't a way even to put a halter on him, let alone start in working with him in the usual way. I could have roped him and snubbed him up to a post, I suppose, but it seemed to me that would only make him more fearful, and I didn't want to do that.

What I did was to block off the passageway through the barn so as to direct him into a stall. I got Mr. King to stand quietly behind the barricade, and when I drove the frightened animal down the passageway and into the stall, he closed the stall door and we had him.

I made sure no one came around that mule but me and made sure I never did anything to spook him. I'd pass by the stall many times a day and speak to him, but go right on by. But each time I passed, I went by a little slower. After a number of times, I began to stand there and visit with him a little. It got where I could stand at his stall for five minutes without bothering him.

Then I started requiring him to look toward me before I'd pour his feed in the manger each time. I just wouldn't pour it until he did. Well, pretty soon he started taking a step toward me sometimes when he looked, and I started holding back his feed until he took that step. Then I started requiring two steps, then three, and so on.

By the end of a week or so he would walk up and let me touch him. He'd let me rub his head while he ate his feed. Pretty soon he'd let me put on a halter and take it off. By then he was ready to work.

When I took him out for the first time, I never pulled him at all. I'd take a step or two, then wouldn't move further until he came up toward me. I was working him pretty good on a slack line even that first time out. After a couple of sessions, I was able to work with him the same as with any of the other mules. Now he's one of my star animals. Mr. King watched a good deal of this as it happened, and I don't think I'd be exaggerating to say he was mighty impressed. He didn't know it, but so was I.

I don't see as much of young Miss King these days. I took your advice to heart and tried to make sure she sees that my interest in her is entirely that of an older friend or brother. I told her a lot about you and about our plans together. She doesn't seem as interested in the mule training as she was at first. But I guess anybody would get a little tired of it after watching me go at the pace I've been on for quite a good while, now.

Maddie, my last waking thoughts are of you every night, and those moments before I fall asleep are the best of the day. I always hope to dream of you, and often I do, and those are the best moments of my sleeping.

I long to see you and hope so much you are doing alright and are enjoying yourself well at home. Thank Goodness the days are speeding by, and soon I will be with you once again.

Your loving and devoted friend,
Hern

September 1, 1857

My Dearest Hern,

How I enjoy your letters! It is the highlight of my week to get one. I'm always interested in your work and how you are getting along with your charges, so never worry that you are boring me with the details of your life—I don't believe you ever could.

I'm happy time is passing quickly for you, and how I wish it could be the same for me! Alas, for me it is just the opposite. Time seems to have stopped its usual progression and resolved itself instead into a single summer day that lasts so long I wonder if it will ever end. After what feels like a decade, I note that another week somehow has finally passed. I try to be encouraged, but regardless of the endless weeks I have endured, the time remaining until I can see you again seems an eternity.

But I must stop this morbid complaining! It can't be the sort of news you want to hear. I must stop it, and I will. I will smile for you now and be cheerful. Do you think it would be too improper if I were to blow a kiss in your direction? I'm going to do it anyway, improper or not. Here it goes, heading east and slightly north. There. I hope you catch it. I hope it lands squarely upon your mouth. And I hope you will remember it.

Oh, there is one new thing going on here these days. I have a new suitor! Now don't go jumping to conclusions and become jealous. There's no need for that. I assure you I have no interest in the fellow. I wish he would give up and stop his visits. I might ask him to do so, but he is an old friend of Papa's, from Hernando.

Papa says I don't have to be interested in the man, but he would appreciate it if I were at least courteous to him, which I have agreed to be.

The man is much older than I, is a widower of almost two years, and has two young children. I assumed at first he had come entirely to visit Papa and paid little attention, uninterested in him as I still am. But after several of his visits I couldn't help but notice he seemed far more interested in me than in Papa or Mama.

His name is William Fast. I wonder if you know him? Probably not. I know what I'll do! I'll ask him if he knows you and your family. I'll tell him all about you and give him a good hint of the connection between us. That will give him something to think about! Maybe then he'll give up on me, and I hope he does.

I've not met his children yet, but he insists I must meet them and says he will bring them to see me soon. I wish he wouldn't–I wish he would just give up–but I don't suppose it will hurt anything to see the children. But enough of Mr. William Fast.

I wish every day that I could be with you, Hern, and think of you many times with fondness and longing. I imagine you walking briskly about with your mules in the sunlight and stretching out aching and tired in your bed at night. I hope you are thinking of me then, as you say you are, for I am surely thinking of you, right at that very moment. Come back to me as soon as ever you can. I will just have to wait until then.

Your loving friend always,
Maddie

Hern received a letter from Maddie in late October containing a passage that placed him, for the first time, in real concern that his extended absence from her might be beginning to threaten their future and the very survival of their relationship.

Mr. Fast has brought his children to visit me several times, now. They really are engaging and delightful children, and they seem genuinely fond of me, as I am of them. It fairly breaks my heart to think of them growing up without having a mother to love them every day, especially since they have said on two occasions that they wish I could come home with them and be their mother, myself.

I have told Mr. Fast quite frankly that my affections are engaged elsewhere. I have told him all about you and about your plans. To my surprise, he showed no resentment but said, instead, that you sound like a very impressive young man. He complimented you on making such a devoted friend of me and wished us both the very best of luck together. But he also tried to convince me—indeed, he has done so repeatedly—that he needs me far more than you do. He has questioned whether a young man as strong and bold as you are could possibly need someone as much as he needs me, and as his children need me to be their mother. I confess these are troubling questions to me. I have not thought quite how to answer them.

November 5, 1857

My Dearest Maddie,

Your last letter has left me in a storm of doubt and worry. I have thought of little else for the past week. I have tried as hard as I could to find the right words to answer the questions that have caused you, and now me, such concern. Here they are. I hope with all my strength that you will find them sufficient.

The main thing I want you to consider is that our relationship to each other is not about need. To me, it doesn't have to do with need but with love, admiration, attraction, respect. I have the strongest feeling I can imagine—an over-whelming conviction—that you are the person with whom I want to make my life, the person I want to be with always, through whatever circumstances may arise.

Our meeting is not to be based on need. We will not come together as one having need and one a willingness to serve. Neither will we come as two having needs and a desire to serve. No, I want our meeting to be a mutual and intimate and beloved acceptance of each of us of the other as equals. I want each of us to bring to the other not need but strength, strength and a host of positive qualities to be shared between us freely and completely. That is my ideal anyway—the sharing of strength and love, not the serving of deficiency and lack.

I do not know Mr. Fast and perhaps should not speak of him,

but the need he proclaims smacks of practical use, like the need for a horse and wagon, for someone to cook and to care for the children, someone to share a house and forestall loneliness. As to his children, I do not doubt they are beautiful, nor that they have need of a mother. But so will our own children be beautiful, Maddie, so will they need a mother, their own mother. They will need you, Maddie. You and no one but you.

My love for you and devotion to you are as strong as they have ever been, Maddie, and they are strong, indeed. Stay with me, Maddie. Do not think of leaving me now. I will be with you in only a little while, and I intend to make you very happy.

Now as ever your loving friend,
Hern

Chapter Twenty-Eight. September, 1857.

On a morning early in the harvest season, Bob Henshaw rode over to Dave Wilson's farm to inquire how the early picking of the cotton crop was coming along. Their own cotton harvest was reaching a stage of production that would allow a wagon load to go to Olive Branch for ginning soon. Bob wanted to check whether Mr. Wilson might have a load ready to go at the same time.

As Bob rode into the yard of the Wilson home, the front door opened, and Peggy Wilson came out onto the porch. Bob had known Peggy Wilson since she was a toddling baby, and through his early teenage years, he had sometimes been amused and sometimes bothered by the degree of the attention and interest the younger girl had displayed in him on many occasions. Bob had not seen Peggy for the past three of four months, and while he had no trouble recognizing her this morning, he saw at once there was something different about her, something new that commanded his attention in a way he had not experienced before. Without his notice, Peggy had turned fifteen years old, had changed, as though overnight, from a girl into a young woman. The transformation was obvious not only in her appearance but in her demeanor, as well.

Peggy had striking blue eyes–how is it he had failed to notice them before? Bob had never seen the Gulf Stream, but he had read an account of it once that described sparkling waters the color of blue ink, a cobalt blue, and of a perfect clarity. That description came to his mind now as he looked into Peggy's eyes. He recalled that the waters of the Gulf Stream were said to contain many wonders beyond the experience of the common landsman, and he thought this must be true, as well, of the depths of her eyes.

"Hello, Bob," Peggy called brightly, "what a pleasure to see you! I trust you find yourself quite well this morning."

"Hello, Miss Peggy," he said. "I do find myself quite well, and doing better by the minute, if I may say so. I needn't ask how you are doing. I can tell at the first look you are doing well, indeed. I think I have never seen you looking so well and so full of life."

"Why Bob, what a nice thing to say! Thank you for saying it." She gave him a big, friendly smile. "What brings you visiting this morning? May I dare hope you have come calling upon me?"

Peggy's breathing, of which he was peculiarly aware, kept swelling the cloth of her white cotton blouse in a way Bob had never noticed before. She seemed to exert a magnetic force upon him. It beckoned him nearer.

"Well, yes ma'am, of course. That is, that's not the only reason I came, but I'm sure glad it turned out that way. In truth, I also had something I wanted to discuss with your Pa, but that can wait. Fact is, I can't remember what it was, now. But I'm sure to think of it again, given a few minutes."

On that same afternoon, Push stood in his dooryard as two riders approached in sedate and steady pace along the ridge from the west. His eyes jumped to sharper focus at a flash of some recognition of posture or form. Still, his surprise was complete as the two came closer and the undeniable visage of Lush-pun-tubby, his uncle, beamed out to him from the face of the lead rider. The riders came into the edge of the yard and dismounted. Push stepped forward to greet them.

"Lush-pun-tubby, my Uncle!" Push cried. "Can it be you are real? I think you must be. It brings great happiness to see you. Yet, Uncle, I must say I'm amazed!"

"Ho-la, my Nephew!" Lush-pun-tubby shouted, smiling with his full face. "It is good to see you again; very good, very good. I should have written to tell you. But then, I thought, I will just go on ahead and when he sees me it will be time enough for him to know I am coming," Lush-pun-tubby said.

"I wished to see the old country again before I begin the Long Journey to the West. I wished to see for myself what has become of my nephew. He reached out his hand to Rube, who stood quietly beside Push. Rube sniffed it respectfully. "You have a fine dog. He is much as you described so many years ago."

Lush-pun-tubby looked back at the young woman who had accompanied him into Push's yard. Push did not quite know her, yet there was something there he recognized. Something familiar and home-like. "I have brought this one with me. She lost her husband some five years ago. She has not found the life she wished in the land beyond the River. She too wished to see again the old land, to see whether there is one who still lives on it in respect of the old ways.

"Perhaps you will recognize her, my nephew. She is Nona; she is the younger sister of your former wife." Lush-pun-tubby was careful to avoid speaking the name of one of the Dead, as was the custom of the Chickasaw.

Push bowed formerly to Nona, she to him. He considered the array of facts laid out so simply by his uncle. They were compelling. But he was not yet caught. Not quite yet.

After supper that night, the three sat around the fire in Push's summer house. He looked over into the face of the woman who sat there so quietly. She had yet to say a single word, and he saw now that she would not–not until he had made the decision for himself. This he respected greatly. He looked into her eyes and, in return, she looked directly into his without any trace of shyness or shame. Her eyes asked for nothing, promised everything. They were soft, deep, gentle. They were the eyes of his wife of so long ago–the love of his youth, the love of his life.

He sensed the closing of a soft trap of great strength. To his utter surprise, he reveled to feel it tightening around him. On the other side of the fire, he saw the trace of a smile etch itself across the stoic visage of Lush-pun-tubby.

Two days later on a perfect afternoon, a wedding party stood assembled before Push's summer house. Mitchell and Bob Henshaw wore jackets and ties. Lush-pun-tubby and Push were elegant in finely dressed hunting shirts of soft deerskin. Nona was a picture of womanhood and grace in a white-tanned, deerskin dress.

Lush-pun-tubby reached forth a choice ear of corn he had chosen from Push's corn house. Push accepted the corn with decorum and held it up for all to see. After a few moments, he turned to face Nona, held the corn before her and, as all watched, carefully broke it into two equal pieces.

Retaining one piece in his left hand, he reached out the other, with his right hand, to Nona. She reached out to receive it in her right hand and drew it to her breast. Then, bowing slightly to Push, she held forth to him a small cake of bread. Returning her bow, Push accepted the cake with his right hand.

Having completed these exchanges, the couple raised their heads. Each looked frankly into the eyes of the other. Then they stepped together onto the porch of the summer house and placed the corn and the cake on a small table beside the doorway. Then, hand in hand, they stepped down from the porch to stand once more before the wedding party.

"My Nephew and my Niece," said Lush-pun-tubby, "may your home always be warm and filled with the things you need."

"Congratulations Push, and Nona," Bob said, reaching out to shake each by the hand. "I know you will be very happy."

Mitchell stepped forward and added his congratulations to the rest.

"My Uncle and my friends, you have done us great honor. We thank you," Push said.

Then, led by Lush-pun-tubby, the wedding party bowed to the wedding couple, who bowed to them in return. Lush-pun-tubby and the Henshaws turned and walked to their horses, mounted, and rode away toward the Henshaw home as Push and his new wife stood smiling in the yard before the porch of their summer house.

Lush-pun-tubby moved into Push's cabin when he returned from the Henshaw's two days later. His old bones were often cold, anyway, he said. He would find the cabin more comfortable. Push and Nona could have the summer house to themselves.

Lush-pun-tubby stayed on for three weeks. He and Push, and sometimes Bob, hunted and fished in the old way and in the old places. They bathed in the bracing water of the cold river and roamed together the wilderness in the country of old.

Then a morning came when Lush-pun-tubby was ready to leave. He had said goodby to Mitchell and Bob Henshaw two days ago. Now Push and Nona and Lush-pun-tubby stood alone in Push's dooryard.

"I have business to attend in the land across the River. It is time I went back and finished it," Lush-pun-tubby said. The three of them knew it was unlikely they would meet again in the Land Beneath the Sky.

"Walk in grace, Daughter of the Chickasaw," Lush-pun-tubby said to Nona. "Take good care of this Son, as he will take good care of you."

"Goodby, my Uncle," she said, "May you walk in grace for as long as you choose to walk."

"My Uncle, you have brought me great pleasure and a great gift," Push said. "May you always walk in peace."

"Push-pun-tubby, my Nephew, your life is a great gift to me. May it always run true."

Chapter Twenty-Nine. December, 1857.

"Here's a bank draft for you, Hern," Mal King said, "one thousand two hundred and fifty dollars for fifty mules trained, and I don't think I ever spent money any better."

"Thank you, sir, thank you very much," Hern said. "I really appreciate the opportunity you gave me, here. I'll never forget it."

"It's been all my pleasure and my good luck you came here, son. I don't need to tell you how much I've been impressed by how hard you worked and how much you accomplished. I hate to see you go. The truth is, you don't need to. Oh, sure you need to go back and visit your folks and all over in Mississippi. But after you do that, why don't you consider coming back here. I ain't getting any younger, Hern, and I could use a partner like you. I'd make you a good deal. We could accomplish a lot together. Make this farm into a breeding center that would draw attention for five hundred miles around. I'd sure like to have you here, and I guess you know well enough it would make Rebecca happy, too."

"That's a fine offer, sir, and I appreciate it more than I can say. It would be good, indeed, to come back and work here with you, but I guess I've got roots sunk back in Center Hill, and I've got a big dream of starting my own business there. Guess I'd never be satisfied until I gave it a good try," Hern said.

"Alright, son," Mal King said, "I can't act like I don't understand that. Still, I wish it could be different. But we'll let that go. Since you're determined to go back to Mississippi, I've got another proposition for you. When you get things set to go over there, you send me word and I'll send you over some stock to get started with, a good breeding Jack and five proven brood mares. I contribute that to the corporation you're starting, and you assign me, say, a thousand dollars interest in your business—whatever portion of the business that's worth when you get it all capitalized."

"Why, that would be a great asset to me, sir," Hern said, "and I sure thank you for your generosity. But you wouldn't be getting enough for the value of your stock. The animals you describe would come closer to costing two thousand than one thousand dollars."

"Nonsense, son. I'm contributing them at wholesale cost, you might say, but alright, you can value them at twelve hundred and fifty, if it's convenient—no more than that. And I'm not doing this just for you, Hern. I got an idea you're going to make big tracks. Only natural for me to want to take a share in it, especially if it can be of help to both of us. I'm satisfied it'll be a help to me. What do you say, will it be a help to you? Be careful, now. Don't let me take advantage of you."

"No, sir. As I said, it's a generous offer. It's just what I need, if you're sure it's what you want to do," Hern said.

"Then it's a deal," Mal King said. "You just send me the word when you're ready."

"Well," he continued, "now that you're finished up, when do you figure on heading back to Mississippi?"

"I think I'll be going tomorrow or tomorrow night, sir, but if you talk to anybody, I'd appreciate it if you'd be pretty vague on what my plans are. I don't want any uninvited company on my trip home," Hern said.

"Yes, that's wise," Mal King said. "It pays to be careful. I'll not say anything of your plans if I can help it. If I get caught in a situation where silence is more suspicious than talk, then I'll be vague, almighty vague."

"Then I'll be saying goodbye, Mr. King. Goodbye and thank you for everything. I already spoke to Miss Rebecca. I'll send a letter soon to let you know how things are coming along. Until then I hope you and all your family will be well."

"Be well yourself, son, and God bless you," Mal King said.

A little after midnight that same night, Hern quietly packed his things in his saddle bags, saddled Gabe, and drifted out a back gate of the King farm. He skirted south of the town of Jackson and cut west toward Memphis. His bank draft was safely hidden away in a special pouch he had fashioned high in the fork on the underside of Gabe's saddle. Not that it would stop anyone getting away with it if they got him. In that case, he'd likely be dead, anyway, and they'd be sure to take both Gabe and the saddle, too, along with his clothes and his boots and even his socks. But they wouldn't find that bank draft right off, and it could be they'd never find it.

He'd not written anyone—not even Maddie—just when to expect him, only that he'd be on his way soon, by what route he didn't say. He didn't like being evasive, especially with her, but a casual word from anyone—even someone with only the best of intentions—might reach the wrong ears and set robbers to watch along his trail.

His letter about his feelings for Maddie and his conviction that need had no place in their relationship had seemed to ease her mind. At least he thought it had and hoped it had. But their latest exchange of letters still left something to be desired. He could tell she was still concerned for the Fast children. He could be certain of her feelings only by being with her again, alone and face to face. How he longed for that! And his urgency to be with her grew as he moved forward now in her direction. Maybe it was need, after all. He guessed you could call it need if you wanted to. Yet that was not the way he cared to think of it.

Well west of the town of Jackson, Hern and Gabe gradually wound their way to the north until they struck the main road from Jackson to Memphis. They took the road, itself, where it ran straight and through open country, but often kept to the right-of-way along the south side. Whenever the surrounding country made it possible, they moved well off the road on the south side and followed a parallel course through the open countryside. They traveled through the night, found a dense copse of woods before daybreak, and moved into it to lay up for a while in seclusion.

Hern awoke at mid morning, ate a couple of cold biscuits, and climbed aboard Gabe. They worked their way back within sight of the road to Memphis and drew up at the edge of the woods to watch. Just past noon two men went by headed west in a heavily loaded wagon pulled by four mules. The man beside the teamster held a shotgun across his lap.

Hern and Gabe waited for ten minutes. No one else appeared on the road in either direction. Then they headed into the open and followed at a walk in the direction of the wagon. Soon they came to the bridge over the Hatchie River. No one seemed to be around. They crossed the bridge at a fast walk and continued down the road across the woods of the Hatchie Bottom. A mile and a half past the edge of the bottom they moved off the road to the north, climbed a wooded ridge running roughly east-to-west and continued west along the ridge top for close to a mile.

They came to a place where a spur of the ridge ran out toward the north. They moved out along the top of the spur for a little over a hundred yards, until it ended in a point above a surrounding wooded hollow. The only easy approach to this position was the route they had taken. Otherwise, an approach required a steep climb from the floor of the hollow. On the other hand, they could fade downhill into the hollow in any direction they might choose, if there was need. It was not an ideal position but as good a one as they were likely to find.

Hern stripped the gear from Gabe and picketed him nearby. He retrieved a double handful of corn from a saddlebag for Gabe, then stretched full length nearby with his head resting against the saddle and his rifle and pistol by his side. His own senses probably would alert him in the event anything came along. In addition, he knew he could rely on Gabe, whose senses were even keener.

Hours later Hern felt a sharp nudge at his shoulder and opened his eyes to find Gabe standing close beside him. Gabe was focused intently toward a spot a few yards away, both his eyes and his ears pointing the direction. Hern looked down the line of Gabe's attention and saw a black bear snuffling about with its muzzle along the underside of a rotting log. The bear was obviously a young one but looked almost full grown. Hern doubted it was still with its mother but took a careful look around to make sure. Concluding the bear was alone, Hern flexed his legs a couple of times in preparation, then rose quickly to his feet, clapped his hands together lightly, and waved both arms in a swift move toward the bear. The bear looked up, mildly startled, stared intently for a moment, then ambled off into the hollow, cautious but unconcerned.

"Good boy, Gabe," Hern said, "it's time we were moving out of here, anyway." It was late afternoon and would be dark in less than an hour. "We could be pretty near home by morning, Gabe, if we have good luck."

They made a good pace along the right-of-way and on the road, itself, where it ran through open country and there was a good chance of seeing what was around it. The night was clear and starlit. Hern's eyes were well adapted to the dark. He could see the countryside well, and he could depend on Gabe's senses even more than his own. Gabe wouldn't be taking any wooden nickels on a night like this. Hern figured he could count on an early warning in case of trouble, and if it came, he doubted there were many riders in the country that could keep up with him on Gabe, running in the dark. There were many places into which they could slip away in the night.

Well past midnight a big sliver of moon rose behind them, and the road became well lit, stretching away into the distance. At a certain moment, Gabe stopped unbidden in mid stride, pointed his ears forward in full alert. Hern quickly urged Gabe deeply into the right-of-way south of the road. They came to a plum thicket and mixed in among the bushes and shadows. Gabe stood quiet and Hern leaned forward along Gabe's neck, reducing his own profile. Among the trunks and canopies of the plum bushes, Gabe couldn't have been said to have a profile at all. Hern held the rifle ready in his hands.

Before two minutes had passed, Hern heard the crunch of horses' hooves on the road, then saw two men ride past in the moonlight, each with a long gun across his saddle. One of the men spoke, and Hern heard the words plainly through the cold, still air.

"What makes you think we'll come across somebody out here tonight, Pete? Hell, it's cold. We ain't found nobody in three tries before and no sign of anybody tonight, neither."

"Maybe not, but I tell you, sometimes you do find 'em. And them as takes the trouble to travel at night is likely packing something worth finding."

"And maybe they're just as likely to blast us through the gizzard as we are them," the other man said.

"Like I told you, Slim, we're out here hunting a stray milk cow, seen its tracks down the road there a ways. No call for anybody to be taking a blast at us. We'll be real friendly, put 'em at their ease. Then we'll move fast when the time comes. Now stop your belly-achin'. We don't find nothing in another hour or so, we'll hang it up for the night," Pete said.

Hern kept still until the footsteps of the horses faded well into the distance, then sat up in the saddle and counted slowly to a hundred. He eased Gabe from the thicket, and they slipped along parallel to the road on the south side for more than a mile. Then they worked carefully back, pulled up beside the road and listened intently for a full minute. Hearing nothing unusual, and sensing no warning from Gabe, Hern headed them into the road again and they continued down it toward Memphis, moving along cautiously, as before.

They traveled for the remainder of the night without incident and crossed the bridge over the Loosahatchie River shortly before sun-up. They were getting close to home now. Soon they would be back in country Hern knew at first hand.

Less than an hour after first light, they turned into a trail and wagon track Hern had been watching for. It headed off due south in a line that would take them within a few miles of home. After making another two miles, Hern guided them into a sheltered area to rest.

They were back on the trail by early afternoon and soon crossed the Wolf River into home country near the community of Rossville, Tennessee. Hern was in a whistling mood as they glided the afternoon away and arrived at the Henshaw farm in good time for supper.

Chapter Thirty. December, 1857.

Hern had arrived at home on a Thursday less than a week before Christmas. When he arose the next morning he learned that it was the very day of a big Christmas party being held by Mrs. Janey at Robertson's Crossroads. No one else in the family planned to attend, but Hern decided he would go alone as a surprise to Maddie, who was certain to be there. He got out his best suit of clothes and Laura pressed them to a condition of perfect readiness. He polished his boots to a fine gloss and left for Robertson's crossroads in the late afternoon. He rode out on his old saddle horse, allowing Gabe another evening's rest to recover from the exertions of the long ride across Tennessee.

Hern arrived at the Janey farm just after the party had started. Several other guests were still arriving as he took his horse toward the barn, turned him over to the Janey's man for stabling, straightened his clothes, and entered the front door. He was greeted warmly by Mr. and Mrs. Janey, then suddenly, there was Maddie, looking so beautiful that Hern's throat swelled so he could hardly speak.

Maddie gave him her hands and her eyes. "Hern, oh Hern, you are back! Thank God you are back safe!" she said.

Hern was still swimming in the light of Maddie's eyes, felt he could live there forever. "Maddie, you are so beautiful," he said, "you can't know how beautiful you are! Maddie, it is so good to see you."

"But when did you get back? Why have you not come to see me? Why didn't you let me know you were coming?"

"I didn't know exactly when I would get away or just when I would get back," Hern said. "I only arrived last night and found out about this party. I came here only to see you, Maddie. It is the first chance I have had."

"Oh, blast this party!" Maddie said. "I would much rather visit with you. But I must help Mrs. Janey as a hostess. I have told her I would do it."

"Oh, that's alright, Maddie. We will still be able to visit," Hern said.

"Well, I hope so," Maddie said. Just then a fashionable young man, dapper to the point of foppishness, appeared at the head of the stairs on the second floor, surveyed the group below with a self-satisfied expression, and began a dramatic descent. "Oh, here comes Mrs. Janey's nephew, Mr. Edmonds," Maddie said. "I promised I would make him feel at home.

"Come with me, Hern, and visit him with me for a moment."

"No, Maddie, you go ahead without me. I'd rather not visit Mr. Edmonds just now," Hern said. "You go ahead. I'll wait on the sidelines until you can get away."

Edmonds looked toward the party with newfound pleasure as he saw an exquisite young woman step from the crowd to approach him from across the room. He immediately foresaw delicious adventures ahead for the two of them, perhaps as early as this very night. He had enjoyed what he viewed as great success with the sophisticated young women of Birmingham. This rural maid, though admittedly delectable, should be easy prey for his proven charms. Edmonds sensed a competitor in the young man with whom she'd been talking a moment before—now watching from the edge of the room—and formed an instant dislike of him.

Hern walked away from the center of the company and waited at its edges for Maddie to disentangle herself and join him. A young man, a boyhood friend whose family had moved to Hernando a few years ago, walked up and greeted Hern. They began a friendly conversation, catching up on old times and recent adventures. At a certain moment, Hern happened to notice that a man standing at the other side of the room seemed to be looking intently at him. He was a friendly looking man, moderately tall, with dark hair and eyes that might have been gray or light blue. As their eyes held contact for a moment across the width of the room, Hern was surprised to see the other man give him a courteous nod of recognition. *Mr. Fast,* Hern thought, in a flash of insight, returning the man's nod in the same instant.

"Oh, I see you are acquainted with Mr. William Fast," said Hern's companion. "Nice fellow, plenty of money, too. Picked up a pile when the railroad came through Hernando."

"No, I don't actually know him." Hern said, "I guess we're aware of each other only because we have a mutual friend."

After a while, Hern's old friend excused himself and drifted away to make other visits amongst the crowd. Having no interest besides Maddie, Hern was content to stand on the sideline and wait for her to detach herself from the lively group in the center of the room; it seemed to be the social focus of the entire party. Hern waited and tried to be patient. Time passed, and passed interminably, and still she made no move to join him. Instead, she continued in high gaiety with the group surrounding the young peacock from Birmingham.

Finally, with a feeling of desperation, Hern forced himself to approach the group in hopes of accomplishing some private conversation with Maddie. Perhaps he could succeed in drawing her away to a quieter part of the room. He longed for an opportunity to visit with her. He wanted a chance for them to share the adventures they had experienced while he was away. He wanted to reassure her–and himself–about the status of their courtship.

Yet, on approaching the group gathered about the hero of Birmingham, Hern was met by bluntness and disinterest by its center of gravity. Ignoring Hern, Edmonds adroitly turned the conversation back to matters they had been discussing previously, leaving Hern in the position of having no idea of what they were talking about. Hern felt slighted and waited in silence, trying to be alert for some opportunity to enter the conversation and thus to regain some semblance of remaining a member of polite society.

As Hern stood in self-perceived awkwardness, feeling half tongue-tied if not half-witted, Edmonds suddenly turned to him and demanded "And you, sir, may I inquire where you come from? I mean to say, do you live here about, in the surrounding community?"

"Why no," Hern said. "I came over from Center Hill, where my family farms, about ten miles away by the roads."

"Where your family farms," Edmonds commented, inserting a disdainful pause, "how impressive, indeed. And of what, may I ask, is Center Hill the center?"

"Why, why I don't know, it's just Center Hill. I mean, it's just a hill in the center–"

"The center of what, pray tell?" Edmonds interrupted. "The center of the county? Surely not. Nor the center of this state. The center of the South, by chance? Hardly the center of society, I dare say!" Edmonds said stridently, breaking into a loud laugh that was joined in, though with less enthusiasm, by the remainder of the group.

But Hern didn't laugh. He could not have smiled for a thousand dollars. He stood silent for a moment, glaring undisguisedly at Edmonds, feeling his red face beginning to shine out at the crowd. "Why, no," he said, "I guess it's just the center of where we live. You gentlemen will please excuse me, and you, please, madam." Then he turned sharply and strode briskly away, trying to get hold of his temper, to sustain his humiliation, trying not to break into a run to be out of there.

"I think that was hardly kind of you, Mr. Edmonds. Indeed, I found it quite rude," Maddie said sharply. But Hern was already several steps away and failed to hear her comment.

"Excuse me, gentlemen," Maddie said, and began to walk away to find Hern. But he had already left the room and the house. He had not even stopped to thank Mrs. Janey or to excuse himself from the party. He had walked as quickly as he could to the barn, saddled his horse, and ridden away at a gallop for Center Hill. Before Maddie had time to realize he had left the party, he was already more than a mile away.

Chapter Thirty-One. December, 1857; January, 1858.

What possesses men to react so aggressively? Maddie thought. *Is that how they want to act, or can they just not help themselves?* She tried to conceive a circumstance that would make her—or any woman of decent upbringing—behave in such a manner. It was just unthinkable. How could he have stomped out and ridden off into the night without a backward glance, without even saying goodnight after not seeing her for six months? Why, he had not even bothered to excuse himself to his hostess, Mrs. Janey!

Of course, Edmonds had been inexcusably rude. But there were better ways to handle it than stomping away in a huff. A deft retort would have sufficed quite nicely.

And to turn against her as he had! Surely he didn't imagine she had condoned Edmonds' behavior. Yet he had gone away without giving her a chance to come to his defense—or to do anything whatever.

Oh, well, Hern is Hern, she thought. *He is full of life. You are drawn to him for what he is. Maybe some things come with the package you don't understand, but maybe you shouldn't try to re-make him the first time he does something you don't like.*

In any case, she was not content to leave things as they now stood. She decided it was appropriate to send him a note, and to do so at once.

My dear Hern,

I felt it important to write you this very day to make certain you understand how much I regret Mr. Edmonds' boorish behavior of last evening. I should have thought you would have known this without the need of a comment, but your manner of departure from me, without a word of goodbye after an absence of six months, has left me in doubt. I hope you will call upon me at home as soon as it is convenient. Let us not allow last night's unpleasantness to grow into a wall that separates us.

As ever your friend,
Maddie

As she prepared the note for mailing, Maddie recalled her encounter with Mr. Edmonds shortly after Hern had gone. She was quite sure it would be her last. Edmonds had approached her with an oily display of self-satisfaction she found sickening. "Ah, my dear," he had said, "now that the awkward young man has run away in a sulk there is nothing to prevent you and me from getting to know each other a good deal better."

"Mr. Edmonds," she had replied, "that young man happens to be a dear friend of mine. I am sorry you saw fit to treat him so unkindly. I have complied, until now, with your Aunt Janey's request that I try and make you feel welcome here. But I find you unable to behave either as a Christian or a gentleman. I wish nothing more to do with you, now, or at any time. It is only left to wish you, sir, a very pleasant evening."

Hern tore open the letter from Maddie and read with intense interest. He was a little stung by the curt tone of the note, but his relief that she had written at all, and so soon, added to the overall message of conciliation, overcame his temporary resentment. *Maybe she would have liked it better if I'd challenged him to a duel,* he thought. But he knew he was wrong. The truth was he *had* overreacted. *I don't know if I could do any better another time—caught off guard like I was—but it would be better if I could,* he admitted. Certainly there was no reason to hold Maddie responsible for Edmonds' rudeness. She'd had no chance to intervene. Hern decided he'd better visit Maddie at the McCall home that very afternoon.

As he rode up to the McCall house, Hern noticed there was an air of unusual quiet about the place, and as he got down from his horse, he was greeted by Jackson Scot, one of the McCall servants. "Afternoon, Mr.

Hern," Jackson called out. "Ain't none of 'em home this evenin'. They's all gone over to Hernando to visit at Mr. Fast's house."

"Well, I guess that's just my bad luck, Jackson," Hern said. He wanted to ask Jackson what the occasion for the visit was but quickly decided it would be unseemly of him to pry into their business. He would find out soon enough, if there was any reason for him to know it.

The fact was, Jackson didn't know why they'd gone, anyway. He'd only seen them driving away in the buggy, and Matthew McCall had called to him that they were off to Mr. Fast's at Hernando. Jackson hadn't seen Mr. Fast's servant arrive from Hernando with the news that one of the Fast children had suffered a bad break of the upper arm and had begged his father to send for Maddie to comfort him. As it had turned out, the entire family decided to go.

"They just left out not two hours ago, Mr. Hern," Jackson said. "I don't see how they could be back before dark, and it may be they'll spend the night over there."

"Guess I may as well turn around and head on back home, myself, Jackson," Hern said. "But I want you to be sure and tell Miss Maddie I was here. Will you do that for me, please? You won't forget, now?"

"Naw suh, I'll be sure to tell her. I won't forget," Jackson said. But he did forget. His cousin came back from a hunting trip in the flooded woods off Camp Creek with a good batch of wild mallards. Jackson was engrossed in the picking, cleaning, cooking, and eating of ducks the rest of that day. By the time the McCalls came home the next afternoon, Jackson's mind had moved on to other things, and Mr. Hern Henshaw's failed visit may as well have been a distant incident in some other lifetime.

Chapter Thirty-Two. February, 1858.

"How much do you figure you'll need to get started, Hern?" Mitchell asked. He and Hern were seated at the dining table. It was just past mid afternoon and they were alone in the room except for Elise, who sat working over her sewing basket in a far corner.

"I can do it for three thousand dollars, if I have to. Counting Mr. King's stock investment as twelve hundred fifty, that would leave me five hundred short as it stands now. But I'd only be able to make a down payment on the land. I'd have only the stock invested by Mr. King to start with. With more investors I'd be able to make a bigger payment on the land and buy some additional stock right off. I could make a faster start," Hern said.

"I can come in with two thousand, if you like, and maybe a little more if we have to have it," Mitchell said. "But I have an idea Red Jameson would like to come in on it, too, if you want to spread it out that far. I think he'd come in for two thousand, as well."

"Why, that would be fine, Pa! That would give us over six thousand to start on. We'd be able to pay out most of the land and buy more breeding stock, too," Hern said.

"We'll need to hold out a cash reserve to cover operating expenses for a while," Mitchell said. "It'll take us two years before we can start generating an income. Besides funding supplies, the corporation will need to pay you a salary for operating the place."

"I hadn't thought much about that, but you're right. I'd need something to live on until we can start turning a profit. And it seems right that the operator should be compensated for his work," Hern said.

"I think the farm boss ought to be compensated at fifty dollars a month," Mitchell said, "against a ten percent cut off the top of the yearly profit, once the operation starts making more than six thousand a year. But that's liable to put the corporation in a strain for cash over the first couple of years. Let's say we credit you with that salary, but you don't start to draw all of it until we start turning a profit. How much do you figure you'd need to get by on?"

"I think I could do fine on twenty a month," Hern said.

"Let's make it thirty a month," Mitchell said. "Could be your expenses might go up a bit. You might want to get married, for instance, start a family."

"Well, Pa, I don't know about that right now. Some things have happened lately. I'm not sure anymore where things stand with Maddie."

Mitchell looked at his son for a thoughtful moment, his own face registering concern and understanding. "I expect everything will turn out alright, Hern. I sure hope it does. You know we all think the world of Maddie," he said quietly.

"Yes, sir, I know you do," Hern said. "So do I."

The two were silent for a few moments, glancing alternately at each other and at the surface of the table before them. "Well, then," Mitchell began again, picking up the conversation, "let's say you draw thirty a month and earn an additional twenty in credit from the corporation. Let's think about how ownership of the corporation is going to be allocated."

"Alright," Hern said, "let's say I put in twelve-fifty, we credit Mr. King with twelve-fifty, pending his delivery of the stock he offered, and you put in two thousand. Shall we figure in Mr. Jameson for two thousand?"

"Let's do," Mitchell said, writing down the figures on a pad in front of him. "Fact is, he and I already talked some about it. You'll just need to go in and discuss the details with him, see if they meet his approval.

"That gives us an initial capitalization of sixty-five hundred," Mitchell continued. "But Red and I already agreed you should be credited with an additional thousand for starting the corporation–Red brought that up, himself–so let's figure shares on that basis."

"That seems mighty generous to me, Pa. Maybe too generous," Hern said.

"No, it's not unusual," Mitchell said. "The man with the idea and the initiative deserves the value of his contribution. Red and I also agreed you should be authorized to make additional investments in the company over the years until you acquire fifty-one percent ownership, based on the initial capitalization–at your discretion, of course."

Hern sat bemused, fascinated as his dream of starting a business acquired the detail of reality. Mitchell finished his calculations. "Alright," he said, "looks like we'll begin operations with ownership shared at 16.66 percent to Mr. King, 26.66 percent to Mr. Jameson and to me, and 30.02 percent to you. I'll write up a statement of the arrangements and you can take it in to Red for his approval. The three of us will sign it and send a copy to Mr. King for his signature. Then we'll put the papers on file with my lawyer in Hernando. He'll make out copies for each of us and likely take care of some other legal details, but we can leave that to him. We'll set up a bank deposit subject to your signature as chief officer of the corporation. Then you can buy your land, Mr. King can make his stock delivery, and we'll be in business."

"Well," Hern said after a moment. "Well, my goodness."

Mitchell rose from the table and held out his hand. Hern rose to join him. Elise got up and came over from the corner smiling, her eyes beaming.

"Congratulations, son," Mitchell said.

Hern rode slowly but steadily along the way toward Olive Branch and Mr. Jameson's hardware store. In his saddle bags he carried his father's statement of the business arrangements he would discuss with Mr. Jameson, but his mind kept returning to the baffling status of his relationship with Maddie.

First, she had remained away from him for an extended time at the party entertaining a foppish stranger, then had stood silent as the stranger humiliated Hern, treating him as a laughing stock. *Well, she may have been as displeased at the outcome as I was,* he admitted. But the memory stung, even so. She had sent him a sharply worded note requesting him to call upon her. *I went as fast as I could,* he thought, *but it did me no good. I didn't even get to see her.* He had left word for her of his fruitless visit, expecting Maddie to respond with word or letter. Yet two weeks passed and he heard nothing from her. By that time he had begun to fear that Maddie's involvement with Fast might be a good deal more serious than he had at first believed. Finally, Hern wrote her a letter.

My dearest Maddie,

 I trust your servant told you, as I requested him to do, of my attempt to call upon you on a day when you and your family were away to visit at Hernando. Yet two weeks have passed since then with no word from you. I no longer know what to think. Have I displeased you so much—or have you become so devoted to another—that you no no longer wish to see me? I can't believe that is true, Maddie. I don't want to believe it. But I don't know what to believe.

 I long to see you Maddie. I long to do anything that is in my power to restore our friendship as it was and as I will always want it to be. Please let me hear from you. I will come running to you as fast as I can. Please send me the word that you want me there. You are the most important thing in my life.

With the love of a true friend, always,

Hern

Hern had sent the letter nearly three weeks ago, and still he had heard nothing from Maddie. He could no longer say he didn't know what to think. He knew what he had to think, now, but he feared it and hated it. He was still able to hope it was not true, but he was filled with doubts.

 Hern was lifted from his dark mood by the jovial boom of Red Jameson's voice, carrying across the hardware store at high volume, as usual. "Hern, Hern! How are you my young friend? How are you? I hope you've come looking for a partner. Ha, ha, ha! Come on, let's go back to my office and I'll give you some coffee."

Chapter Thirty-Three. February, 1858.

Hern's letter was picked up by Jackson Scot at the general store at Robertson's Crossroads two days after it was mailed. Jackson stuck the letter in a pocket of his jacket, completed his chores and visiting in town, and returned to the McCall farm. A week from the following Sunday, wearing the same jacket again, he discovered the letter still there in the pocket. Realizing he was over a week late in his delivery, and that the fact would be all too obvious, Jackson eased into the McCall living room the following day. Finding no one around, he slipped the letter beneath an old issue of Godey's Lady's Book on a corner table, where it remained undiscovered and unread for two more weeks.

Maddie leaned back against the front seat of William Fast's buggy and took a full breath of the cool February air. The weather was fair and mild, more that of early spring than late winter. It was a perfect day for the outing William Fast had promised his injured son as soon as the broken arm had mended sufficiently. Maddie had promised the boy weeks ago she would accompany him on his holiday.

As they drove through countryside just awakening to spring from winter slumber, Maddie's thoughts returned to the subject that had occupied them frequently for weeks–Herndon Henshaw, from whom she had heard not one word since the Christmas party. She had been certain he would respond promptly to the note she sent on the morning following the party. Perhaps she had been unnecessarily snippy in her phrasing, but she had felt justified in her displeasure at his behavior that night. She had not suspected at the time that the breach between them was nearly so serious as she now feared it was. She had not understood his behavior that night, and understood still less his silence over the many weeks since. Despite her wishes to the contrary, she had begun to fear that Hern had found the breach a welcome event. Certainly, he seemed to have taken advantage of it as a reason to keep his distance from her. She didn't want to believe this—everything she knew of Hern proclaimed this was not within his character—but she was unable to discount the fact of his extended and apparently willful absence.

Maybe he's still not ready to marry, even though the reasons he gave for waiting have been satisfied, she thought. *I was ready long ago and he wasn't.* Yet she was certain he cared for her deeply, as she cared for him. Maybe she wasn't able to appreciate fully the responsibility a man like Hern might feel at the prospect of taking a wife. *Maybe it's only the responsibility that backs him away, not a lack of feeling for me,* she thought. Yet this, too, seemed unworthy of the Hern she knew. In the end, she simply didn't know what to think.

Every other day for weeks she had sat before her writing paper thinking of what she might say that would bring Hern back to her—that would bring him to his senses. The problem was she couldn't be sure he wasn't well within his senses already. *Maybe he's doing exactly what he wants. If not, then why is he doing it? I know it's not what I want. I didn't sit waiting for him to act. I took the first step. I wrote him the very next morning. With the way he charged off into the night, that was the earliest I could have made a response. Yet he's done nothing—has made no response at all.* If her idea that he was shying from responsibility were accurate, his reluctance might only be increased if she assumed the aspect of a pursuing woman. *He has said quite plainly that he admires strength, that he wants no weakness between us.* Very well, she would show strength, at least for as long as she was able to do so. Surely Hern would come back if she kept patience, if she gave him time enough to do it on his own. But she was filled with doubts.

Maddie was brought back to the present moment by the sounds of laughter and excited talk from the children in the back seat. They were in high spirits, and she turned in her seat to join them in their pleasure of the bright day and varying scenery and the gliding passage of buggy through it all. William Fast had kept his silence while Maddie brooded, not wishing to intrude on her thoughts. Now he watched in admiration as she immersed herself in the pleasure of his children. After a time, she turned again to the road before them and looked over at him, a smile still on her face.

"You are wonderful with the children, Maddie. It must be obvious how much they adore you," he said. "But I fear I may have stressed that point too much in the past. I must be sure you know it is not only the children who adore you. My feelings for you are just as strong–and of quite a different nature.

"I care very much for you, Maddie. I care for you as a man cares for a woman. I want to be with you as a man wants to be with a woman. I want you to be my wife. I will love you now, and I will keep loving you across the years. You can make me the happiest of men, Maddie. Please tell me you will consider it. I know you may not be ready just now, but I hope you can tell me you will consider it when the time comes. I want to be with you. I want you to be with me, now and always."

Maddie had not expected this. William had not made this sort of appeal before. Neither, until now, had he asked her directly to be his wife. She sat in silent thought, looking at him. Finally, she spoke.

"You do me great honor, William," she began, "and you bring honor to yourself by your sincere and frank declaration. You are a fine man, and I am not blind to the fact that you are an attractive one. I care very much for the children, and I esteem your friendship and hope I may always have it. But I must tell you in all honesty, William, that my heart belongs to another. He was secure in his possession of it long before I met you. I'm no longer certain he wants it anymore, but I think he may have it always, whether he wants it or not. In any case, it is true that I can never give up on him so long as there remains a chance we can be together.

"And so I thank you for your gracious offer with all my heart. And I wish for you all happiness, which I believe you surely deserve. But I must tell you honestly I can see no hope of fulfilling your wishes with me."

William drove on in silence a little way, his eyes on the road before him. Then he turned again to Maddie.

"I thank you for your honest answer, Maddie, and for your good wishes. You will always have my friendship, for as long as you want it, and even if a time should come when you don't. I admire your loyalty to the man you have chosen and pray he will prove himself worthy of such a treasure. And if the situation regarding you and me should in future change, I pray you will give me sign of it."

"Thank you, William. You will always have my friendship, and my admiration," Maddie said.

Hern stepped into the afternoon sunshine on the porch of Jameson's Hardware. He was feeling pretty good. Mr. Jameson had approved the business arrangements Hern had come to discuss, had done so enthusiastically and with his usual good humor. Assured, as he was, that Mr. King would approve them as well, Hern knew he had assembled his partnership. He was in business at last.

He took a deep breath of satisfaction, looked out over the town square, and felt his heart spring into his throat. Immediately before him across the width of the square, he saw Miss Madelyn McCall come out onto the terrace before Gartrelle's Store. She had not yet seen him, and hesitating only a moment, he stepped off the porch and started toward her. Then William Fast appeared in the doorway behind her, and Hern stopped dead in the street. William Fast stepped up beside Maddie and offered his arm. As Maddie reached to take it, she glanced out across the square to see Hern looking directly into her eyes. Maddie's face brightened in immediate recognition, but Hern's expression clouded over. Maddie smiled and raised a hand in greeting.

Hern stood in a turmoil of emotion. What he did next surprised even himself. He reached up his right hand to his hat brim, gave it a sharp tug toward Maddie, and turned directly away to where his horse stood hitched. He mounted without looking back and began to ride away.

No, Hern, no, Maddie silently plead, *please don't do this. Please, please don't.* But she watched helplessly as Hern continued to ride away toward home, offering only his back. Maddie's eyes were filled with tears as she finally turned to William Fast, still standing at her side. She made no attempt to hide them. "I fear I have served you poorly, Maddie," he said. "I am sorry. I had no way to know."

"It is alright, William. Please don't feel bad about it. Neither of us did anything wrong," she said.

Chapter Thirty-Four. March, 1858.

"Mitchell, I am afraid something is terribly wrong in Limestone County."

"But how can you possibly know that, honey?" Mitchell said.

"I have no idea how I know it, I only know that I do," Elise said. "It is a terrible feeling, a feeling of dread. It is not fear—not an apprehension that something bad might happen. Something has already happened. I only dread to hear what it is."

"And you feel it's coming from Alabama?" he said.

"Yes, from our old home. I don't know how it comes, or why, but it is strong, and it is definite."

"Do you think you would feel better if I rode to Olive Branch and found out if there's been any news?" he asked.

"I don't think anything will make me feel much better about it, Mitchell, but at least then we will have done everything we can do," she said.

Mitchell had checked in Olive Branch, but they had heard nothing at Gartrelle's Store, which also served as the local post office. Three days later a letter arrived there addressed to Mitchell and posted from Limestone County. They were concerned enough at the store that they hand-delivered the letter to the Henshaw Farm.

Mitchell opened the letter with trepidation while Elise sat in a chair nearby with her head down and her hands clasped. Mitchell's brother

Robert had been killed, with his wife Nancy, in a freak wagon accident. Their daughter Daisy was now an orphan.

"Hern and I will be off in the morning at first light," Mitchell said. "We should be back here with Daisy in less than two weeks. You'll be alright here in the meantime. You'll have Bob to help watch over things. Ed Oakley and Dave Wilson are nearby if you need them, and you have George and Price right here on the place."

"I'm not worried about us. We'll be fine here. I'm worried about you and Hern. It's a dangerous trip to make—all the way to Alabama and back over those back-country roads," Elise said.

"Then take comfort that we'll have Push with us. He and his dog Rube will be a lot of help if we run into a difficulty. They work together like two wolves in a pack. Any badman that goes up against them had better look to the Lord for mercy—he won't find it in Push, or that dog, either.

"By the way, I told Nona to come to see you while Push is away. She may want to stay over here on some of the nights. I hope you don't mind."

"On the contrary, I'd be glad to have her company. I'm awfully glad Push is going with you. I won't worry. But please be as careful as you can," Elise said.

"We will, Lise. We'll be careful every minute."

Mitchell and Hern rode in single file below tall, wooded hills that rose steeply on both sides of the trail. Their route, suggested by Push, ran parallel to the main road from Memphis to Muscle Shoals, Alabama, but lay some five or six miles to the south. It was a Chickasaw trail and not widely known, used for the most part only by local people with intimate knowledge of the countryside.

Hern was mounted on the mule, Gabe, and led a saddled horse lightly loaded with supplies. If need be, Daisy could ride this horse on the return trip. Push and Rube followed along behind, keeping a distance of some fifty yards between themselves and Hern. They were close enough to give support but far enough back that it would be difficult or impossible for robbers to cover both elements of the group at the same time. Push kept in constant touch with their back trail as he rode, but with Rube in close company, he had little concern that a stranger could approach without Rube's giving warning.

They were well into their second day's travel from Center Hill, and in the northeastern extreme of the state of Mississippi. Soon they would be across the line into Alabama. But there was no way to mark just where the line lay on the local ground.

The three men rode with rifles across their saddles and revolving pistols at their belts. Push also had a hunting bow ready-strung, suspended from the saddle and riding beneath his left calf. Rube had only his teeth, but they had never failed him.

They turned aside from the trail in the early twilight and moved off to the north toward the slope of a nearby hill. A stream ran along the flat just at the foot of the hill; they crossed it and continued along it toward the east until they came upon a level bench a few yards above the stream. Here they set about to pitch camp. Push and Rube moved out first thing to explore the woods above camp. They returned a few minutes later after Push had assured himself they were alone in the vicinity, and after he had noted several avenues of egress should they require an escape route. Rube was released from duty to range in pursuit of his evening meal.

The men finished their supper and cleaned up the dishes. Mitchell soon excused himself, pleading tiredness, and went off to bed early, leaving Hern and Push alone at the fire. Rube rested at the edge of the circle of light, his head on his forelegs. He appeared to doze, but occasionally his ears pricked, his eyelids lifted, and he glanced from side to side without moving his head.

Push and Hern sat in silence for several minutes. Then Push spoke in a quiet voice. "I wonder if you'd care to speak of it Hern?" he said. "It is more than the deaths of your uncle and aunt, though that is enough, I suppose."

"Yes, that is enough, but you are right. There's something else, too," Hern said.

"I haven't seen the McCall girl around in quite a few weeks, now," Push said. "Have you seen her lately, yourself?"

"No, no," Hern said, "you are right again. I have not seen her lately, and I don't know when I may see her again."

Push nodded and sat quiet, waited for Hern to speak again.

"I can tell you about it, Push, but it will just sound foolish," Hern said. "It seems foolish enough to me. Yet I'm afraid it has ruined things between Maddie and me."

Hern told the story as simply and accurately as he could.

"That's the way things were left between us," he concluded. "It seems likely she wants no more to do with me. It seems she has settled on my rival, instead, and I've lost the girl I thought would be my wife." Hern came to an abrupt stop.

"And you've been able to reach this conclusion without once talking directly with Maddie since the night of the Christmas party," Push said. "Think about that for a minute, Hern. Don't you find it remarkable?"

"Well, I tried to talk to her. I wrote her a letter. She just doesn't seem interested," Hern said. "Anyway, the situation seems clear enough to me."

"And you've not once talked to Maddie about it," Push repeated.

"Well, no. No, I haven't," Hern said.

"And what would you say has prevented you from doing so?" Push asked. "Don't you think Maddie deserves that? Don't you think you deserve it, yourself?"

"But I've reached out to her and she's done nothing in return, Push. I have a little pride left. I won't throw myself at her feet."

"It seems to me your pride is expensive. Tell me, do you find it worth the expense? Do you find it serves you so well?"

"No! It does nothing for me. Nothing at all. But it is all I have."

"If it does nothing for you, then why not drop it? It is all you have only because it is all you care to see. But you can change your attitude."

They sat for a few moments.

"You are caught in a tide of emotion," Push said. "Maybe you don't mind being caught. Maybe you like drifting like a helpless leaf in the current. It lets you keep your pride. It protects your self-pity.

"The fish of the river live within the current. Yet they swim about from side to side. They move upstream against the current as they wish. You can do it, too. All you need to do is flex your tail a little." Push concluded and sat silent.

"Well, thank you, Push," Hern said after a while. "You've given me something to think about."

Elise stood at the counter in Jameson's Hardware, behind which stood Red Jameson. A rudely-dressed man stared from across the store, strode quickly forward and stepped up a little closer than Elise thought was strictly polite. Then, boldly, he broke in on their conversation.

"Mrs. Henshaw, I hear your man and your oldest boy have gone rambling off clear across the state. Tell me, ain't you scared to be left at home with those young nigger men right there behind your house?" He had spoken out loudly, as though proud of making a point.

"Good afternoon, Mr. Briggs," Elise said. "How kind of you to be concerned for my welfare. But you needn't trouble yourself. No, I'm not afraid to be at home with George and Price nearby. But I might be if they weren't. Good day to you sir, and my compliments to your wife."

Early on the fourth day out from home, the riders from Center Hill pulled into Muscle Shoals and caught a ferry across the Tennessee River.

"You fellas look like you're about serious business," the ferryman said as they swung out into the stream.

"It's serious enough to some people," Mitchell said.

The ferryman stood expectantly, waiting to hear more. Mitchell said nothing else, and time stretched for a few seconds. Then Push spoke out in a loud voice.

"We're heading to the state prison over in Georgia," he said. "They got my brother over there. They done got him on a bad charge some years ago. I ain't saying he done what they say he done, but whether he done it or not, he's done paid for it now, and it's done past time for him to step into free light again. When he does we'll be there to meet him. I couldn't advise anybody else to try to meet him, though. He really ain't what you'd call a sociable man."

The ferryman stared open-faced at Push, then looked to Mitchell and Hern. But they appeared to have heard nothing remarkable and seemed satisfied with Push's proclamation. The ferryman glanced at the saddled horse that had no rider. Then he looked back to the stream and to the ferry's passage across it. He spoke again only when they reached the far shore and his passengers disembarked.

"You fellas have a safe trip, now," the ferryman called as they departed.

"Thank you, friend," Push called back, "thank you kindly."

The riders turned their horses into the yard of Robert Henshaw's home outside the town of Athens, Alabama. Before they could get down, a lithe young woman of sixteen years threw open the front door, flowed down the steps from the porch, and stepped quickly to meet them as they dismounted. A long stream of hair swept out behind her in a shimmering wave. It was of a light brown color, almost exactly like Hern's. Her lively brown eyes recovered something of their usual shine as she threw open her arms to greet her kinsmen. Mitchell enveloped her in a bear hug and held his chin to her shoulder.

"My dear girl, my dear Daisy. What you have been through!" he said into her ear.

"Uncle Mitch! Oh, it is good to see you. I'm so glad you are here," Daisy said as she hugged him.

Mitchell released her and she turned to Hern, who took both her hands in his and looked frankly into her eyes. "Hern, you are so handsome and grown up," she said, "but I would have known you anywhere, despite how tall and grown you are. I'm glad you came with Uncle Mitch. I'm so glad to see you."

They hugged. "I'm glad to be here at last, Daisy. It is where all of us have wanted to be since we heard what happened. We wanted to be here with you."

Daisy reached to take Mitchell's hand in one of hers while retaining Hern's hand in her other. "And now you *are* with me! It is so good to have both of you here. It means more than I can say," she said.

"Daisy, I want you to meet our good friend, Push—short for Push-pun-tubby. He came along to give us extra company and extra protection on the trip," Hern said.

"They didn't need any protection, Miss Daisy," Push said, "but I was glad to provide the extra company. I'm very pleased to meet you."

"I'm very pleased to meet you, too, Mr. Push. I have heard many good things about you in letters. I hope we will be good friends."

"Yes, ma'am," Push said, "I'm sure we will be."

"You got our letter, Daisy?" Mitchell said, "You know the whole family wants you to come home with us, to be our daughter and our sister?"

"Yes, Uncle Mitch," Daisy said with tears brimming her eyes, "and that is just what I want to do, more than anything in the world."

Mitchell and Hern sat over coffee with Steven Wills, husband of Nancy Henshaw's sister, brother-in-law of Robert Henshaw. "How did it happen, Steve? Robert knew how to handle a horse and wagon when he was ten years old. What in God's name went wrong?" Mitchell said.

"I don't guess we'll ever know for sure, Mitch," Steven said. "No one saw the accident. Maybe if someone had they could have done something to help them. But I don't think it would have mattered. I don't think there was anything anyone could have done.

"Near as we can figure it, something must have happened to spook the horse. Somebody said maybe a big snake had crawled out on the bridge to get the sun. That seems like as good a guess as any.

"They were pulling across that high bridge over Fox Run Creek. Looked like the horse started to jumping around right in the middle of it. The right front wheel of the wagon must have been thrown 'way off the track-runners onto the support planks. Two of the planks–maybe first one, then another–must have snapped off under the wheel. The wagon must have lurched off at a sharp angle–maybe the horse jumped that way, too. Anyway, the wagon went off quick and turned over. It fell ten feet to the creek and came down on Robert and Nancy. They were trapped under the box, but maybe they were already unconscious by then. It must have all happened fast, in just a second or two. Took the horse, too. He was tangled up in the harness and drowned."

"My God, how do such things happen?" Mitch said after a few moments.

"I guess nobody can say, Mitch. But they happen. And when they do, there's just nothing anybody can do about it."

"You just never know," Mitchell said. "You never know."

Chapter Thirty-Five. March–April, 1858.

Hern sat with Daisy on the front porch as dusk deepened in the spring evening. Early tomorrow they would begin the journey back to Center Hill–a new journey for Daisy, a watershed in her life. She looked forward with enthusiasm.

"I'm so glad to be going home with you, Hern," she said. "I'll not only be with you and your family, but I'll be near Maddie again. She has been my best friend since I was a little girl. I haven't seen her in a few years, but we have written each other all along. She's written a lot about you, Hern. I was so happy to hear of the friendship between you."

"My God, Daisy! Somehow in all this I forgot to think that you're Maddie's cousin, too. She's lost her Aunt Nancy, too, and somehow I never even thought of it."

"No doubt you had enough on your mind worrying about your own family," Daisy said. "I'm sure Maddie will understand."

"I hope she will," Hern said, "but I'm afraid that is only one of the problems I have with Maddie."

"Why, from Maddie's letters, I thought you and she would be ready to marry any day now!" Daisy said. "I can't believe there are problems between you! Please tell me about it, if you can."

"I can tell you, Daisy, but it makes a sorry tale, I'm afraid."

Hern told the tale as Daisy sat in rapt attention and concern. When he had finished, she hesitated only a moment.

"But that doesn't sound in the least like Maddie, Hern! It doesn't add up right. Something must be left out. Something you don't know. Maddie would not act as you have described."

"I think I've told it just as it happened, Daisy," Hern said.

"I'm sure you told it truly, as far as you know the situation. What I'm saying is there must be some things you aren't aware of. I think it must look quite different to Maddie.

"I know her as well as a sister. I think it would not betray her confidence in me if I tell you her feelings for you are of the strongest and most serious kind. I can't believe they would be altered so easily. I'm sure there is something you don't know, and I am going to find out what it is just as soon as I can."

"I sure hope you're right, Daisy. I'd give a lot to believe it."

"You can believe it, Hern. We are going to see to the recovery of this situation. It will turn out alright. I'm going to see that it does."

Mitchell came out of the house and walked out to the edge of the porch. "Pleasant evening, isn't it?" he said. "Looks like we'll have good weather for a few days. Push says so, too.

"Daisy, I believe you'd have an easier time over the trails on a man's saddle. We have one that should fit you alright. But I expect we can turn up a side saddle, if you prefer one."

"Thanks, Uncle Mitch, but I prefer riding a man's saddle," Daisy said. "I've ridden one since I was a girl. Pa always thought side saddles were silly. He said they made riding twice as hard as need be."

"That's what I thought, but I'm glad to hear you confirm it. Very well. I think we can be off for home in the morning."

"I suggest we consider passing Muscle Shoals on the north side and heading up into Tennessee, instead," Push said. "We can cross the river over to the west at Savannah. Far as I know, no one paid us undue attention on our way out here, but it troubles me to go back by the same route we came out on. I'd rather step off into country where we know nobody's seen us at all."

They had finished their supper at the end of the first day of the journey homeward. Push, Mitchell, Hern, and Daisy were seated around a small campfire well off the trail they had traveled through the afternoon. Their stock was picketed on grass nearby. Rube lay quietly at the edge of the firelight, as usual.

"That sounds like good thinking to me, Push," Mitchell said, "but then, I'm likely to agree with whatever you suggest about this trip. You have any thoughts on the matter, Hern?"

"Why, thanks for asking, Pa, but I'd never disagree with Push about such things," Hern said with a smile.

"Why, that's very wise of you, Hern," Push chuckled, "very wise of you, I must say."

"We'll be passing through an area this afternoon where we need to be especially careful," Push said the following day at their noon break. "We'll cross the Natchez Trace right near the corners of Alabama and Mississippi. It's a place where highwaymen can take their choice of three states. They can be in Tennessee or Alabama without having to cross the river. If they keep a Jake-leg ferry hid out, they can get across into Mississippi. Makes it a convenient place for them to operate.

"Early afternoon is a good time to go through," he went on. "If there are any bad characters around, they may be laid up taking a nap. Rube and I will hang back a mite farther than we've been doing. You may not see us all the time, but we'll see you. Any trouble comes up, we'll be there directly."

"Alright, Push. We'll keep on the alert," Mitchell said.

"Likely as not we won't even see anybody," Push said.

The highwaymen came out of the woods from two sides of the trail as the travelers crossed a small creek. Five men held guns of various types covering Mitchell, Hern, and Daisy. Two men remained mounted while the other three stood on the ground, their horses behind them.

"Alright, pilgrims, just sit easy there, and you won't be harmed," one of the mounted men called out. "We only want your money and horses. No need for anybody to get hurt. You men just throw down those weapons. Let us take what we need and we'll be on our way. We got no call to hurt anybody. Keep your heads and you'll only lose your property."

Mitchell sat his horse easily. "What do you think Hern? Think we'd better do as he says?" he asked.

"*He's stalling,* Hern thought, *he's taking time for Push.* He felt his grip on the rifle across his saddle.

"I think they won't be satisfied with the property," Hern said. "I think they'll kill us. I think they'll take Daisy." As Hern was speaking, his mule Gabe moved to the side on mincing feet, drifting away from Daisy and causing Hern's rifle to come in line with the three men in view to his left. Any fire directed at Hern would now be drawn away from Daisy.

"Now keep your head, young fellow," the lead robber said. "I told you there's no need for anyone to be hurt here."

"Boys, I'm a ring-tailed coon," Mitchell said loudly.

As his father began speaking, Hern swung his weapon slightly and fired into the nearest dismounted man on his side of the trail. The man went down hard, and from the corner of his eye, Hern saw a quick movement as Mitchell raised his rifle and fired.

Hern jumped Gabe toward a point between the remaining two men on his side as he drew the revolving pistol from under his coat and fired. He saw the shot take the second unmounted man low in the abdomen above the left hip, then turned to fire repeatedly at the mounted man, who was having trouble with a plunging horse. There was firing on all sides now. Some of it came from the woods near Hern. More robbers came out of the trees on horseback, at least two more on each side of the trail.

Mitchell was down! Hern kept firing the pistol. Just then the wild scream of a panther rang from the woods nearby. The nearest robbers wheeled their horses toward the sound of the scream, and Hern saw one of them jerked almost out of his saddle as the shaft of an arrow appeared, digging deeply into his right shoulder. Almost immediately a second arrow sprang forward, striking another of the robbers high in the left thigh near the groin. Suddenly a dog or a wolf burst from the cover of the woods, leaped high, and dragged a man from his saddle. The high scream came again and an arrow sliced through a man's cheek.

"Hell, boys it's an Indian attack!" the lead robber shouted. "We got to get out o' here, now!" The leader and the others still mounted wheeled their horses and scrambled to ride away. One man hobbled from the ground toward his horse. Two others crawled toward theirs and struggled most of the way into their saddles. Then they were gone and it was suddenly quiet.

Daisy leapt to the ground and ran to Mitchell, where he lay sprawled on his back. "Uncle Mitch, Uncle Mitch," she cried as she knelt to lift his head.

Then Push was there, kneeling over Mitchell's other side, holding his arrow-strung bow in one hand and reaching toward Mitchell with the other. Hern stood with his back to Mitchell's feet, looking in quick glances from one side to the other while working to re-charge his pistol, then his rifle.

Mitchell struggled to sit up, then slumped again to his back. Push saw a bloody hole through the shirt high on the right side of Mitchell's chest. He took his knife and cut the shirt away from the area of the wound. They could see that it was closer to the right shoulder than to the chest. Push went to his saddle bags and brought back a tightly woven, slick-finished cloth. He sprinkled the cloth with a powder he poured from a pouch, then sprinkled more powder into and around the edges of the wound. Cutting the point from one of his arrows, he used the shaft to work the cloth into the wound to staunch the flow of blood.

"Let's help him sit up, Daisy," Push said. "Try to take a good breath, Mitch. See if you can get your breath." Mitchell did so, with gratifying results. "That's good, Mitch, that's real good," Push said. "I don't think it got the lung. Maybe it ain't as bad as I thought at first."

Mitchell sat there blinking his eyes. He took a few more breaths. "I think now I might live," he said.

"We can't stay here, Mitch," Push said. "We got to be riding out of here as soon as you can move."

"I can move right now, I think," Mitchell said. "Give me a hand and I'll get on that horse."

Push led them another mile of so down the same trail they had been riding, then took them into the woods on the north side of the trail. They went along parallel to the trail for a quarter mile, then went back to it and crossed directly to the south side. Push dismounted and went back to brush out their tracks as well as he could where they had crossed the trail to the south.

"We'll move along well to this side of the trail for a while," Push said. "I think it's the least likely place they'd expect to find us. That is, if they come looking, which I don't think they will. I think they've had enough of us."

"I don't think we killed any of them, Push, at least not right off," Hern said.

"No, and that's good," Push said. "I doubt you fellas had the time to give it consideration, but I had it in mind. A dead man is no trouble, but a wounded man has to be tended to. From the looks of 'em as they dragged out of there, I'd say they got a considerable amount of tending to do. Should keep their minds occupied for the time being.

"I'd like to push on another mile or two, Mitch," he said, "but we can stop anytime you need us to."

"I can make it a while longer, Push. Don't worry about me. Just take us to where we need to be," Mitchell said.

"Good. Then we'll go on a little farther. More distance we put between ourselves and that gunfight the better. Then we'll find us a good place to lay up, and we'll give that bullet wound some proper attention."

"The bullet almost came through, Mitch. I think I can see where it lies beneath the skin. I should be able to get it without trouble," Push said.

Mitchell lay face down on his blankets as Push examined his back. "That's good, Push. Go ahead with what you need to do," he said.

"It won't quite be painless, Mitch. But with any luck I won't have to carve you up much."

"Fire away," Mitchell said.

A short time later he was sitting back against a tree sipping at some broth Push had made from jerked venison. Push had bound up the wound, wrapping it snugly around both sides of the shoulder. It felt a good deal better.

"Hern, if you'll stay here and keep a handle on things, I'd like to slip out a ways and try for some fresh meat for supper," Push said. "It would do Mitch good to have some. I'll leave Rube here with you, and I won't be far away."

"We'll be fine, Push. Go ahead, and take your time about it," Hern said.

Push returned before nightfall with a good-sized turkey hen. He'd killed her with his bow, so there was no report of gunfire to reveal their presence.

"I'll cut this bird up in pieces we can roast over the fire, Daisy," Push said. "We ain't carrying a pot big enough to stew it in."

"Save a few small chunks for me, Push, and I'll stew them with some dumplings in the small pot," Daisy said.

"Now you're talking," Push said. "At a girl."

"We'll just laze around here a while in the morning," Push said after supper. "Let Mitch get some rest. Take time to give a good listen to the country around. We don't need to cover much ground for a few days. Just let Mitch get plenty of rest and get his strength back. We'll amble along a little every day. Keep working toward home. Take it in easy stages."

Mitchell and Hern sat at their ease in the soft afternoon. Push was out scouting around for food and Daisy was washing out some clothes in a stream nearby. Rube had accompanied Daisy to the stream, and lay beside the spot where she worked, his head resting on his paws.

"I've been thinking about your new business, Hern. You'll need help from the beginning. I want you to take Zak for the job. I'm going to sign him over to you," Mitchell said.

This had not been mentioned before, but Hern had thought about it, anticipating his father might do something such as he had just suggested.

"That's mighty generous of you, Pa, and I appreciate it more than I can say. But I'm troubled by the idea of slavery. I can't feel easy about it. I think I got that from you, Pa," he added. "From you and Mama."

Mitchell nodded but said nothing, and Hern went on. "I don't feel like I want to own anybody, Pa. Zak least of all. I was raised with Zak. He's my friend. I can't make him my property."

"Well, the fact is, Zak is a slave, Hern. Something has to happen to him. Don't you think he'd rather be with you than anything else that's likely to happen?" Mitchell said.

"I want his help, Pa, and I need it. But I don't want to be his owner."

"I've thought the same thing before, myself," Mitchell said. "But this is a country of slavery. It's not a simple thing to give a slave his freedom. Lot's of people don't take kindly to it. And that can cut two ways, Hern, and worse for Zak than for you."

"I've thought about that too. But aside from the fact that it's none of their business, what if they didn't know about it?

"What if we keep it strictly between ourselves? Zak is smart. He'll see the need of it. He can work for me, same as if I owned him. But I'll pay him a fair wage. If the company does well, so will he. Only he and I need know he's a free man."

"What if he wants to go, wants to leave as a free man?"

"I don't think he will, but if he does, I can take him up the river to Illinois or Ohio. He can travel as my slave and walk away free, with the papers to prove it."

"Alright. Say he stays with you. He's likely to want a wife someday. What then?"

"He can pick one out and I'll buy her for him. Better yet, he can save up and buy her, himself. Only I'll be his front man."

They sat quiet, Mitchell looking closely at his son. "By the Creeping Judas!" he said at last. "It might just work! It sounds good, the more I think about it. Let's try it! If it works, I'll see about doing the same with George and Price. Aunt Lucy, too, if she's not too old for such ideas.

"But it's not without risk, Hern. I think you should consult Red Jameson about it. If he's part of the company, he'll be part of this, too. And he has to live in the same community as we do."

"Yes, that's clear. I'll do that, Pa. I'll speak to him as soon as we get home."

Chapter Thirty-Six. April, 1858.

Push led them home without further high adventure, six days after the gun battle. The remainder of the journey was routine, except for the care taken for Mitchell's recovery. The first thing Daisy did at Center Hill, after greeting everyone properly, was to sit down and write Maddie a letter.

My Dear Maddie,

Thank you for your beautiful letter about Mama and Pa. I will always treasure the thoughts you expressed. They helped me through some hard days.

Now listen, Maddie. I just arrived in Center Hill! I am going to live with the Henshaws! Won't that be wonderful? Uncle Mitchell, and Hern, and Push came all the way to Alabama and brought me here on horseback! But there is even more important business for today, and I must get to it at once.

As you would expect, I asked Hern about you at the earliest opportunity. He told me a long story. He is distraught, Maddie. He is almost convinced he has lost you. It is plain he loves you very much. I told him that his story doesn't add up. Something is missing and I am intent on finding out what it is.

Hern came to visit you the very day he got your letter follow-ing the Christmas party. Did anyone tell you he had been there?

After hearing nothing from you for two weeks after that, he wrote you a letter. Did you ever get it?

I tell you now if I had a young man like Hern dying of love for me, I know what I would do. I would not wait a minute! I would come this very day and get him! I would get over here and settle things just as soon as I could move.

And I hope that is just what you will do.

Your most loving friend and cousin,

Daisy

When Daisy finished the letter, she called her Uncle Mitchell aside and told him what she intended. She asked if there was someone they could send to Robertson's Crossroads with the letter the first thing in the morning. Mitchell sent for Zak to come up to the kitchen.

"Zak, this is Miss Daisy Henshaw," Mitchell said. "I'm sure you already know who she is and where she fits in this family. She has an important errand that needs doing, and I'm going to entrust it to you."

"Hello, Zak, I'm pleased to meet you," Daisy said.

"Thank you, ma'am, I'm pleased too," Zak said, and stood waiting.

"Zak, I have a letter here for Miss Madelyn McCall. It is such an important letter that it must be hand-carried to Robertson's Crossroads and put directly into Maddie's hands. I want you to take it to her as early as you can leave here in the morning. This letter is very important to Hern, Zak, and important to everyone in this household. I want you to promise me you will deliver it directly into Maddie's hands."

"Yes, ma'am, I understand," Zak said. "I will deliver it directly to Miss Madelyn, herself. I will tell her it comes from you and that you said it's important. You can depend on me, Miss Daisy."

Late the next morning, Hern sat with Red Jameson in his office at the hardware store in Olive Branch. "Approve it, approve it?" Mr. Jameson said. "I surely do approve it! I wish I'd thought of it myself. You bet I approve it!

"I've been congratulating myself on joining your business, Hern, and this makes me even prouder than I already was. I'm proud of your thinking. Proud you've known me all your life. That way I can claim an influence on how you turned out. Ha, ha, ha!

"You've brought good news, today, Hern. Excellent news. By God, I don't see how you could have brought better."

Hern returned the horse to the barn and walked up the path toward the back porch of the Henshaw home. Maddie came through the back door and down the steps, came walking directly to Hern, just as she had done on the Fourth of July in the square at Olive Branch almost two years before. Hern stood in utter amazement. Maddie came to a stop just one step in front of him. Then she spoke for the first time.

"Mr. Herndon Henshaw, I entreat you: Withhold from me no longer that friendship which is so dear, upon which I stake my belief in the future. Whatever my failures to you in the past, I implore you, please forgive me."

Hern reached out to grasp her hands, then fell to his knees at her feet. "Maddie, Maddie," he said, "I've acted the fool. I've been filled with useless pride. I have sulked like a child against imagined wrongs. I should have come to you weeks ago, Maddie. It is I who beg your forgiveness.

"I want you to be my wife, Maddie. I want to marry you now, at once, just as soon as we can arrange it. I want to be with you always, Maddie. Please say you will marry me."

It was a moment before Maddie could speak. Her eyes were full. "Hern, I have been miserable and now I am so happy. You've made me happier than I thought I could be. I promise I will make you happy, too.

"I will marry you, Herndon Henshaw. The wedding cannot come soon enough for me."

Hern rose, took her in his arms and held her. He could hear the smile in her voice as she spoke into his ear. "It is time we fed the ducks, Henshaw," she said. "This time we will feed them as they should be fed."

Unnoticed by the pair, Daisy had slipped out onto the back porch. Behind her in the open door stood Mitchell and Elise.

Hern and Maddie held their embrace. They kissed; then again, and again. Then Daisy could contain herself no longer. She came bounding down the steps toward the new couple, clapping her hands, laughing with tears in her eyes. She reached Hern and Maddie, and they expanded their embrace to include her. "Oh my cousins, my dear cousins," she cried. "I'm so happy for you both!"

Author's Note.

Much of the action portrayed in this book is fictional, but the places where it occurs are real, and I have drawn upon numerous family stories and local tales of old times in DeSoto County, Mississippi. A number of the book's main characters are based on members of my family who lived there at the time. Mitchell and Elise Henshaw are based on my great, great grandfather and grandmother Achilles Moorman Haraway and Julia McCargo Haraway. Herndon Henshaw and Madelyn McCall are based on my great grandfather and grandmother David Herndon Haraway and Martha (Mattie) McGowan Haraway.

Achilles Haraway lived on at Center Hill, Mississippi until September 12, 1891. His wife Julia followed him to the grave seven days later. Family legend says she died of a broken heart. David Herndon came through the Civil War, and he and Mattie lived for forty-six more years at Center Hill. They both died in the year 1911. Mattie departed first on April 3; Herndon went on to join her a little less than seven months later.

Lush-pun-tubby is based on a historical character of the same name. Early deeds of land sales in the area of Olive Branch and Center Hill show Lush-pun-tubby as the original seller. The character *Push-pun-tubby*, however, is entirely a fictional creation.

The community of Center Hill still goes by the same name today. The city of Olive Branch was known first as Cowpen—a way station for drovers traversing between Memphis and Holly Springs, Mississippi–and Watson's

Crossroads, after a popular Methodist minister in the community. The name *Olive Branch* refers to the branch brought back by the dove in the Bible story of Noah and the Flood. The community known as Robertson's Crossroads actually went by that name during the time of the novel but is now known as Pleasant Hill. The name of the county seat was and is Hernando, named, as is the county, for the explorer Hernando DeSoto.

About the Author

Maury M. Haraway is a fifth-generation native of DeSoto County
Mississippi. He received his Ph.D. from the University of Mississippi
and served for many years as Professor of Psychology at the University of
Louisiana, Monroe prior to retiring to his hometown of Olive Branch,
where he now lives with his wife Cathy.

CPSIA information can be obtained at www.ICGtesting.com
Printed in the USA
237732LV00001B/112/P

9 781456 765514